P. C. Doherty was born in Middlesbrough. He studied History at Liverpool and Oxford Universities and obtained a doctorate at Oxford for his thesis on Edward II and Queen Isabella. He is now the Headmaster of a school in North-East London, and lives with his wife and family near Epping Forest.

P. C. Doherty's previous Hugh Corbett medieval mysteries – SATAN IN ST MARY'S, CROWN IN DARKNESS, SPY IN CHANCERY, THE ANGEL OF DEATH, THE PRICE OF DARKNESS, MURDER WEARS A COWL and THE ASSASSIN IN THE GREENWOOD – are also available from Headline.

Acclaim for the Hugh Corbett medieval mysteries:

'Wholly excellent, this is one of those books you hate to put down' *Prima*
'I really like these medieval whodunnits' *Bookseller*
'A powerful compound of history and intrigue' *Redbridge Guardian*
'Medieval London comes vividly to life . . . Doherty's depictions of medieval characters and manners of thought, from the highest to the lowest, ringing true' *Publishers Weekly*
'A romping good read' *Time Out*
'Historically informative, excellently plotted and, as ever, superbly entertaining' *CADS*

Also by P. C. Doherty

Hugh Corbett medieval mysteries

The Song of a Dark Angel
Satan in St Mary's
Crown in Darkness
Spy in Chancery
The Angel of Death
The Prince of Darkness
Murder Wears a Cowl
The Assassin in the Greenwood

Satan's Fire

P. C. Doherty

HEADLINE

First published in 1995
by HEADLINE BOOK PUBLISHING

First published in paperback in 1996
by HEADLINE BOOK PUBLISHING

10 9 8 7 6 5 4 3 2 1

ISBN 0 7472 4905 9

Printed and bound in Great Britain by
Cox & Wyman Ltd, Reading, Berks

HEADLINE BOOK PUBLISHING
A division of Hodder Headline PLC
338 Euston Road
London NW1 3BH

To my baby son, Little Paul [Mr. T. T.]

Prologue

On the shores of the Dead Sea, where the djinns and devils rested from their constant war against man, stood the rocky, yellow-stoned eyrie of Am Massafia; the stronghold lair of the Sheikh Al-Jebal, the Old Man of the Mountain. The trackways to the Old Man's lair were narrow, winding and secret, the shadow of vultures' wings a constant presence. The final path, a perilous journey along a roped bridge above a yawning gorge, was guarded by Sudanese swordsmen with broad, razor-edged scimitars clasped to their waists. Once across this bridge of hell, however, and through the iron-studded gates, a visitor would enter a palace with mosaic floors. Cool courtyards, with fountains spouting ice-cold water, offered shade against the setting sun. Peacocks strutted and gaily coloured parrots shrieked amongst the rose gardens or rustled the leaves of the dark mulberry trees. Around the courtyard, wooden lattices, built against the wall, were covered with rare and exotic flowers which turned the dry air heavy with perfume, whilst thuribles, in corners or on shelves, poured amber smoke to the ever-blue sky.

Beneath the fortress, however, lay a different place: dark, hot passageways; galleries without light or air; only the occasional torch flickering against the blood-red rock. The dungeons of the Old Man of the Mountain housed many prisoners. Some had long died, the flesh falling off their bones which now turned yellow in the heat. Others had gone insane and crouched like animals in their narrow chained dungeons, crawling around like dogs, their eyes mad, their tongues

1

constantly baying against the darkness. But, in one cell, the Unknown, the infidel knight with corn-coloured hair and light-blue eyes, squirmed on rotting straw and dreamed of vengeance. For only this, burning brightly within him, held back the Stygian blackness and the demons ever ready to carry away his soul. Hatred, anger and a burning desire for vengeance kept his wits together and body and soul as one. He refused to dwell on the silent horrors around him but lived constantly in the past, on that dreadful night when the great city of Acre had fallen to the Turks. Again and again he would recall the constant beat of the kettledrums as the Muslim hordes poured through the breach in the wall of the city. The armoured regiments of Mamelukes streaming across the ruined moat, over the bodies and broken engines, pressing back the wounded knights, forcing their way into the streets. The prisoner blinked and, lifting his arm, stared closely at the white scabs forming on his arms and legs. He closed his eyes and called on God for life: not a cure for his leprosy but length of days and the opportunity to wreak his revenge.

In the opulent, breeze-filled chambers far above the dungeon, the Sheikh Al-Jebal, the Old Man of the Mountain, sat overlooking a walled garden with marble fountains which tossed sparkling wine into the perfumed air. The Old Man, his eyes heavy with opium, stared down at the silk-carpeted pavilions and beautifully tiled porticoes, where his young men lay sprawled with their Circassian girls and dreamed hashish-filled fantasies of Paradise. So it was, every day, a time of Paradise until the Old Man issued his orders. Once the die had been cast, these young men, dressed in their white robes, red girdles about their waists, scarlet, gold-tipped slippers on their feet, would leave the fortress and go down into the valleys to wreak their master's will. No one could ever oppose him. No one ever escaped his death sentence. Two daggers pressed into the pillows of their intended victim's bed and, on the table beside it, a flat seedcake, a warning from the Old Man of the

Mountain that his Assassins were about to do his will.

The Old Man turned, shifting his body on the purple silk divan between the naked, golden bodies of his concubines. They murmured in their drug-filled sleep whilst he stared up at the ceiling of the chamber, hard cedarwood, inlaid with gold and fresh diamonds. He felt restless and sat up, gazing round the room at the inanimate birds fashioned out of gold and silver with enamel feathers and brilliant ruby eyes. The sheikh's hand went out to the table next to the bed where gold dishes and amber cups stood, filled with the sweetest wines or ripest fruit. He let his hand fall. He had drunk and eaten enough. He was bored and the affairs of men required his attention.

'What does it profit a man,' Sheikh Al-Jebal murmured, quoting the Christians, 'if he gains the whole world but suffers the loss of his immortal soul?'

Yesterday messengers had arrived bringing news of the outside world; whispers from the busy markets of Alexandria, Tripoli, and even further west, from the land of the infidels. From Rome, Avignon, Paris and London. The sheikh got off the divan. He stretched and a slave, standing in the corner, hurried across, a white gauze cloak in his hands, he carefully wrapped this round his master's shoulders. The Old Man ignored him as if the slave didn't even exist. He walked across to a small alcove, pulling back the double-edged curtain of gold-embossed leather and stared down at the ivory chessmen.

'It is the will of Allah!' He murmured. 'It is the will of Allah that I intervene in the game.'

He picked up the figure of the king and, cradling it against his cheek, went and sat on his throne-like chair. He thought of the infidel kings of the west: Edward of England, Philip of France, as well as his inveterate enemies, those monk-soldiers, the Templars, with their red crosses, great castles and immense power. He played with the figure of the king and smiled lazily.

'It is time to go down,' he murmured, 'among the sons of men.'

3

England and France were on the verge of signing a great peace; the Templar order, ever ready, might exploit this peace and turn the eyes of the Western kings and princes to the regaining of Jerusalem and its Holy Places. Once again the fleets of Venice, Genoa and Pisa would be seen off the Palestine coast. The Templars would reprovision their castles and the great iron-mailed knights of the West would pour ashore to plant their standards above Acre, Damascus, Tripoli and Sidon, turning the whole coastline into a sea of blood. And there were other whispers. Strange stories, things the Old Man of the Mountain could hardly believe but hoped to act upon. He closed his eyes and whispered the three sacred messages of the Assassins, always dispatched to every one of their victims.

KNOWEST THOU, THAT WE GO FORTH AND RETURN AS BEFORE AND BY NO MEANS CAN YOU HINDER US.
KNOWEST THOU, THAT WHAT THOU POSSESSES SHALL ESCAPE THEE IN THE END AND RETURN TO US.
KNOWEST THOU, THAT WE HOLD YOU AND WILL KEEP THEE UNTIL THE ACCOUNT BE CLOSED.

He opened his eyes. Few men escaped such a message. Only one, Edward of England, whilst crusading in Palestine in the months before he became king: a poisoned knife plunged into his shoulder but, through God's grace as well as the attentions of his wife, Edward had recovered from the poison. The Old Man of the Mountain played with the rings on his fingers. He must act on the secrets he'd learnt. But how, he wondered, could assassins be sent to Edward's cold, misty isle? He toyed with the rings, watching the light dance on the precious stones, then lifted his head: there were more ways to sting a man than use a scorpion.

'Bring up the prisoner!' he whispered into the scent-filled

air. 'Release the Infidel, the knight we call the Unknown. He will do my bidding!'

Some three months later, Dames Cecilia and Marcia of the Order of St Benedict were journeying along the old Roman road leading to the gate known as Botham Bar at York. The daylight had died. Darkness was beginning to shroud the damp forests on either side of the road. The two good sisters, swathed in their brown, woollen robes, each riding one of their convent's best palfreys, gossiped to hide their own concern. They were not truly frightened. Their guide, Thurston of Guiseborough, striding ahead in front of them, was a burly, thickset peasant. He carried a short, small buckler on his back, sword and dagger were clasped to his belt, and his burly fist held a club which would have dimmed the brains of an ox. Nevertheless, the two good sisters liked to frighten each other. Now and again, they would glance hurriedly sideways at the damp trees and recall the tales about how the Romans had built this road. How, in the cold, wet forest beyond, the ghosts of these ancient people clustered in the vine-covered ruins where the owl, fox and badger made their nests.

The good sisters' fears became more real as daylight disappeared and the undergrowth on either side of the road became alive with night creatures. A boar crashed across the road, his wicked tusks scything the air. Vixens yipped at the rising moon and, from some hamlet hidden in the trees, a dog bayed dolefully against the night. The two good sisters edged their palfreys closer. Secretly they comforted themselves. Who would harm two women consecrated to God? In actual fact they put their faith in Thurston's thick club as well as the king's impending arrival in York. Because of that, the highways and forest tracks had been cleared of outlaws and vagabonds. Moreover, the presence of so many sergeants of the great Templar Order also kept the villains, rascals and wolves heads well away from the city of York. It was the Templars about whom the two good sisters chattered: those iron-clad men with their sunburnt faces, their chainmail covered by great white cloaks of wool bearing a six-sided blood-red cross. The sisters had just passed the great Templar manor of Framlingham and its shadow-shrouded buildings had prompted their conversation about these strange men. The Templars were soldier-monks, virgins dedicated to war, but also the holders of great wealth as well as mysterious secrets. The two good sisters had learnt all this whilst staying at their mother house in Beverley. In the refectory there the sisters had gossiped about how the great Templar lords had swept into the convent courtyard demanding provisions for themselves and their horses. How they had guarded so securely a covered wagon bearing a six-locked coffer which, so Mother Perpetua informed them, must carry some great relic of tremendous force.

'Why else?' Mother Perpetua had concluded, 'had the wagon been closely guarded by knights, foot-soldiers and crossbowmen all wearing the insignia of the Order?'

Dames Cecilia and Marcia had spent their long journey speculating on the many rumours about the Templars. Now, as the owls began to hoot, they wondered if these same Templars had brought a curse upon the land.

'We are definitely living in dreadful times,' Dame Marcia declared. 'Look you, Sister; where else have we had rain at seed times to smother the young crops and rot the wheat in the ear of corn?'

'Aye,' Dame Cecilia replied. 'There's talk of famine and hunger. How the poor are mixing chalk with their flour.'

'And other stories.' Dame Marcia chattered on. 'Outside Hull, a vicar saw three witches come riding towards him, a yard and a half above the ground.'

'And at Ripon,' Dame Cecilia interrupted, eager to show her knowledge, 'the noon-day devil was glimpsed under the outstretched branch of the yew tree, glaring, with horrid eyes, at the priory gates.'

The two sisters heard a sound on the road ahead of them. Dame Cecilia gave a small scream and reined in. Thurston strode on, cursing under his breath at these chattering women. He stopped and peered down the road.

'It's nothing,' he murmured in his broad Yorkshire burr, 'though . . .' He hid his grin and scratched his tousled beard.

'What?' Dame Cecilia snapped.

'Well,' Thurston replied slowly, thoroughly enjoying himself, 'there have been rumours . . .'

'Rumours about what?'

'Well, ever since those Templars came back to York,' Thurston continued, staring into the darkness, 'there've been stories of devils, in the form of weasels, riding huge, amber-coloured cats along these roads.'

The two good nuns drew in their breath sharply.

'Or there again,' Thurston continued, his voice dropping to a whisper, 'outside Walmer Bar, the Lord Satan himself has been glimpsed. He was clad in a purple gown with a black cap upon his head.' He walked back and stared up at Dame Cecilia's wrinkled face. 'His face was terrible,' Thurston continued hoarsely. 'He had the nose of a great eagle, burning eyes, his hands and legs were hairy and he had feet like a griffin.'

'Now that's enough,' Dame Marcia interrupted. 'Thurston, you are frightening us. We should be in York.'

Aye, Thurston thought, and we'd have been there an hour ago if it hadn't been for your constant gabble and chatter about imps, Templars, demons and magic. He looked up at the starlit sky.

'Don't worry, good sisters,' he called back over his shoulder. 'Two more miles and we'll be at Botham Bar; even sooner if you can make those palfreys trot a little faster.'

The two nuns needed no further urging. They dug their heels in, shouting at Thurston not to walk too far in front of them. Their guide strode on, quite pleased at teasing these plump, well-fed gossips who, ever since they had left Beverley, had spent more time talking about Satan than their devotions. Thurston stopped abruptly. A country man, a born poacher, Thurston knew the forest and could distinguish between what sounds and smells spelt danger and what to ignore. Now something was wrong. He lifted his hand, even as his neck went cold and his heart began to beat faster. A strange smell in the night air of smoke, fire and something else, smouldering human flesh. Thurston recognised that smell. He'd never forgotten the time they'd burnt the old witch in the market place at Guiseborough. The village had stunk for days afterwards, as if the old crone had cursed the air at the very moment of dying.

'What's wrong?' Dame Cecilia shrilled, fighting hard to control her usually meek palfrey which had now become restless, as it too caught the smell.

'I don't know,' Thurston replied. 'Listen!'

The two nuns obeyed. Then they heard it: the mad galloping of a horse coming along the trackway ahead. Thurston moved them quickly to the side of the road just as the horse appeared, pounding along, neck out, ears flat against its head. Thurston wildly wondered whether he could stop the charging animal. The horse saw them and, skittering on the trackway, turned sideways then up, back on its hind legs, before charging on. As it did, Thurston's blood ran cold: the severed legs of the horse's former rider were still clasped firmly in its stirrups.

'What is it?' Dame Cecilia whispered.

Thurston crouched on the edge of the road, his hands across his stomach.

'Thurston!' Dame Marcia yelled. 'What is wrong?'

The guide turned and vomited on the grass. He then grabbed the wine skin slung over the horn of Dame Cecilia's saddle. He ignored their protests, undid the clasps, almost throwing the wine into his mouth.

'We'd best move on.' He put the stopper back, thrust it at Dame Cecilia and, without a backward glance, continued along the trackway. They rounded the bend and fearfully approached the fire burning so fiercely on the edge of the forest. Dame Marcia gagged at the terrible stench, her palfrey, unwillingly, drew close to the flames. Dame Marcia took one look at the fire greedily consuming the upper, severed part of a man's corpse; she screamed and fell like a sack from her saddle, swooning in terror at the hideous sight.

Chapter 1

York. Lady's Day, 1303

'The Lord knows I need it!' Edward of England ran a hand through his iron-grey hair then brought his fists down on the refectory table in the priory of St Leonard outside York. The crash echoed round the long whitewashed room. 'I need money!' the king yelled.

The commanders of the Temple, the principal officers of Christendom's monastic fighting order, however, were not frightened by the English king's play-acting. Indeed, all four looked to the other end of the table where Jacques de Molay, Grand Master of their Order, recently arrived from France, sat in his high-backed chair, hands linked together as if in prayer.

'Well?' Edward barked.

De Molay spread his hands; his sunburnt face was impassive, his clear grey eyes betrayed no fear at the English king's terrible rage.

'Well?' Edward snapped. 'Are you going to answer or bless me?'

'My lord King, we are not your subjects!'

'By God's teeth, some of you are!' Edward roared back. He straightened in his chair, jabbing his fingers down on the table. 'On my way here, I passed your manor of Framlingham with its elegant gatehouse, fields, pastures, stewponds and orchards. Those lands are mine. The cattle and sheep which graze there are mine. The sparrows which nest in the trees and the pigeons in your dovecotes are all mine. My father gave you that manor. I can take it back!'

'All we have,' de Molay answered quietly, 'comes from God. They were given to us by noble princes like your father, so we can continue our fight against the Infidel and win back the Holy Places in Outremer.'

Edward of England was tempted to reply that, so far, the Templars had made a poor job of it, but then he glanced across the room: the dark-haired clerk who sat in a window embrasure caught the king's gaze and shook his head slowly. Edward breathed out noisily through his nose. He stared up at the polished hammer-beam roof.

'I need money,' Edward continued. 'My war in Scotland is nearly finished. If I can only catch that bastard, that will-o'-the-wisp Wallace . . .!'

'You have no war with France,' de Molay interrupted. 'You and His august Majesty, Philip IV, are about to sign a treaty of eternal peace.'

Edward caught the sardonic note and hid his own smile.

'Your son,' de Molay continued, 'your heir apparent, the Prince of Wales, is set to marry Philip IV's daughter Princess Isabella. She will bring a grand dowry.'

John de Warrenne, Earl of Surrey, seated to the left of the king, belched noisily. His watery blue eyes never left de Molay's face. Edward pressed his boot on de Warrenne's toes.

'The good earl,' Edward intervened, 'may not be elegant in his response but, Seigneur de Molay, you taunt us. Isabella is only nine years old. It will be three years before she can marry. I have to fill my coffers in the next few months. I need a new army in Scotland by mid-summer.'

Edward looked despairingly at each of the four Templar commanders. Surely, he thought, they will help? They are English. They know the problems which beset me. Bartholomew Baddlesmere, his head bald as a pigeon's egg, his grizzled, weather-beaten face showed no compassion. Next to him William Symmes, his face a patchwork of scars: one black patch covered his left eye, his blond hair hung in lank tendrils to frame a narrow, mean face. No hope there, Edward thought: both of them are Templars born and bred. All they care for is their bloody Order. Edward tried to catch the eye of Ralph Legrave who, twenty years ago, had been one of the king's household knights. Now he wore the white surcoat of the Templars emblazoned with their red-pointed cross. Legrave's open, boyish face, however, skin smooth as a maiden, showed no concern for his former lord. Across the table from Legrave sat Richard Branquier, tall and stooped, the Templar's grand chamberlain in England. He just wiped his dripping nose on the back of his hands. His short-sighted gaze refused to meet the king's; instead he glanced down at the accounts book before him, a doleful look on his face.

Just like some bloody merchant, Edward thought, he regards me as a poor prospect. Edward stared down at his hands clenched in his lap. I'd like to break their heads, he thought. Beside him de Warrenne shuffled his feet, moving his head slowly from side to side. Edward caught the earl's wrist and gripped it. De Warrenne was not the brightest of his earls and Edward recognised the signs: if this meeting went on too long and the Templars grew more obdurate, de Warrenne wouldn't think twice about name-calling or even resorting to physical violence. Edward glared across at the man sitting in the window-seat, staring down at the courtyard below. Moody bastard! Edward thought. Sir Hugh Corbett, Keeper of the King's Secret Seal, should be over here sitting at his right hand, instead of staring out of the window, mooning over his flaxen-haired wife. The silence in the priory refectory became oppressive. The Templars sat like carved statues.

'Do you want me to beg?' the king snapped.

Edward scratched at a stain on his purple surcoat. Out of the corner of his eye he watched Branquier lean over and whisper in de Molay's ear. The grand master nodded slowly.

'The King's Exchequer is in York?' de Molay asked.

'Yes, my Treasury's here but there's sweet bugger-all in it!' Edward retorted.

Branquier brought his hand from beneath the ledger book and sent a gold coin ringing down the table. Edward deftly caught it. He stared down at the coin, his heart skipping a beat. He grimaced at de Warrenne.

'Another one!' he whispered, passing it to his companion.

The earl looked at it curiously. As large as a shilling, the gold coin seemed freshly minted, with a crude cross stamped on either side. He weighed it carefully in his hand.

'Well?' Edward taunted. 'Is this all you are going to give me?'

'You say you have no treasure.' Branquier leaned on the table. He pointed one bony finger at the coin de Warrenne was now tossing from one hand to the other. 'Yet, Your Grace, those coins are appearing all over York. Freshly cut and neatly minted. Are they not issued by your own Treasury?'

'No, they are not,' Edward replied. 'Since my arrival outside York, scores of such coins have appeared, but they are not from our Mints.'

'But who would have such bullion?' Branquier asked. 'And how can they circulate such precious coinage?'

'I don't know,' Edward retorted. 'But, if I did, I'd seize the gold and hang the bastard who made it!' He took a wafer-thin shilling out of his own purse and tossed it down the table. 'That's what my own Mints are producing, Sir Richard: so-called silver coins. They have as much silver in them as I have in my . . . er . . . hand!' the king added quickly.

'But who would counterfeit such coins?' de Molay insisted. 'Who has the bullion as well as the means to fashion such precious metal?'

'I don't know,' Edward shouted. 'And, with all due respect, Seigneur, that is my business. The counterfeiting of coins in this realm is treason. I can't see what this has got to do with the business in hand.'

'Which is what?'

'A loan of fifty thousand pounds sterling,' Edward retorted. The Templars stirred, shaking their heads.

'Could you not,' Baddlesmere declared, staring across at Branquier, 'ask Philip of France for a loan? To be put against the dowry settlement on his daughter? After all, Philip's envoy Sir Amaury de Craon is now feeding his face in the priory buttery.'

Edward glanced across at Corbett. The clerk, at the mention of his inveterate enemy and political opponent, was now listening intently to what was being said.

'What do you think of that, Sir Hugh?' Edward called out. 'Shall I send you to France and ask my brother in Christ to empty his Treasury?'

'You might as well send me to the moon, Sire: Philip is even more bankrupt than yourself.'

'What is it you really want?' de Molay intervened. 'A loan or a gift?'

Edward beamed from ear to ear. He winked at Corbett: the Templars were about to negotiate.

'If you offer me a gift, de Molay,' Edward teased back, 'then I'll take it.'

'Let me explain,' the grand master continued. 'If you confirm all Templar possessions in England and Gascony . . .'

Edward was already nodding vigorously.

'. . . Free passage for our merchants; confirmation of our Templar church in London. Confirmation,' de Molay continued, 'of all our possessions, both movable and immovable.'

The king was now beside himself with pleasure. 'Yes, yes,' he murmured.

'And a quarter of this gold,' de Molay concluded.

Edward sat up in his chair. 'What gold?'

'You mentioned a counterfeiter,' de Molay continued. 'Whoever it is must have a mass of gold. We want a quarter of it.'

'Agreed!' Edward snapped.

'And finally,' de Molay leaned forward, clasping his hands together; 'twelve years ago, Acre, the last fortress in Outremer; our door to the Holy Places, fell into Infidel hands.'

'God knows,' Edward murmured piously. 'But the city of Acre still weighs heavily on my soul.' He pressed the toe of his boot on de Warrenne's foot, just in case the Earl began to snigger.

'Yes, yes, I am sure it does,' de Molay observed sarcastically.

'I fought in the Holy Land,' Edward retorted. 'Thirty-three years ago I went there with my beloved wife, Eleanor. You may recall how the Old Man of the Mountain sent an assassin to kill me.'

'And you were cured by a Templar physician,' de Molay interrupted.

'My lord King, you were cured for a purpose. We want you to take the cross.' He watched the smile fade from Edward's face. 'We want you to swear an oath that you will go on Crusade and join the Temple in liberating Acre with one great, holy war against the forces of Islam. Do that and our Treasury in London, through its Italian bankers, will deliver to your Exchequer, by the feast of St Peter and St Paul, fifty thousand pounds sterling.'

'Agreed!' The king shouted.

'We want your oath now.'

'Impossible!' Edward replied. 'I am still fighting the Scots!'

'When that war is over, will you take the oath?' William Symmes called, touching the patch over his eye. 'The war in Scotland will soon be over. We have agreed to your gift. You must agree to our request.'

The Templar's one eye gleamed fanatically. Edward regretted his impetuosity. You are all in this together, he thought. You had this planned before we ever met. He glanced across at Corbett and saw the I-told-you-so look in his clerk's eyes.

'Tomorrow morning,' de Molay continued. 'You will enter

York to hear Mass at the abbey church of St Mary's. We would like you to take your oath after receiving the Eucharist. Swear, your hand on the sacrament, that when the war in Scotland is finished, you will support our Crusade.'

'And I get the money?'

'Will you swear?'

'Yes, yes, I intend to enter York tomorrow by Micklegate and go through Trinity to Mass in the abbey. I'll take the oath but will the money be paid?'

'As I have promised,' de Molay replied. He leaned back in his chair. 'When this meeting was arranged, my lord King, you said there were other matters.'

Sir Hugh Corbett continued to watch the juggler amusing the royal troops in the courtyard below. The man was throwing skittles in the air and deftly catching them, whilst a scraggy-haired bear, with a monkey on its shoulder, danced a shuffling gait to the reedy tune of a piper. He heard de Molay's remark about 'other matters' and sighed. He got to his feet and walked back to sit on the chair to the right of his royal master.

'For God's sake, stop dreaming!' the king hissed. 'You could have been of more help!'

The Templar commanders, pretending to chatter amongst themselves, glanced slyly up the table.

'More like a monk,' Branquier whispered, staring at Corbett's cropped, black hair with flecks of grey at the temples, the smooth, olive-skinned face and deep set eyes. The king's dramatic whisper had been heard and the Templars now waited to see what this most enigmatic of clerks would reply. Corbett leaned his elbows on the table; pushing his face only a few inches away from Edward's.

'My lord,' he whispered. 'You don't need my help. As usual, you have a skill even the devil would admire, though for what . . . ?'

The king stared back in mock, hurt innocence.

'You got your money,' Corbett continued. 'The clerks of the

Exchequer will draw up the agreement and you will swear whatever you like.'

'You are not going home,' Edward hissed spitefully. 'I want you here, Hugh. Now, tell our guests just what our problems are.'

'Seigneur de Molay,' Corbett began. 'Commanders of the Temple.' He rose to his feet. 'What I say to you is a matter of secrecy. The king mentioned his enemy, the Old Man of the Mountain. You know, as men who have lived and fought in Outremer, how the Old Man heads a sect of dangerous assassins.'

His words were greeted by murmurs of agreement.

'This sect,' Corbett continued, 'prides itself that no man is beyond its reach. Seas, mountains, deserts pose no obstacles to them. They follow the same ritual: two daggers, each wrapped in red silk with a piece of seedcake, are always left in some prominent place as a warning to their intended victims.' He paused, his fingers drumming the table-top. 'Our lord the king has received such a warning. Ten days ago,' Corbett explained, 'two daggers, a seedcake nailed in between, were found thrust into the doors of St Paul's Cathedral in London.' Corbett plucked a piece of parchment from his wallet. 'Each dagger had a red sash tied to it. To one of the daggers was pinned the following notice:

KNOWEST THOU, THAT WE GO FORTH AND RETURN AS BEFORE AND BY NO MEANS CAN YOU HINDER US.
KNOWEST THOU, THAT WHAT THOU POSSESSES SHALL ESCAPE THEE IN THE END AND RETURN TO US.
'KNOWEST THOU, THAT WE HOLD YOU AND WILL KEEP THEE UNTIL THE ACCOUNT BE CLOSED.'

Corbett paused; his words had caused consternation amongst

the Templars. Chairs were scraped back; no longer the calm, impassive warriors, the very mention of their inveterate enemies – as well as the sheer impudence of the message – had the Templars clutching daggers and muttering threats.

Grand Master de Molay, however, still sat as if carved out of stone.

'How could this be done?' Legrave shouted. 'The Assassins live in the deserts of Syria: they have no house in Cheapside.'

His words created a ripple of laughter.

'In London,' Baddlesmere shouted out, 'such an assassin would stand out like a hawk amongst pigeons!'

Corbett shook his head. 'You mentioned Sir Amaury de Craon? True he is here, being attendant upon the king over the marriage negotiations for Philip's daughter.' Corbett paused to choose his words carefully. 'But yesterday de Craon also brought messages from France. A similar message was pinned to the doors of Saint Denis. A short while later, whilst Philip was hunting in the Bois de Boulogne, a mysterious archer tried to kill him.'

The refectory had now fallen silent, all eyes on Corbett.

'Sir Hugh, you have still not answered our question,' de Molay said quietly. 'How could an assassin walk through the cities of Paris and London yet not be seen?'

'Seigneur, aren't there links between your Order and the Assassins?'

De Molay silenced the protests of his companions.

'We have had dealings with them, as your king has with different caliphs and sultans, not to mention the Mongol lords. Say what you are going to.'

'Monsieur de Craon,' Corbett continued, 'believes the assassin is an apostate, a turncoat, a member of your Order!'

Now the Templar commanders jumped to their feet, chairs and stools were knocked over. Baddlesmere drew his dagger. Symmes pointed at Corbett, his face mottled with fury.

'How dare you?' He spluttered. 'How dare you accuse us of

treason? We are Christ's monks. We spend out lives and our blood defending God's holy creed.'

'Sit down!' de Molay shouted. 'All of you!' His sunburnt face had now turned an ashy grey and a murderous fury blazed in the grand master's eyes.

'You'd best sit down!' de Warrenne ordered. 'To draw sword or dagger in the king's presence is treason.'

'I have heard rumours about what happened in Paris,' de Molay declared. 'And I reject them as scurrilous scandal until the full facts are known. What proof does de Craon have for his assertions?'

'Quite considerable,' Edward intervened. 'On the day the assault was launched on Philip, a soldier, wearing the Templar livery, was seen fleeing from the Bois de Boulogne. Secondly, Templars are in London and in Paris. Thirdly, the Templars know the rites of the Assassins: the dagger, the red silk, the sesame seedcake and the three-fold message. Fourthly,' Edward straightened in his chair and pointed a finger at de Molay. 'You know, Monseigneur, how there are many in your Order, perhaps even seated round this table, who believe that the Temple was driven out of the Holy Land due, or so they claim, to a lack of support from the kingdoms in the West. Finally,' Edward looked up at the ceiling. 'Yes, finally, and I will say this. Thirty years ago the Assassins tried to kill me. They failed and I brained the man responsible with a stool. Very few people know about that attack. Most of the lords who were with me at the time are now dead, but the Templars knew.'

'And are there other matters?' de Molay asked wearily.

Corbett, ignoring the rancour his words had caused, continued in a matter-of-fact tone.

'Since the reign of the king's father, the Templars have owned the manor of Framlingham on the Botham Bar road, outside York. Usually it is left in the care of bailiffs and stewards. However, over the last two weeks, since the arrival of your good selves in York, petitions have come in about strange happenings: fires are seen glowing at night in the woods. Certain rooms and passageways are strictly forbidden . . .'

'This is nonsense!' Branquier interrupted. 'We are a religious Order. We have our own rituals. Sir Hugh, the Templars are an enclosed community: we would not let any jack-in-the-puddle know what we are doing, no more than the king or yourself allow the common sort to wander through the Chancery rooms at Westminster or the Treasury chamber of the Tower.'

'There are other matters,' Corbett continued. 'Sir Richard Branquier, you showed us a gold coin, certainly not from the Royal Mints. Now, with all due respect, these gold coins appeared during the last month: the very time you and your companions took up residence at Framlingham Manor.'

The Templar commanders objected vociferously, beating their fists on the table, shouting denials at what Corbett had said. De Molay remained impassive, gently clapping his hands, exercising that iron discipline for which the Temple was so famous.

'You'd best finish, Sir Hugh,' he declared resignedly. 'What else are we held responsible for? Surely not the strange death on Botham Bar road?'

Corbett smiled thinly. 'Now you mention it, Monseigneur; two good sisters, Cecilia and Marcia, accompanied by their guide Thurston, came before the mayor and aldermen of this city and swore that, as they approached York, a horse, bearing the lower half of a man's body, charged wildly by them. Further along the trackway, they discovered a corpse being eerily burnt to death by a fire for which they could see no source.'

'Yes, we heard that,' Baddlesmere declared. 'The story is all over York. The man's body was burnt beyond recognition.'

'Not exactly,' Sir Hugh interrupted. 'Only the top half of the man's corpse was burning, the bottom part of his torso and legs . . .' He shrugged. 'Well, you have heard the story.

What is strange is no one knows who he was, why he was attacked, the identity of the killer, or where the strange fire came from.'

'I object.' Branquier spoke up, turning to de Molay. 'Monseigneur, we have been brought here and our generosity has been exploited. We have always served the Crown of England well and have just agreed to the bestowal of a most generous gift. Now the king's senior clerk, his Keeper of the Secret Seal, stands in our presence and whispers the most scandalous allegations.'

De Molay placed his elbows on the table, steepling his fingers. 'No, no.' De Molay shook his head. 'You are not saying that, are you, Sir Hugh? You do not really believe the Templars are guilty of such horrid acts?'

'No, Monseigneur, we do not.' Corbett stared bleakly at Branquier. 'But remember, sirs; first, we have not gossiped behind your backs but bluntly informed you about what others have whispered to us. Secondly, there is a remarkable coincidence between your arrival here and those strange happenings. Thirdly, and most importantly, the Templars are a kingdom in themselves. You have houses which stretch from the borders of Scotland to the toe of Italy. From Rouen in the West to the borders of the Slavs. Now gold coins, burning corpses . . .' Corbett shrugged. 'These matters can be dealt with, but treason against our lord the king is another matter. You can use your knowledge and power to acquire information. You listen to the rumours of courts.'

'In other words,' de Molay intervened, 'you would like us to search out why the Assassins have decided now to reawaken old grievances against your king?'

'Exactly,' Corbett replied. 'We do not intend to threaten you.' He turned and bowed to Edward. 'The king has already agreed to the confirmation of your rights and privileges. We simply seek your help in this matter. We would be grateful for what you discover.'

'And it does not affect what we have agreed?' the king asked.

'No,' de Molay replied. 'It does not.'

The king heaved a sigh. 'Then in the abbey church tomorrow, I will take the oath.'

After that the meeting broke up. De Molay and his commanders bowed and took their leave. Edward, de Warrenne and Corbett sat in the refectory, listening to the mailed footsteps of the Templars fade in the distance. The king grinned slyly at Corbett.

'I got what I wanted, did I not?'

'And so did the Templars, my lord. Your oath will be a public statement of support for them.'

'It was a pity,' Edward pushed back his chair, 'that you had to lay such allegations before them.'

Corbett smiled as he began to clear his writing tray from the desk.

'My lord, you have been threatened. These are matters which could be laid at the Templars' door. By raising them, you are warning the Templars that, perhaps, their Order does not enjoy the support it once did.'

'Do you think there is any truth in the Assassins' threat?' De Warrenne asked.

'The knives were found,' Corbett exclaimed. 'Thirty years ago His Grace was attacked by the same sect. We also have the warnings brought by Monsieur de Craon.' He shrugged. 'But it's all too vague.'

'In other words,' Edward declared, getting to his feet and stretching till his muscles cracked, 'not serious enough to hold you here at York, eh, Hugh? So you can scuttle off, back to your manor at Leighton, to the lovely Lady Maeve and Baby Eleanor.'

'It has been three months, Sire. You did promise I would be released from your service at Candlemas, some seven weeks ago.'

Edward glanced down at him. 'Affairs of state, Sir Hugh.' The king held up his long, scar-studded fingers. 'We have a council in York and the French envoy is here. We have the marriage negotiations for my son. There's the business of the counterfeit coins and the matter of the Templars.' He gripped Corbett's shoulder. 'I need you here, Hugh.'

'And my lady wife needs me at home.' Corbett retorted. 'You gave your word, Sire. You, Edward of England, whose motto is, "My word is my troth".'

The king shrugged. 'Well, sometimes it is . . .' He picked up his cloak from the back of the chair and swung it round his shoulders. '. . . and sometimes it isn't.'

'We'd all like to go home to our wives and families,' de Warrenne exclaimed, glaring like an angry boar at Corbett. Deep in his heart the earl could never understand why the king tolerated this clerk's bluntness. Corbett bit his tongue. He felt like reminding the earl that if he was married to Lady de Warrenne, he'd spend as much time as he could as far away as possible from her. He looked at the king.

'So, when can I leave, Sire?'

Edward pursed his lips. 'By mid-April. I promise you, by the feast of Alphage, you will be released. But, meanwhile,' Edward strode to the door, snapping his fingers for de Warrenne to follow, 'I want that counterfeiter unmasked. I want you to keep an eye on the Templars. There are also over a hundred petitions from our good burgesses at York. You and that green-eyed rapscallion clerk of yours, Ranulf, can deal with them.' The king paused, one hand on the latch. 'Oh, and to show there's no ill-feeling between myself and the grand master; go to the vintner, the master taverner Hubert Seagrave. He owns the largest tavern in York, just off Coppergate. Ask him for a tun of his best Gascony. Tomorrow, after I have sworn the oath, take it out to Framlingham. A gift from me to him.'

Corbett turned in his chair. 'And will you go on Crusade, Sire?'

Edward looked innocently back. 'Of course, Hugh. I have given my word. Once all the affairs in England are settled, then you and I, de Warrenne and all the rest, will go on Crusade to Jerusalem.'

And, chuckling softly to himself, the king swept out of the chamber, de Warrenne plodding behind him. Corbett sighed and got to his feet. He stared round the refectory, the huge, black cross hanging on the far wall and the brightly coloured triptych above the fireplace. He went back to the window and stared down into the courtyard. The king's soldiers had persuaded two blind beggars to have a duel with wooden swords. The two hairy, ragged men lurched and struck at each other, staggering about, their wooden swords beating the air. Now and again the circle of soldiers pushed them back into the ring with roars of laughter.

'Didn't you have enough?' Corbett whispered to himself. 'Didn't you see enough humiliation and bloodshed on the Scottish march?'

He sat in the window-seat. Since the end of January the king had been in his northern shires, launching raids across the Scottish border, trying to bring to battle or capture the elusive Scottish leader William Wallace. Corbett had become sickened by the hamlets and villages left as a black, smouldering mess, the corpses strewn about in pools of scarlet across the damp, broken heather. The columns of grey smoke, the stench of death and putrefaction, the gibbets full of corpses naked as worms. Cattle and sheep slaughtered, their bloated bodies fouling streams and wells, all consumed by the sea of fire which Edward, in retreat, had lit to burn everything behind him.

Corbett didn't just want to go back to Maeve and Eleanor because he was missing them; he was also sickened by Edward's ruthless drive to bring the Scots to heel; and by the intricacies and subtleties of court intrigues; by nobles like de Warrenne who believed they were lords of the soil and every other man and woman had been born to serve them. The two beggar-men were now crying. Corbett was tempted to ignore them but, rising, he thrust open the window.

'Stop it!' He yelled.

One of the soldiers was about to make an obscene gesture back, but his companion immediately recognised Corbett and whispered in the soldier's ear. Corbett called over to a serjeant.

'Take the beggars to the almoner!' He shouted. 'Give them bread and wine and send them on their way!'

The grizzled veteran nodded. 'The lads are just amusing themselves, sir.'

'There has been amusement enough!' Corbett snapped. 'Make sure your lads pay for their enjoyment. Organise a collection for the beggars!'

Corbett waited for the serjeant to carry out his orders then closed the window. He heard a rap on the door.

'Come in.'

Ranulf, his manservant, now a fully fledged clerk in the Chancery of the Green Seal, swaggered in, his red hair tied in a knot behind his head. Proud of his clerkly tunic of light blue edged with squirrel fur, Ranulf stuck his thumbs in the broad swordbelt fastened round his waist. His cat-like eyes twinkled in a smile.

'Are we going home, Master?'

'No!' Corbett snapped, 'we are not.' And he went back to the table.

Ranulf quickly made a face at the blond-haired, bland-faced Maltote, Corbett's messenger.

'Good,' he whispered.

Corbett whirled round. 'What holds you at York, Ranulf?'

'Oh, nothing, Master.'

Corbett studied him carefully. 'Do you ever tell the truth, Ranulf?'

'Every time I open my mouth, Master.'

'And you have no lady-love here? No burgess's buxom wife?'

'Of course not, Master.'

Corbett turned back to his writing tray. Ranulf pulled a face behind him and quietly thanked God that Corbett hadn't questioned him about the burgess's buxom daughters.

'So, we are staying?'

'Yes,' Corbett wearily replied. 'We'll take lodgings in St Mary's Abbey. Meanwhile, we have work to do. You have the petitions?'

Maltote hurried across, carrying a thick roll of vellum. 'This is what the clerks have received.'

Corbett gestured at his servants to sit on either side of the table.

'We'll work for two more hours,' he declared.

As Corbett reopened his writing case, Ranulf looked across at Maltote and raised his eyes heavenwards. 'Master Long Face', as Ranulf had secretly nicknamed Corbett, was not in the best of humours. Nevertheless, both men helped as Corbett began to work through the roll of vellum containing all the petitions the council had received, once the good burgesses of York knew the king was visiting their city. Every town had the right to petition the Crown, and Edward took such matters most seriously. The Chancery clerks would collect individual petitions, write them out again in a fair hand on sheets of parchment which were then sewn together. One of Corbett's functions, whenever he was at Court, was to deal with such requests. This collection of petitions covered a multitude of affairs: Francesca Ingoldsby complained against Elizabeth Raddle for assaulting and beating her with a broomstick on a pavement in the presence of their neighbours. Matthew Belle complained against Thomas Cooke for assault and striking him in the face with a poker at the Green Mantle tavern. Thomasina Wheel sought a licence to go beyond the seas to St James's Shrine at Compostella. Mary Verdell alleged she'd lost a cloak and believed Elizabeth Fryer was the culprit. John de Bartonon and Beatrice his wife complained against the vicar of their church who constantly trespassed upon their property. On and on the petitions went. Corbett ordered some of them to be sent to the city council, others to the sheriff, or the mayor; a few he kept for the king's consideration. One, in particular, he did scrutinise: it was from Hubert Seagrave, 'king's vintner in his own city of York', seeking permission to buy two messuages of land adjoining his tavern.

Corbett smiled across at Ranulf. 'We can deal with this one ourselves,' he muttered. 'I am to collect a tun of wine from Seagrave and take it to the Templars at Framlingham.'

Ranulf, busily writing down his master's decisions, just mumbled a reply. Corbett returned to the roll, noticing how a growing number of petitions from individual citizens, as well as some from the commonality of York, complained about the strange and mysterious events happening at the Templar manor at Framlingham. One man, John de Huyten, complained of lights burning late in the manor house, with hymns being sung at the dead of night. A batch of further petitions complained about how, since the Templar commanders had arrived at Framlingham, the gardens and estates of the manor were very closely guarded, and ancient rights of way across the Templar estates were now closed. A petitioner, Leofric Goodman, carpenter, declared how he had been ejected from Framlingham. He had been hired to work in the manor: he had gone upstairs to repair a shutter on a window but a Templar soldier had accosted him and driven him away with threatening and violent language.

Corbett put his pen down and went out to stand by the window. Daylight was fading: already lamps and torches had been lit, and even Ranulf was muttering that the light was too poor to read by. Corbett tried to marshal his thoughts. He wished to return to Maeve but there was a deep feeling of unease, a sense of growing menace: the warnings against the king in London, the daggers left pinned in the doors of St Paul's; that strange, macabre murder on the road outside York. Who had been that unfortunate rider? Who had cut his body in two then mysteriously burnt the top half? Why was Jacques de Molay in England? And what did the Templars have to hide? Outside in the priory grounds, an owl hooted, proclaiming its coming hunt through the night. Corbett recalled an old soldier he had known in his fighting days along the Welsh march.

'When the owl hoots before dusk,' the man had warned, 'the devil is about to walk!'

Chapter 2

At the manor of Framlingham, Guido Reverchien, Keeper of the Templar Estates in Yorkshire, was making his daily, lonely pilgrimage along the pebbledashed path of the great maze. Guido made this pilgrimage, as usual, on his hands and knees, chanting the Divine Office of the Church in atonement for his sins. Guido, now in his sixtieth year, his hair and beard white, his skin almost burnt black by the sun, still believed he carried a great burden of sin. He had been a Templar knight, a warrior of Christ: one of those who had defended the walls of Acre in 1291 until the Mameluke hordes had swept across its walls and turned that Templar city into a sea of blood. Guido had escaped: shoulder to shoulder with his comrades, he had fought his way down from the quayside to one of the few remaining boats waiting to take him and other refugees out to the Christian fleet. Oh, Guido had fought! At times the narrow, dusty streets of Acre became ankle-deep in blood: yet, still, the city had fallen and he, Guido Reverchien, had been saved. Ever since that terrible night, Guido had suffered nightmares. Every minute of his sleep seemed to be trapped in the destruction of Acre.

As the years passed, Guido had reached the conclusion that he should have died in Acre. He should have fought on until the enemies of Christ had killed him and so given others the opportunity to escape.

'Instead,' Guido had whispered to his father-confessor, 'I came back to England. I was given a comfortable benefice supervising the granaries, granges, fields and meadows of the

31

Templar Order. Father, I am a traitor to Christ, I failed God. I must go back and be saved.' Time and again his father-confessor had advised him that this was out of the question.

'You are needed in England,' he whispered back from behind the lattice screen. 'You have your duties here.'

But Guido would not be comforted until his father-confessor had mentioned the maze. This lay to the side of the Templar manor: a great sea of high, cruel, privet hedge with narrow paths leading to its centre, where a huge wooden cross stood bearing the image of the crucified Christ.

'You cannot go to Jerusalem,' Father-confessor had confided. 'But, Sir Guido, if you must atone for your sin; if you seek to do reparation; every day, just before dawn, go on your knees through the maze chanting the psalms.'

Now Guido did that. The pebbles dug deep into his knees but Guido saw this as his path to heaven as he shuffled along, the battered, wooden rosary beads slipping through his gnarled fingers. He knew the maze like the back of his hand. Every secret corner, each blind path. Sometimes Guido would deliberately take the wrong turnings intensifying his pain, feeling a release from his self-inflicted tortures. At last he reached the centre. His knees were now bloodied, the pain in his shoulders and arms intense. The sweat ran like water down his face.

'I am in Jerusalem,' he whispered, staring up at the cross. 'I have kept faith!' He crawled on his hands and knees to the stone base of the crucifix and looked up at the stricken face of his Saviour. 'Domine,' he murmured, striking his breast. 'I have sinned before heaven and before Thee!'

Guido took a tinder from his pouch and lit the three squat yellow candles which stood in their iron spigots on the steps before the cross. He moved his knees away from the pools which had formed amongst the pebbles and watched the flames of the candle flicker in the dawn breeze. He stared up at the crucifix.

'Just like Acre,' he whispered. 'A grey dawn, flames flickering.'

Guido narrowed his eyes; even the smell of that damned burning city seemed to haunt him. The candle flame grew stronger, suddenly there was fire all around him. Guido opened his mouth to scream just as a sheet of flame engulfed his body.

Edward of England was entering York with banners and pennants flying. Heralds walked in front of the long procession which wound its way under Micklegate Bar. Behind the king trundled a long train of carts and pack animals, lines of pike men and archers marching on either side. The city had been busy as an upturned beehive, because only at the last minute had the royal heralds proclaimed through which gate the king would come. Now all of York had turned out to greet him: the burgesses in their fur robes and ermine-lined cowls; their wives and daughters, clothed in the most costly sarcanet and samite dresses, their brows plucked, their lustrous hair covered by the most ornate head-dresses and veils. Parish priests in colourful chasubles had brought their parishioners as well as stoups of holy water and asperges rods to bless the king as he passed. The city council had done its best. The streets and sewers had been cleaned, the sore-ridden beggars driven away, the stocks emptied and the gibbets and their iron cages taken down. The Guilds of Corpus Christi and Trinity were well represented under their great many-coloured banners.

The mayor and his aldermen had met the king outside Micklegate Bar and handed him the keys of the city on a purple cushion. They'd widened the king's smile even more with purses full of gold and silver coins. Edward had expressed his thanks, accepting their protestations of loyalty and thrust the purses into de Warrenne's hand.

'Keep your eye on them,' he whispered. 'I don't want a penny to go amiss.'

Just within Micklegate Bar, they stopped and listened as a

choir of boys in white surplices sung a three-voiced hymn welcoming the king, praising his rule and extolling his victories. Then the royal progress had continued into the city itself, along the narrow streets, past the great houses with their beams painted a polished black, the plaster between gleaming a brilliant white in the morning sun. Despite the city ordinances, all the colourful underworld of York was also present. The whores and prostitutes in their low-cut gowns and orange and red wigs eyed the soldiers and tried to catch the eye of the mounted knights and sergeants-at-arms. The masterless and penniless alley folk were also there, sheltering in the shadows away from the sunlight, ready to flee at the approach of any city bailiff. The cripples, the song-chanters, the cut-throats, the foists and pickpockets had gathered around looking for easy prey. The stalls had been put away and the merchants and their apprentices, each in the colour of their guild, stood gawping, eager to catch a glimpse of their great king.

Edward did look the image of the Conquering Prince: a gold circlet round his iron-grey hair, his coat of chainmail, which Corbett had insisted he wear, covered by a golden samite surcoat. Edward rode his great destrier, Black Bayard, and its saddle and harness were of dark purple leather edged with silver. The king rode easily, one hand holding the reins, the other bearing a magnificent snowy-white hawk from Paris. Beside him, John de Warrenne, Earl of Surrey, dressed in half-armour, carried the king's personal banner, a golden lion rampant on a field of blood. Corbett rode just behind the king, restless and worried: his eyes constantly surveyed the crowds and the open windows on either side of the procession. Now and again he would feel the hilt of his dagger and glance anxiously sideways at Ranulf. His manservant, however, was more interested in smiling and blowing kisses at the wives and daughters of the burgesses. Every so often the procession would pause and the gloriously garbed heralds blew a silver fanfare before advancing further into the city, behind the fluttering banners bearing the arms of England, Scotland, Wales, France and Castille.

At the corner of Trinity, the king paused to watch a pageant. A scene from the Last Judgement; a massive tapestry from the Corpus Christi Guild, had been hung between two long poles on a frame mounted across three great carts. In garish colours the tapestry depicted the fate of sinners: legislators who had made bad laws were dressed in burning cloaks of sulphur, whilst corrupt lawyers were impaled and broken on the wheel. Edward chuckled at another scene depicting a group of monks, their pates shaven, being led by a monkey-faced demon to a boiling hot pit filled with venomous serpents. In front of this makeshift stage were groups of young women, all dressed in white, with green chaplets on their heads, singing a sweet carol welcoming the king. Edward listened attentively whilst stroking the hawk on his wrist. He then threw silver coins in front of the cart, kissed one of the young girls, and ordered the procession to continue. Corbett glared as Ranulf tried to imitate the king's example, reaching out to seize one of the young maids by the arm.

They had just turned into Trinity when Corbett heard the whistle of the crossbow bolt flying by his head, between him and the King. One of the men-at-arms, walking alongside, dropped his spear and collapsed screaming and gurgling on the blood spurting out of his mouth. Corbett raised himself in the stirrups and yelled at the men-of-arms who ran forward: under Corbett's and de Warrenne's instructions, these circled the king, raising their shields to form a wall of iron around him. Corbett glanced quickly at the houses on either side.

'There!' Ranulf yelled.

Corbett followed his direction to the top-storey window of a tavern on the corner of an alleyway. He saw the casement and wooden shutter being pushed open again, a cowled figure lurking there and the thick snout of a crossbow. Again there was a whirr like a hawk falling to the kill, but this time the bolt smashed against one of the upraised shields.

'Follow me!' Corbett urged.

He dismounted, drew his sword and, with Ranulf and Maltote following behind, forced his way through the crowd, ignoring the chaos breaking out around them. They reached the shadows of the houses. Corbett looked up and cursed. He had lost his way. Then he saw the corner of the alleyway: a hooded beggar squatted there, hands extended. Corbett knocked him aside as he ran towards the entrance under a garish tavern sign swinging from its jutting pole. Yelling at Ranulf to go down the alleyway and guard the back entrance, Corbett entered the narrow, dark hallway. The people gathered there had no idea what was going on. Most of them were tapsters, scullions and maids. Corbett ordered them out of the way and ran up the narrow, shaky, wooden stairs. By now he was covered in sweat and had to grip the sword more tightly: he desperately wondered what he would do if he met the assailant. He tried to recall the window.

'It's at the top,' he muttered to himself, and gingerly climbed the next flight of stairs. He was half-way up when he saw the smoke seeping out from under a doorway in a recess at the top of the stairs. He turned round.

'Maltote!' he ordered, 'go back! Tell the taverner his house is on fire!'

Corbett, pinching his nostrils, tried the garret door. It was locked. He stepped back and kicked it open. Smoke curled and twisted, though most of this was pouring out of the open window. There was a chair just under the sill on which an arbalest lay, a collection of bolts beside it. On the floor next to this sprawled the corpse of a man blackened and burning. For a while Corbett could only stare, horrified by the eerie blue and yellow flames which danced over the blackening corpse.

'God save us!' Maltote muttered, coming up behind him. 'Master, what kind of fire is that?'

Coughing and spluttering, Corbett broke from his reverie. He wrenched off a heavy curtain, tattered and holed, which hung on the back of the door and, urging Maltote to help, threw it over the burning corpse, dousing the flames. Others came up: the landlord and his helpers carrying pails of water. They threw these over the blanket and around the rest of the room. Corbett, however, noticed that, apart from some scorching, the fire had not caught either the walls or floorboards. At last the fire was doused. Nothing to show except the stench, scorch-marks, and a horrid sizzling as the water seeped through the curtain covering the corpse.

'Clear the room!' Corbett urged. 'Maltote, get them all out!'

The landlord, a pot-bellied, balding fellow, began to protest as Ranulf burst into the room.

'I saw no one!' He gasped. 'No one at all! What happened here?'

'Clear the room!' Corbett shouted. 'You, sir –' he pointed at the taverner – 'wait for me below!'

Maltote and Ranulf shoved them from the room. Corbett pulled back the heavy curtain then gagged at the terrible stench. Maltote turned away to vomit on a pile of straw in the corner; Ranulf coolly squatted down beside the remains.

'How did this happen?' he asked, pointing to the crossbow and bolts on the stool.

'I don't know,' Corbett replied. 'Here we have a man full of life and malice. He takes a crossbow, shoots two bolts in an attempt to kill the king and then, a few minutes later, is a burning cadaver. He is consumed by a strange fire which does not spread to the walls or floorboards.'

'It would have done,' Ranulf retorted. 'Eventually, the wood would have smouldered and then burst into flames. Our arrival here stopped it. The question is, who is he; and how did he die?'

Corbett forced himself to examine the corpse. The face and upper torso were all burnt. The eyes had turned to water. Any hair on scalp and face was now flakes of ash. Corbett swallowed hard.

'Look.' He pulled the blanket further down. 'The top half of the body has been terribly burnt.' He pointed to the hose and boots the man wore. 'Yet these are only scorched.'

Corbett eased himself up and went across to the bed. A battered leather saddlebag lay pushed just under the dirt-stained bolster. Corbett pulled this out, cut the straps and emptied the contents on to the woollen coverlet: a Welsh stabbing dagger; a purse full of silver coins, and the soiled white surcoat of the Templar Order with its red cross on either side.

'A wealthy man, at least for a soldier,' Corbett observed.

He opened the neck of the purse and shook the coins into his hands. He put the silver on the bed and unrolled the scraps of parchment he'd also found. One was a very crude diagram which Corbett immediately recognised as a rough map of the road leading from Micklegate Bar up through Trinity. The other was a list of provisions bought by one Walter Murston, serjeant of the Templar manor at Framlingham. Corbett sat down on the bed.

'Ranulf, put everything back into the saddlebag. For God's sake,' he waved at the blackened remains, 'cover that. Here we have,' he continued, 'Walter Murston, a member of the Templar Order, who tried to commit treason and regicide. He fired two bolts at our king but then, in a matter of minutes, is consumed by a mysterious fire.'

'God's punishment,' Maltote intoned.

'If that was the case,' Ranulf jibed, 'most of York would burst into flames.'

Corbett got up and stared out of the window. The royal cavalcade was now on its way. The crowd was staring up at the tavern. A curtain of men-at-arms, shields locked together, lances out, now ringed the tavern. On the stairs outside there was a heavy footfall and a deep voice cursing every taverner as 'fatherless, misbegotten spawns of Satan'. Corbett grinned.

'My lord of Surrey is about to arrive,' he murmured.

The chamber door crashed back on its leather hinges.

'Poxy knaves! Ingrate bastards!' de Warrenne shouted, his red face covered in sweat. He lumbered into the room like an old bear. 'Well, Corbett, you bloody clerk! What do we have here?' The earl pulled back the ragged coverlet and stared down at the corpse. 'Fairies' tits! Who's he?'

'Apparently a serjeant, probably an arbalester of the Temple Order,' Corbett replied. 'He came into this chamber with his crossbow and tried to slay our king.'

'And who killed him?'

'We were just debating that, my lord. Maltote thinks it was God, but Ranulf believes that if every sinner in York was to be so punished, the whole city would be a sea of fire.'

De Warrenne hawked and, going back to the door, bawled down the stairs. A group of royal archers came up.

'Take that out!' de Warrenne ordered. 'I want it dragged to the Pavement in York and hung from the highest gibbet!'

The archers neatly stripped the bed and wrapped the corpse in soiled sheets. De Warrenne looked out of the corner of his eye at Corbett. 'Oh, and get some bloody lazy clerk to write out a notice: SO DIE ALL TRAITORS. Fix it around the bastard's neck!'

De Warrenne hustled the archers and their grisly burden out of the room, slamming the door behind them. 'And the bastard's name?'

'Walter Murston.'

'The king will want an answer to all this.' De Warrenne snapped. 'I don't trust those bloody fighting monks!' He came over and kicked the ash away with his boot, spurs jingling on the wooden floor. He stared through the window. 'I am frightened, Corbett.' He whispered. 'I am terrified. I was with the king thirty years ago when the Assassins tried to kill him. A man pretending to be a messenger.' The old earl narrowed his eyes, breathing heavily through flared nostrils. 'He got so close, so quickly. The king was quick. He brained him with a stool. Now they are hunting him again.' He gripped Corbett's arm; the clerk stared unflinchingly back. 'For God's sake, Hugh, don't let them do it!' De Warrenne glanced away. 'We are all dying,' he murmured. 'All the king's old friends.'

'Tell His Grace,' Corbett replied, 'that he will be safe. Say that I will join him at the abbey of St Mary's.'

De Warrenne stomped across the room.

'Oh, my lord Earl?'

'Yes, Corbett.'

'Tell the king I will not return to Leighton Manor.' He forced a smile. 'At least, not until this present business is finished.'

He paused and listened as de Warrenne stamped down the stairs, hurling abuse at everyone in the tavern below. Ranulf and Maltote were standing in the corner watching open-mouthed.

'What's the matter, Ranulf?' Corbett asked. 'If you don't close your mouth, you'll catch a fly.'

'I've never heard de Warrenne call you Hugh,' Ranulf replied. 'He must be very frightened . . .'

'He is. The Assassins' boast is never hollow.' Corbett closed the window. 'But let's leave. This place stinks. Ranulf, bring that saddlebag.'

'Who are the Assassins?' Maltote asked.

'I'll tell you later. What I want to know is why a member of the Templar Order is carrying out their instructions!'

They walked back down the stairs and into the taproom, a low, dank chamber, its ceiling timbers blackened by a thousand fires. At the far end, near the scullery door, sat the landlord surrounded by his slatterns; he was gulping wine as if his life depended on it. He took one look at Corbett's face and slumped to his knees, clasping his hands before him.

'Oh, Lord have mercy on me!' He wailed, staring piteously, though Corbett's grim face did nothing to ease his panic. He almost grovelled at the clerk's feet. 'Master, believe me, we had nothing to do with it!'

Ranulf drew his sword and brought the flat of its blade down on the man's shoulder. 'If you had,' Corbett's red-haired servant taunted, 'within a week you'll hang, then you'll be quartered and your pickled limbs dangled above Micklegate Bar.'

The landlord grasped Corbett's cloak. 'Master,' he groaned, 'mercy!'

Corbett knocked away Ranulf's sword and pushed the man back on to his stool.

'Get your master a cup of the best wine. The same for me and my companions,' he ordered one of the slatterns. 'Now, listen sir,' Corbett pulled a stool up and sat close, his knees touching the landlord's. 'You have nothing to fear,' he continued, 'if you tell the truth.'

The landlord could hardly stop shaking. Ranulf's sword was one thing, but this soft-spoken clerk was absolutely terrifying. For a while he could only splutter.

'You are in no danger,' Corbett reassured him. 'You can't be held responsible for everyone in your tavern.' He took the wine a servitor had brought and thrust it into the man's hand. Corbett sipped from his own then put it down: the wine was good but the sight of a fat fly floating near the rim turned his stomach. 'Now, who was the man?'

'I don't know. He came here last night. A traveller. He gave his name as Walter Murston. He paid well for the garret: two silver coins. He ate his supper and that's the last I saw of him.'

'Didn't he come down to break his fast?'

'No, we were busy preparing for the king's entry to York.' The landlord groaned and put his face in his hands. 'We were going to have a holiday. One minute we are by the doorway cheering the banners and listening to the trumpets, the next...' The man's hands flailed helplessly.

'And no one else was with him?' Corbett insisted. 'No one came to visit him?'

'No, Master, but there again the tavern has two entrances:

41

front and back. People come and go, especially on a day like this.' The man's voice trailed away.

Corbett closed his eyes and sat, recalling how he had struggled through the crowds. He had knocked that beggar aside as Ranulf had gone down the alleyway. Corbett opened his eyes.

'Wait there,' he ordered, and went out of the tavern.

'What are you looking for?' Ranulf hurried up behind him.

Corbett walked to the mouth of the alleyway and stared down. It was a narrow, evil-smelling tunnel between the houses, full of refuse and wandering cats. Two children were trying to ride an old sow which was lumbering amongst the litter, but there was no sign of the beggar.

'Master?' Ranulf asked.

Corbett walked back into the taproom.

'Master taverner, in London, and I suppose York is the same, beggars have their favourite haunts: certain corners or the porch of some church. Does a beggar-man stand on the corner of the alleyway, on the other side of your tavern?'

The landlord shook his head. 'No, Master, no beggar would stand there. It's well away from the stalls, and the alleyway really goes nowhere.' He smiled in a display of red, sore gums. 'After all, my customers are not the sort to part with a penny.'

'In which case, Master taverner, go back to your beer barrels. You have nothing to fear.'

Corbett beckoned at Ranulf and Maltote to follow and they walked back into Trinity Lane.

'Sir.' A serjeant of the royal household came up, one hand on the hilt of his sword, the other cradling his helmet. 'The Earl of Surrey told us to stay here until you were finished.'

'Take your men, Captain,' Corbett ordered. 'Rejoin the king at the abbey. Tell my lord of Surrey I will be with him soon. Our horses?'

The soldier raised his hand and an archer came forward, leading their three mounts.

'You'll have to walk them,' the soldier observed. 'The streets are now packed.'

Once they had left Trinity, Corbett was forced to agree. Now the royal procession had swept on, Micklegate was thronged. The stalls had been brought out and it was business as usual: traders, hawkers and journeymen trying to earn a penny in the holiday atmosphere of the city. Corbett walked his horse, Ranulf and Maltote trailing behind: they made slow progress. Outside St Martin's church, a troupe of players had erected a makeshift stage on two carts and were depicting, to the crowd's delight, a play about Cain and Abel. As Corbett passed, God, a figure dressed in a white sheet with a gold halo strapped to the back of his head, was busily marking Cain with a red cross. If only it was so easy, Corbett reflected: if the mark of Cain appeared on the forehead of every assassin or would-be murderer.

'Do you think that Templar acted by himself?' Ranulf asked, coming up beside him.

'No,' Corbett replied. 'How long, Ranulf, did it take us to leave the king's side and reach that garret room?'

Ranulf paused as a group of children ran by, chasing a wooden hoop; a mongrel followed, the corpse of a scrawny chicken in its mouth, hotly pursued by an irate housewife, screaming at the top of her voice.

'They talk strangely here,' Ranulf declared. 'Faster, more clipped than in London.'

'But the girls are just as pretty,' Corbett replied. 'I asked you a question, Ranulf; how long do you think it took us?'

'About the space of ten Aves.'

Corbett remembered pushing through the crowds, losing his way, then entering the tavern and going up the stairs.

'You think there were two, don't you?' Ranulf asked.

'Yes, I do. The door to the room was locked, probably by the crossbowman's accomplice as he left. I noticed the key was missing.'

'So it was the beggar you went looking for?'

'Perhaps, though that doesn't explain it,' Corbett continued. 'Murston must have fired those two bolts. Yet how could a professional soldier be killed in such a short time, offering no resistance? And then his body be consumed so quickly by that terrible fire?'

'The other person could have killed him,' Ranulf replied, 'then ran downstairs and pretended to be the beggar you knocked aside.'

'That's only conjecture,' Corbett replied.

He gripped his horse's reins more tightly as they entered the approaches to the bridge across the Ouse. The bridge was broad; stalls had been set up alongside the high wooden rails where traders could offer fish 'Freshly plucked', so they shouted, 'from the river below.' Corbett stopped, told Ranulf to hold the horses, and went to look through a gap between the palings. To his right, he could see the great donjon of York Castle then, turning to his left, he glimpsed the towering spires of York Minster and St Mary's Abbey.

'What shall I tell the king?' he murmured to himself, ignoring the curious looks of passers-by. He looked down at the river swirling past the starlings of the bridge, and the fragile craft of the fishermen bobbing there. These rowed against the tide, struggling to hold their nets, whilst avoiding the mounds of refuse which swirled about, trapped by the great pillars of the bridge. Corbett couldn't make sense of the Templar's death: a fighting man, so expertly reduced to burning ash! He walked back towards Ranulf and, as he did so, a little beggar boy ran up, a penny in one hand, a piece of parchment in the other. He chattered to Corbett. The clerk smiled and squatted down.

'What is it, boy?'

The smile on the urchin's thin face widened. He thrust the dirty piece of parchment into Corbett's hand. The clerk unfurled it and the boy ran away. As he read it, despite the bustling crowds and the warm sunlight, Corbett's blood ran cold.

KNOWEST THOU, THAT WHAT THOU POSSESSES SHALL ESCAPE THEE IN THE END AND RETURN TO US, the message read. KNOWEST THOU, THAT WE GO FORTH AND RETURN AS BEFORE AND BY NO MEANS CAN YOU HINDER US.

KNOWEST THOU, THAT WE HOLD YOU AND WILL KEEP THEE UNTIL THE ACCOUNT BE CLOSED.

Corbett studied the scrawl on the parchment: the sequence of the verses was slightly changed but the threat was just as real. He glanced up: the boy was gone, impossible to follow. Somewhere in the crowds the Assassin had been watching them, tracking their every footstep. The dead Templar had not been alone, he had merely been a pawn – and the game was only just beginning.

Chapter 3

Edward of England sprawled in the great wooden bath in the private chamber of the archbishop's palace. The tub's surroundings had been covered by a purple buckram cloth, filled by a troop of servants carrying buckets of scalding water, then sweetened by rose-hips and other herbs. The king sat with his arms out on either side, allowing his body to float in the sweet-smelling, soapy water. He glared over the rim at Corbett who was sitting next to de Warrenne. The clerk was trying to keep his face straight: not that Edward lost any of his royal dignity in taking a bath, the clerk was more amused by the pretensions of the archbishop, the owner of this tub, whose coat of arms, not to mention a few crosses, were painted on the bath.

'Do you think it's amusing?' Edward snarled. 'I have just been promised a loan of fifty thousand pounds sterling by the Templars. I have taken their bloody oath to go on Crusade: now you say the bastards are trying to kill me!'

'It wasn't a loan,' Corbett retorted, 'it was a gift. If you go on Crusade, Your Grace, then with all due respect, that tub will sing the Te Deum.'

Edward rose to his feet, shaking himself like a dog. He stepped out of the bath; de Warrenne placed a woollen cloth round his shoulders.

'I enjoyed that,' Edward declared. 'I wish I didn't have to wait until mid-summer for the next.' He padded over to Corbett, shaking the water from his hair. 'You bathe once a week, don't you?'

'An Arab physician, a student of Salerno, said it would do me no harm.'

'It makes you soft!' Edward grumbled.

The king went across to a small table, filled three gold-encrusted goblets with wine and brought them back, thrusting one each into de Warrenne's and Corbett's hands.

'So, this Templar loosed two arrows at me then burst into flames?'

'Apparently, my lord, though there must have been someone else there,' Corbett replied. 'The same person followed me through York and delivered that warning message.'

'But why should the Templars want me dead?' Edward asked. And does this attack have anything in common with that poor bastard those two nuns found burning on the road outside York?' He breathed in deeply. 'You still look fresh, Corbett. I want you to go out to Framlingham.' He slipped a ring from his finger and dropped it into Corbett's hand. 'Show that to de Molay. He'll recognise it.'

Corbett looked at the amethyst sparkling on the gold ring.

'The Templars gave it to my father,' Edward explained. 'I want it back, till then it's your authority to act. You are to investigate, Corbett! Use that long nose and sharp brain, ferret out the assassin and, when you do, I'll kill him!'

'Is that all, my Lord?'

'What more do you want?' Edward sneered. 'The archbishop's tub to sing the "Te Deum" for you? Oh,' he called out as Corbett rose, bowed and made his way to the door, 'I want you to stay at Framlingham until this business is finished. However, to show my friendship to the grand master, take that tun of wine I promised.'

There was a rap on the door and it was abruptly pushed open, almost knocking Corbett over. Amaury de Craon, Philip IV's envoy to the English council, stalked into the room all afluster. He scarcely seemed aware of de Warrenne, but immediately sank to one knee before the king.

'Your Grace,' he murmured. 'I heard about the attack on you.' He raised his red-bearded, foxy face. 'On behalf of my own master I give thanks to God for your safe deliverance. I pray that your enemy will soon be brought to destruction.'

'As he will be. As he will be.'

Edward stretched his hand out for the French envoy to kiss. De Craon did so, then rose to his feet.

'Our dear and well-beloved clerk, Sir Hugh Corbett, Keeper of our Secret Seal,' the king continued, 'will search out the truth.'

'As I have done on other occasions,' Corbett added, closing the door and leaning against it.

De Craon turned. 'Sir Hugh, God save you!' And, going over, he grasped the English clerk by the arms and kissed him, Judas-like, on his cheek. 'You look well, Sir Hugh!'

Corbett stared at his inveterate enemy: Philip's spy-master and the source of all his intrigues. He admired the Frenchman's ostentatious dress: the damask tunic, edged at the neck and cuffs with gold; the hem over shiny red leather boots, studded with miniature gems.

'And you, Sir Amaury, have not changed.'

De Craon smiled, though, keeping his back to the king, his eyes betrayed a deep antipathy for this English clerk he'd love to kill.

'Congratulate me, Sir Hugh. I am married and my wife is already with child.'

'Then you are twice blessed, Sir Amaury.'

'But I did not come to share pleasantries.' De Craon turned. 'Nor even to rejoice in His Grace's narrow escape.'

'Then what?' Corbett snapped.

'Warnings from my master,' de Craon continued. 'You heard of a similar attack on him whilst hunting in the Bois de Boulogne?'

'Continue,' Edward said softly.

'The culprit was found,' de Craon explained. 'A Templar, a

high-ranking serjeant from their fortress in Paris. My master's agents arrested him. He made a full confession after a short sojourn in the dungeon of the Louvre.'

'And?' Corbett asked.

'Apparently there are high-ranking Templars who view their expulsion from the Holy Land as the fault of the Western kings, the Holy Roman Emperor, even the Pope himself; more especially, Philip of France and Edward of England.'

Corbett walked across. 'And so you bring warnings?'

'Yes, Sir Hugh, I bring warnings. England and France are about to sign a great treaty of peace. It will be cemented by a royal marriage between the two houses. Both our countries have had their differences. However, this is a common danger which threatens us both and could shatter that peace.'

'And what else did this serjeant confess?' Edward asked.

De Craon plucked a parchment from his sleeve and thrust it at Corbett. 'See for yourself!'

Corbett unrolled the parchment and read it; as he did so, he realised that his suspicions about de Craon were, on this occasion, apparently unfounded.

'What does it say?' the king asked, sitting down on a bench.

Corbett studied the manuscript, taking it over to a window for better light. 'It's a confession,' Corbett explained. 'By a serjeant based in the Temple at Paris. He admits to trying to kill Philip in the Bois de Boulogne. Apparently, the serjeant was carrying out the orders of a high ranking officer known only to him as "Sagittarius" or "The Archer".'

'And Philip's torturers wrung this out of him?' Edward asked.

'No,' Corbett looked up, 'not the royal torturers.' He saw de Craon's smile of satisfaction. 'No less a person than the grand inquisitor.'

'And you know,' de Craon intervened, 'the Holy Inquisition is a law unto itself.'

'Apparently,' Corbett continued, studying the manuscript

carefully, 'certain artefacts were found in the Templar's possession: a pentangle, a picture of an inverted cross, and other tools of the black magician.' He glanced up. 'Which is why the Inquisition took the matter over. The serjeant maintained that he and other Templars were part of a warlock's coven, participating in Satanic practices, the worship of demons and a disembodied head.'

Corbett glanced at the bottom of the paper. He studied the blood-red seal of the Holy Inquisition as well as the personal signature of the master grand inquisitor and his two witnesses.

'So,' Edward leaned forward, 'this is a serious threat.'

De Craon nodded tersely. 'My master has already written to Pope Boniface the Eighth demanding the order be investigated.' He rose and sank to one knee before the king. 'But I shall inform my master about your safe deliverance. And,' he added slyly, glancing out of the corner of his eye at Corbett, 'your sacred vow to go on Crusade.'

'In which,' Corbett intervened, 'my master will call on other Western princes to join him.'

De Craon got to his feet and bowed at Corbett. 'You shall not find Philip of France lacking. He is ready to spill his blood, as his grandfather did, to win back God's fief.' And, making further obeisances, de Craon left the room as swiftly as he had arrived.

'It must have been hard,' Corbett declared, going over to make sure the door was closed. 'For de Craon, once in his life, to tell the truth.'

'Go to Framlingham,' Edward declared. 'Take up residence there. Tell their grand master that if any Templar is found outside the grounds of that manor, he will be arrested on suspicion of high treason!'

Ranulf and Maltote complained bitterly at being pulled away from their game of dice with the royal archers. Their wails grew even louder as Corbett told them where they were going.

'Stop moaning,' their master ordered. 'First, it's only a matter of time before the archers realise you cheat. Secondly, Ranulf, a period of abstinence from chasing the ladies will do your soul the world of good.'

As they later rode through the streets of York, Corbett did not bother to look, though he knew Ranulf was scowling behind him and muttering under his breath about 'Master Long Face' and his killjoy actions. Maltote was more resigned. As long as he was with horses and able to know what the great lords of the soil were planting, he was content. So, he let Ranulf mutter on whilst trying to manage a vicious sumpter pony who deeply resented being plucked from a comfortable stable and taken through the noisy, dusty streets of York.

Ranulf, who had got to know the city well, eventually pushed his horse alongside Corbett's.

'Master, surely we should be going in the other direction? Framlingham lies beyond Botham Bar to the north of the city.'

Corbett paused just before they entered the Shambles, York's great meat-market.

'We have business, Ranulf, with Master Hubert Seagrave, King's vintner and proud owner of the Greenmantle tavern in Coppergate. We are to take the grand master a present.'

Corbett stared down the narrow streets ahead of him. He saw the blood and offal which coated the cobbles in a bloody mess; from the stalls on either side of the street hung the gutted carcasses of sheep, lambs and pigs. He pulled his horse's head round.

'Let's find another way.'

As he turned, an arrow bolt whirred by his face, smashing into the plaster wall of the house alongside. Corbett stared open-mouthed: Ranulf seized the reins of his horse, pulling it into a gallop down a narrow alleyway leading into Coppergate. Tradesmen, apprentices, beggars, children, scavenging dogs and cats fled before the pounding hooves. The more quick-witted picked up fistfuls of refuse and threw it at these three riders, for Maltote had quickly followed suit. Once in Coppergate, Corbett reined in.

'Who fired that?' he demanded.

Ranulf wiped the sweat from his face. 'God knows, but I don't intend to go back and find out.'

Corbett hurriedly dismounted, ordering Ranulf and Maltote to do the same.

'Keep the horses on the outside!' he urged.

They walked down Coppergate. A trader ran up, protesting at their feckless ride. Ranulf drew his sword, shouting that they were on the king's business, so the fellow backed away.

'What was it, a warning?' Ranulf asked.

'I don't think so,' Corbett replied. 'If I had not turned, that arrow would have found its mark.'

'Shall we go back?' Maltote asked. 'Perhaps—'

'Don't be stupid!' Ranulf snarled. He gestured at the houses on either side. 'Windows, doors, alleyways, nooks and crannies; you could hide an army in York.'

Corbett walked on. He just wished his stomach would stop heaving. The narrowness of his escape made him feel light-headed, and the sweat coating his body was turning cold. He tried to distract himself by looking at the crowds on either side, the different colours, the shouts and cries, but he was afraid. He felt like drawing his sword and dashing into the crowd. He also found he could not stop thinking about Maeve and his baby daughter Eleanor. They will be cleaning the rooms, he thought, now spring was here; Maeve will turn the house inside out. Oh God! he thought. Would she be doing that when the messenger came riding up the manor path? Would she run down to meet him? How would she take the message sent by the king that his trusted and well-beloved clerk, her husband, was dead, killed by some assassin in York? He heard, as if from far off, his name being called.

'Master? Sir Hugh?'

Corbett stopped and glanced at Ranulf.

'What is it?' Corbett rasped. His throat and lips were bone dry.

'Do you know where we are going?' Ranulf asked quietly, alarmed by Corbett's pallid face.

'I made a mistake, Ranulf,' Corbett confessed. 'I am sorry. We should have left York.'

'Nonsense.' Ranulf leaned over and gripped his master's hand, ice-cold to the touch. 'We are going to the Greenmantle tavern,' Ranulf said quietly. 'We'll collect the tun of wine, Master, and go on to Framlingham. We'll tell those Templar bastards they cannot leave the place: then you'll ask your questions. You'll sit and you'll brood like you always do. And, before Ascension Day has arrived, you'll have dispatched another felon to his well-deserved fate. Now, come on,' Ranulf urged. 'Cheer up. After all, I am leaving Lucia.'

'Lucia?' Corbett asked.

'Master, she's the most beautiful girl in York.' Ranulf walked on. 'She has hair as black as midnight, skin like white silk and eyes,' he pointed to the sky between the overhanging houses, 'bluer than that.' He looked over his shoulder at Maltote. 'And she has a sister. Indeed,' Ranulf chattered on, 'the two of them remind me of a story I heard about the bishop of Lincoln who had to take refuge in farmhouse at the dead of night . . .'

Soothed by Ranulf's chatter, Corbett found himself relaxing. They paused at the corner of Hosier Lane where Ranulf hired a young lad who led them down into the courtyard of Master Seagrave's tavern.

The Greenmantle was a spacious, four-storeyed mansion with wings built on either side, standing in its own grounds off Newgate. The courtyard at the front was bounded by a curtain wall: the tavern was really a small village in itself, with outhouses, smithies, stables, a small tannery, and workshops for coopers and carpenters. Its owner, Hubert Seagrave, came out to greet them. He was dressed like a merchant rather than a landlord, in pure woollen robes. A straw hat was perched on his balding head against the heat of the day. He swaggered across the courtyard, swinging his cane.

'Just like a bishop in his palace,' Ranulf whispered.

Seagrave was apparently used to meeting royal officials, but his harsh face and gimlet eyes became more servile when Corbett introduced himself.

'I am sorry, sir, I did not realise,' he stammered. 'Usually servants from the royal household come . . .'

'The king wants a tun of your best wine, Master Seagrave,' Corbett remarked casually. 'And I mean your best. It's his gift to the Templar grand master.'

Seagrave's face became worried.

'What's the matter?' Corbett asked. 'Are you out of wine?'

Seagrave plucked Corbett's sleeve, pulling him closer as if they were fellow conspirators.

'No, no,' the vintner whispered. 'But the rumours have swept the city, of strange doings at Framlingham as well as the attack on the king this morning.'

Corbett gently detached his arm. 'Aye, tell a taverner,' he said. 'And you have told the world. But you shouldn't listen to every bit of tittle-tattle.'

Seagrave agreed. 'I have a cask,' he declared, 'from the best year in Gascony. Ten years it has been in my cellar. I hoped to give it to the king. My servants will pull it out but, come, you wish some refreshment?'

'In a while, Master Seagrave, there is another matter: the two messuages of land you wish to purchase.'

Seagrave became even more servile, rubbing his hands together as if he sensed a profit. He insisted on taking Corbett, a cynical Ranulf and an awe-struck Maltote, on a tour of his domain: the stores and smithies in the courtyard, the deep cellars where Seagrave pointed out the tun of wine he had selected. He then took them up through sweet-smelling rooms where the scent of fresh rushes mingled with the cooking smells from the kitchen, and out into the pleasant garden beyond. This was bounded on all four sides by a high bricked wall covered by creepers and lichen. The garden itself was divided into small patches where, Seagrave explained, the tavern grew its own herbs and vegetables for the kitchen.

Ranulf impatiently asked about the two messuages, so Seagrave led them over to a small postern gate. Corbett paused just before this and stared at the sheet which covered a great yawning hole near the wall.

'You are building again, Master Seagrave?'

'Aye. We intend to build arbours, small drinking places screened against the wind, where select customers can sit and eat during the pleasant days of summer.'

Corbett nodded and stared round. The garden was beautiful; a small dovecote stood at the far end with beehives on either side. He closed his eyes, smelt the fragrance of the flowers, and listened to the gentle hum of the hunting bees.

'A pleasant place, eh, Sir Hugh?'

'Aye, it makes me homesick.' Corbett opened his eyes: Ranulf was still looking at him curiously. 'But come, Master Seagrave, let me see the land you wish to buy.'

The taverner opened the gate and led him through. The area beyond was nothing more than a common where wild grass and brambles grew, a broad triangle of land stretching between the tavern and the back of houses on either side.

'Who owns this?' Corbett asked.

'Well, at first I thought the city but, on examination of the deeds, I discovered it was granted to the Order of the Templars. They own many such plots throughout the city.'

'Ah!' Corbett sighed. 'And, of course, such sales can only be made with the permission of the king.'

Seagrave drew his bushy brows together. 'Of course, Sir Hugh. No land granted to a religious Order can be resold without royal permission.'

They returned to the tavern. Corbett gathered from Ranulf's

hungry look that they should accept Seagrave's offer of refreshments, so they stayed for a while sharing a dish of lampreys and succulent chicken slices. Seagrave himself served them a white wine specially chilled in his cellars. After they had eaten, the taverner's ostlers fastened the small tun of wine on to the sumpter pony and they made their farewells. They went up Colney Gate through Lock Lane, up Petergate and under the yawning, cavernous mouth of Botham Bar. Corbett rode ahead. Ranulf and Maltote felt better after eating what they described as the best meal they'd been served since arriving at York.

The afternoon was now drawing on, and Corbett wondered how he would manage his meeting with the Templars.

'Do you think they'll know?' he called out over his shoulder.

'What, Master?'

'Do you think the Templars have heard about the attack on the king?'

'God knows, Master.'

Ranulf pulled a face at Maltote. Despite all the banter on their journey to Framlingham, Ranulf was anxious. Corbett was determined to leave the royal service and go back to Leighton Manor. The recent attack would only strengthen his resolve. But what, Ranulf wondered, would happen to him? Leighton could be beautiful, particularly in summer. However, as he had often told Maltote, one sheep tends to look like another, whilst trees and hedgerows do not contain the same excitement as the crooked alleyways of London. He now began to discuss this with Maltote, as the houses and small cottages gave way to green open fields and they entered the open countryside which Ranulf disliked so much. He watched Corbett tense in the saddle and Ranulf himself grew uneasy as the trackway narrowed. Thick hedgerows rose high on either side, and the trees leaned so close that their branches entwined to form a canopy over their heads. Now and again a wood-pigeon's liquid cooing would be offset by the raucous cawing of hunting rooks. Ranulf tried to ignore these, listening for any sound, any movement which could presage danger. He relaxed as the hedgerows gave way and the road became broader. Corbett, however, would stop now and again, muttering to himself. He would look down at the trackway and then ride on.

'For the love of God, Master!' Ranulf shouted. 'What's so exciting about stones and mud?'

Corbett reined in. 'The severed, burning corpse,' he remarked, 'was found near here.' He dismounted, ignoring Ranulf's protests. 'That's right.' He pointed to the trackway. 'There, just before the corner near the small copse of trees: that's where the good sisters found the remains.'

'Are you sure?' Ranulf asked.

'Yes, their guide said they were approaching a bend in the road. The horse came pounding round and passed them. When they turned the corner, they found the corpse, or part of it, burning like a torch.' He remounted and grinned at Ranulf. 'Let's see if my memory fails me. The good sisters did say that, within half an hour of leaving the spot, they reached Botham Bar. We have travelled the same distance.'

In the end Corbett was proved right. They rode on into the small copse of trees. Corbett stared into the darkness, then down at the pebble-covered soil, and pointed to the great scorch-mark.

'Why are you so interested in this murder?' Ranulf asked.

Corbett dismounted, crouched down, and ran the scorched earth through his fingers.

'Here we have a traveller to York. We don't know who he was, where he was going or what he was doing on this lonely road. But, apparently, he was attacked by a master swordsman.'

'How do you know that?' Ranulf asked.

'Only a professional soldier, someone capable of using a great two-handed sword could slice a man through his waist: the horse careered off, leaving the decapitated upper part of the torso to be consumed by a mysterious fire. And where did that come from, eh?'

'The Templars?' Ranulf interrupted. 'They carry two-handed swords.'

Corbett smiled. 'Now you understand my interest. So, stay where you are.' Corbett drew his sword. 'Right, Ranulf, you are the victim and I am your assailant.' He grasped his sword hilt with two hands, ran forward and gently smacked the flat of the blade against Ranulf's stomach.

'Is that how it was done, Master?'

Corbett resheathed his sword. 'Possibly. But why should the victim ride on to the sword? Why didn't he turn his horse and flee?'

'It was night,' Ranulf remarked.

Corbett shook his head. 'It doesn't make sense. Why cut a man in half then burn the upper part of his body? And, if you are the victim, some innocent traveller, why not flee?'

'How do we know he was innocent?' Ranulf asked.

'Well, no other weapon was found.' Corbett stared back along the trackway. 'So there was little resistance.'

'Was the victim going to or from York?' Ranulf asked.

Corbett shook his head. 'According to what I have seen, not one petition has come in asking about the whereabouts of any citizen, nor has anyone been reported missing.'

'What makes you think,' Maltote asked, 'that the assailant was a Templar knight?'

Corbett patted his horse's neck. 'That's what I like, Maltote. Good, searching questions. I think it was a knight,' he continued. 'As I've said, for a man to cut through another man's body requires terrible force as well as skill. You must think, Maltote, of this murderer running towards his victim, sword in hand, then he brings it back, like a farmer's scythe, and cuts straight through the middle just above the crotch. Now only a trained knight, an experienced warrior, could swing a sword with such position and force. I have seen it done in Scotland and Wales. Such skill only comes after years of experience in war.'

'But why a Templar?' Maltote insisted.

'Because of their skill and their proximity to Framlingham. Also, as far as I know, the only other knights capable of such a blow were with the king.'

'So, the murder on this lonely trackway, and the death of the assassin in the city are linked?' Ranulf asked.

'Yes, both men were killed and their bodies burnt. But why, and by whom, is a mystery.'

'What happens if the victim was a Templar?' Maltote asked, now preening himself at Corbett's praise.

'Possible,' Corbett replied. 'And that could explain why no one has come forward to claim the remains, as well as why the whereabouts of the horse and the rest of the poor victim's body remain a mystery. But,' he added slowly, 'somehow I think he wasn't a Templar.' He shrugged. 'But there again I have no proof.' Corbett stared down at the scorch-mark then into the green darkness of the trees. 'We will see,' he murmured and, mounting his horse, they continued on their journey.

For a while they jogged along in silence, Corbett assessing in his mind the sea of troubles mounting against him. Who was the victim on the lonely trackway? Why was he killed, then his body set alight? Why didn't anyone recognise the corpse? Why had that Templar serjeant tried to kill the king and, in turn, been consumed by a mysterious fire? Was the Templar Order so rotten with intrigue and greed? Was there some dark coven plotting the destruction of princes through murder and black magic? Who was Sagittarius? Corbett closed his eyes, letting his horse find its head. Then there was this business of the coins: who had the means to issue good gold coins? Where had the precious metal come from? How was it distributed? Was that, too, linked to the Templars? Had they discovered the secret of alchemy, of transmuting base metals into gold? Corbett opened his eyes. And what could he do at Framlingham? He carried the king's ring in his pouch and the royal authority in his wallet, but how would the Templars react? They could scarcely reject him but, there again, there was no guarantee that they would cooperate. Corbett found his mind whirling round and round like a little dog turning a kitchen spit. So engrossed was he in the problem, he was startled to find himself on the trackway leading down to the gates of Framlingham Manor. As soon as he and his companions approached the heavy, iron-studded gates, Corbett knew there was something wrong. The small watch-tower above the gates were manned and a troop of crossbowmen stood on guard, resplendent in their white livery and great red crosses.

'Stay where you are!' a voice rang out.

Corbett reined in, lifting his hand in a gesture of peace. A Templar soldier walked forward, his face almost hidden by the chainmail coif and heavy helmet with broad noseguard. Questions were asked. Only when Corbett produced the king's ring and warrants were the gates opened and he was allowed on his way. Two of the soldiers went before him, up the shady path which wound between the trees. Now and again Corbett could hear the bracken on either side of him crackle, and the barking of a dog nearby. Ranulf pushed his horse alongside.

'What's happening?' he whispered. 'The gates are fortified. Templar soldiers with war dogs are in the trees.'

'Is anything wrong?' Corbett called out.

One of the soldiers stopped and came back. 'Haven't you heard?' the Templar asked. 'Sir Guido, the keeper of the manor, was killed early this morning. He died at the centre of the maze, consumed by fire.'

'Fire?' Corbett asked.

'Aye. Whether from heaven or hell we don't know. The grand master and all the commanders are now in council.'

He led Corbett on, they turned a corner and entered the great, grassy area which stretched in front of Framlingham Manor. This was a large, four-storeyed building, as huge as any merchant's, greatly extended, with two wings coming out on either side. It was shaped in the form of a horseshoe: a rich, palatial residence. The bottom storey was built of stone, the upper storeys consisted of black beams, the plaster between painted a dull gold. The roof was tiled with red slate. The windows were filled with glass gleaming in the afternoon sunlight. Nevertheless, the silence and sense of oppression made itself felt. The serjeant took them round the manor into the stableyard: the grooms and ostlers looked frightened. They scurried forward as if desperate for something to do to break the tension. Corbett told Ranulf and Maltote to guard the sumpter pony and followed the serjeant in through a back door along wainscoted passages.

The knight whom Sheikh Al-Jebal had called the 'Unknown' slipped from the saddle of his horse outside the Lazar hospital near the church of St Peter-Le-Willows just inside Walmer Gate Bar. For a while the Unknown rested against his horse, one hand on the high saddle-horn, the other on the hilt of his great two-handed sword which hung from it.

'I am dying,' the Unknown whispered.

The terrible sickness raging within him had manifested itself in more great open sores. He had tried to hide these behind the cowled cloak which shrouded him from head to toe, the gauntlets on his hand and the black band of cloth which covered the lower half of his face. The old war horse which he'd bought at Southampton snickered and whinnied, its head drooping in exhaustion.

'We are both finished,' the Unknown murmured. 'God be my witness, I can go no further.'

He had spent days journeying around York, then out through Botham bar towards Framlingham Manor. He had seen the Templar commanders and their seigneur, Jacques de Molay, as he'd sat hidden in the shadow of the trees. The sight of their surcoats, flapping banners and pennants had tugged at his heart and brought tears to his fading eyes. Since his release, the Unknown had found his thirst for vengeance had faded. Before he died, he wanted to make peace with his brothers and with

God. Death was very close. For years, in the dungeons of the Old Man of the Mountain, the Unknown had evaded death, but now, out in God's sunlight, back in a country where church bells tolled across lush green meadows, what was the use of vengeance? God had already intervened . . .

'Can I help?'

The Unknown turned, his hand dropping to the dagger thrust in his belt. The kindly face of the aged friar didn't flinch as the Unknown dragged down the black, silk mask over his face.

'You are a leper,' the brother whispered. 'You want help?'

The Unknown nodded and stared into those gentle, rheumy eyes. He opened his scarred mouth to speak, his horse jerked and the Unknown grew dizzy; the friar was hazy, the walls of the lazar hospital behind him seemed to recede. He closed his eyes, sighed, then crumpled into a heap at the friar's feet.

Chapter 4

At Framlingham, the Templar serjeant led Corbett up the dark mahogany staircase and along a bare, hollow-sounding gallery. Crosses and shields bearing the escutcheons of different knights hung on the walls, interspersed by the stuffed heads of wolves and stags which stared glassily down at him. Only a window at the far end lit the gallery and gave it an eerie atmosphere, where light and darkness mixed so mysteriously. On corners and in doorways, men-at-arms stood on guard, silent as statues. They went up another short flight of stairs and into the council chamber. Oval-shaped, the walls were bare apart from two great banners bearing the Templar insignia. There was no fireplace, just an open stone hearth with a flue high in the roof; it was a bleak, awesome room, bereft of furniture and carpets, the windows mere arrow-slits. It smelt strangely of sizzled fat, which curdled Corbett's stomach and brought back memories of the burning villages in Scotland. The Templar commanders, sitting in heavy carved choir-stalls formed in the shape of a horseshoe, fell silent as he entered. De Molay, in the centre, waved Corbett forward to a stall on his immediate right. The clerk made his way past a table which bore a corpse covered by a sarcenet, gold-edged pall and ringed by purple wax candles. A ghastly sight, the source of the sour smell, made rather pathetic by the dirty boots peeping out from beneath the cloth.

'We thought you'd come, Sir Hugh.' De Molay gestured at the table. 'We are holding a coroner's court according to the rule of our Order. The keeper of the manor here, Sir Guido

Reverchien, was mysteriously killed this morning, burnt alive in the centre of the maze.'

Corbett glanced round at the Templar commanders; they looked alike with their stony, sunburn faces. Not one of them made a gesture of welcome.

'Every morning, just before dawn,' de Molay continued, 'whatever the weather, Sir Guido did his own private pilgrimage to the centre of the maze. Over the years he'd come to know it so well, he could find his way in the dark, chanting psalms and carrying his beads.'

Corbett looked down at the burial pall. He'd heard about the construction of such mazes, so those who were unable to perform their vow to go on pilgrimages or Crusade, could make reparation by following the tortuous path of a carefully contrived maze to a cross or statue of Christ in the centre.

'How could a man meet such a death in the centre of a maze?' Corbett asked.

'That is why we are assembled,' Legrave explained. 'Apparently Sir Guido reached the centre. He had lit the candles at the foot of the cross when this mysterious fire engulfed him.'

'And no one else was present?' Corbett asked.

'Nobody,' Legrave replied. 'Very few people knew the mysteries of that maze. His old friend Odo Cressingham, our archivist, used to stand on guard at the entrance. No one had gone into the maze before Sir Guido, and no one followed him. Odo was sitting on a turf seat, as he did every morning: Sir Guido's knees and legs would be sore by the time he left the maze and he always required help to go back to the refectory. Odo said it was a beautiful morning; the sky was lighting up when he heard Sir Guido's terrible screams. Standing on the turf seat, Odo could see a heavy pall of smoke rising from the centre. He raised the alarm. By the time he and some serjeants reached the centre, this was what they found.' Legrave got up and lifted back the pall.

Corbett took one look and turned away. Reverchien's body had been reduced to a cinder. From the frizzled scalp to those pathetic boots, the fire had burnt away all features and reduced flesh, fat and muscle to a cindery ash. If it hadn't been for the shape of the head and the holes where the eyes, nose and mouth had been, Corbett would have thought the corpse was a blackened log.

'Cover it!' de Molay ordered. 'Our brother Guido has gone. His soul is in Christ's hands. We must decide how he died.'

'Shouldn't the corpse be handed over to the city coroner?' Corbett asked.

'We have our rights,' Branquier snapped. 'Approved by the Crown.'

Corbett wiped his lips on the back of his hands.

'And why are you here?' the treasurer continued harshly.

'Let's be courteous to our guest,' William Symmes intervened.

Sitting next to Corbett, he smiled across the choir-stall, but then the clerk started as a small, furry bundle leapt from Symmes's lap into his. Corbett's consternation eased the tension. Symmes sprang to his feet apologising, and deftly plucked the little weasel from Corbett's lap.

'It's my pet,' Symmes explained.

Corbett peered over the stall at the weasel's small, russet body, its white pointed features, twitching nose and the unblinking stare of those little black eyes. Symmes cradled it as if it was a baby, stroking it gently.

'He's always like this,' Symmes explained. 'Curious but friendly.'

De Molay rapped his fingers on the side of the stall and all eyes turned to him.

'You are here, aren't you, Sir Hugh, because of recent happenings in the city? The attack on the king!'

'Aye, by a serjeant of your Order, Walter Murston.' Corbett ignored the indrawn hiss of breath. 'According to the evidence,

Murston fired two crossbow bolts at the king as the royal procession was moving up Trinity.'

'And?'

'By the time I reached the tavern garret where Murston was lurking, he, too, had been killed by a mysterious fire which consumed the top half of his body.'

'How do you know it was Murston?' Legrave asked.

'We found his saddlebag, Templar's surcoat and a list of provisions in his name. I am sure,' Corbett added, 'that if you search, you will find the serjeant gone and your armoury lacking an arbalest.' The clerk stared across at Branquier. 'And you will not be sitting in judgement on his corpse. Sir John de Warrenne, Earl Marshall of England, has ordered it to be gibbeted on the Pavement in York.'

De Molay leaned back in his choir-stall. Corbett saw how his saintly, ascetic face had now turned an ashen grey. Dark rings under the grand master's eyes showed he had slept very little, and betrayed the anxieties seething within him. You know, don't you, Corbett thought; you know there's something rotten here. Something festering within your Order.

De Molay drew his breath in. 'Murston was one of my men,' he explained. 'A member of my retinue. He was of Gascon birth and belonged to the French chapter of our Order.'

'Why should he try to kill our king?' Corbett asked.

De Molay tapped the side of his head. 'Murston served in Outremer: the heat there can boil a man's brain. He was a good serjeant but his wits were slightly addled.'

'The same could be said of many in York, but they do not try to commit treason and regicide.'

'There are those in our Order,' Legrave spoke up, 'who claim the Western princes' lack of support cost Christendom the city of Acre. The Templar Order lost many good knights at Acre, not to mention treasure, as well as their foothold in the Holy Land. If Acre had been relieved . . .' Legrave wrinkled his brow. 'If Edward of England had done more,' he continued, 'perhaps that tragedy would never have occurred.'

'But that was twelve years ago!' Corbett exclaimed.

'Some wounds fester,' Baddlesmere snapped. 'Others heal quickly. Murston was one of those who felt betrayed.'

'In which case,' Corbett continued, 'there are others, aren't there? Somebody else was with him.'

'What proof do you have of that?' Symmes shouted.

'I simply don't believe that fire consumes every would-be murderer, even if their intended victim is a crowned king.'

'But you have no proof,' Legrave said.

'No, I don't. But I do possess proof that, as I came through York earlier today, I received the Assassins' warning as well. A message thrust into my hand. Someone scrawled it out then paid a beggar to give it to me. A short while later,' Corbett continued, 'a crossbow bolt narrowly missed my head. This was not imagination, I have all the proof I need.' Corbett held up his hand bearing the king's ring.

'I see it,' de Molay remarked softly. 'You act for the king in this matter?'

'So, let's not sit here engaging in tittle-tattle,' Corbett said. 'Some days ago, a grisly murder occurred on the road outside York near Botham Bar. A man's body was cut into two, the top half consumed by fire. Only a trained knight, with a two-handed sword, could have performed such a terrible feat.' He glanced at de Molay. 'You have recently all come from France, Grand Master.'

De Molay nodded, running his fingers through his beard.

'We attended a grand chapter there,' Branquier explained.

'Aye, and shortly afterwards,' Corbett replied, 'a Templar serjeant tried to kill Philip of France.'

'Rumour,' Branquier scoffed. 'More of your tittle-tattle, Master Clerk.'

'You will hear the truth soon enough,' Corbett replied. 'We have news from France. This Templar serjeant has been captured and handed over to the Inquisition. He confessed that there's a coven within your Order of high-ranking knights who dabble in black magic and wage a secret war against God's anointed princes.'

Corbett's words created an uproar. Legrave and Symmes sprang to their feet. The latter still stroked his pet weasel, so lovingly that Corbett idly wondered if it could be his familiar, but he dismissed the thought as both unfair and superstitious.

Richard Branquier put his face in his hands: he glared through his fingers at Corbett with such intense hatred that the clerk wished he had brought Ranulf and Maltote with him. Old Baddlesmere just sat shaking his head. Only when de Molay brought his high-heeled boots crashing down to the floor and shouted for silence, did the knights resume their seats.

'We heard about this attack,' he announced. 'Sooner or later the Temple in Paris will send us the truth of these matters, though Edward of England's own emissary would never lie. What else do you know, Sir Hugh?'

'The French Templar confessed that members of this coven are led by a high-ranking officer who calls himself Sagittarius, or the Bowman.' Corbett turned and jabbed a finger at de Molay. 'You, Sire, know there is something wrong. It's written on your face: that's why your soldiers now patrol the grounds and heavily armed men stand guard in the galleries outside. What do you fear?'

'Nothing but superstition,' de Molay snapped back, 'of course.' He shrugged. 'There are Templars who are bitter at what happened at Acre and elsewhere, just as there are English barons who do not want peace with France.'

'Is that why you acceded so quickly to the king's demand for money?' Corbett asked. 'Are you trying to buy his protection?'

This time Corbett knew he had hit his mark. There were no dramatic outbursts or cries of disapproval.

De Molay smiled faintly. 'Sir Hugh,' he replied. 'Templars are fighting monks. All of us here are warrior-priests. We came into this order for one purpose, and one purpose only: to defend

Jerusalem and the Holy Places. To protect Christ's fief from the infidel. Now look at us ... Merchants, bankers, farmers. Of course, we hear the rising tide of protest. They call us idle, time-wasters! But what can we do? Men like Guido Reverchien, Murston, myself; all the knights in this room who would love to give our lives on the walls of Jerusalem and spill our blood so the likes of you can kneel and kiss the ground in the Holy Sepulchre. It is politic,' he added slowly, 'for us to seek out friends in high places, whether it be Philip of France or Edward of England.'

'We are the king's loyal subjects.' Legrave's boyish face looked even more youthful.

'Then you can prove it,' Corbett replied. 'Where were you all, today, between the hours of ten o'clock and two o'clock, the time of the attacks on both the king and myself?'

'Why single us out?' Baddlesmere snapped. 'We are not the only Templars.'

'You were in France and Philip was attacked. Murston was from Framlingham Manor. He carried a purse of silver, far too much for a common serjeant. Above all, the murderous attack outside Botham Bar was, I believe, carried out by a knight. More importantly, the only people who knew which street the king would use in going to the archbishop's palace were me, John de Warrenne and yourselves.'

'Nonsense!' Baddlesmere exclaimed.

Corbett shook his head. 'No, sir, the only time that route was mentioned was when you were present in the priory yesterday afternoon. I deliberately arranged it so that the king could take four, even five routes through the city. The decision to go up Trinity was reached just before the king met you. It was announced publicly only very shortly before the king entered York, yet Murston was in that tavern from the night before.'

The Templars now looked frightened. Baddlesmere shuffled his feet, Branquier fingered his lips, Legrave stared in outrage at Jacques de Molay, whilst Symmes sat, head bowed, stroking and muttering under his breath to his pet weasel.

'If what you say is true,' de Molay remarked, 'the traitor must be in this room.'

'You are forgetting one thing, Master Clerk,' Branquier pointed down to the corpse covered by the pall. 'Guido Reverchien was killed this morning just before dawn. Concedo, there is a link between the death of the stranger outside Botham Bar, that of Murston, and the mysterious death of Guido Reverchien. However, you cannot prove any person here was present on the road outside Botham Bar or with Murston. On the other hand, we can prove, every man in this room, that when Sir Guido Reverchien died we were lodged at St Leonard's Priory.' He saw the surprise on Corbett's face. 'Didn't you know that, Clerk? We stayed there overnight. We arrived back here, shortly before you did, to discover the tragedy.'

'And, before you ask,' de Molay intervened, 'this morning we were in the city. We had business there with our bankers.'

'Together?' Corbett asked, trying to conceal his confusion.

De Molay shrugged. 'Of course not. Legrave came with me, my colleagues went hither and thither. There was business to be done.'

'So, any one of you,' Corbett asked, 'could have been with Murston? Or written that message or loosed a crossbow bolt at me?'

'Sir Hugh,' de Molay almost shouted, raising his voice over the cries of protest, 'you have no proof of these matters!'

'I returned here just after noon,' Branquier protested, 'to speak to Brother Odo our archivist.'

'And the rest?' Corbett asked.

Different replies were given; clearly all the Templars had been back at Framlingham shortly before Corbett's arrival.

'We heard about Guido's death,' Branquier explained. 'We deemed it mysterious. The gates were locked, the guards doubled and this court held.'

'You may well be innocent,' Corbett replied, 'but I act on

orders from my king: no Templar may leave the grounds of Framlingham Manor until this matter is resolved. None of you is to enter the city of York.'

'Agreed,' de Molay answered quickly. 'And I suppose you and your companions are to be our guests?'

'Until these matters are resolved,' Corbett replied. 'Yes, we are.'

'In which case Ralph,' de Molay gestured at Legrave, 'will show you to our guesthouse.'

Corbett pointed to the corpse. 'And your companion's death?'

De Molay pulled a face and got to his feet. 'Either an act of God or . . .'

'Murder,' Corbett added.

'Yes, Sir Hugh, murder. In which case we can use your skills. After Legrave has shown you your chambers, you are free to go into the maze. A rope has been laid, as a guide, from the centre to the entrance. Use that and you'll not get lost!'

Corbett followed Legrave to the door.

'Sir Hugh!' De Molay came forward. 'Tomorrow morning, the brothers will sing a Requiem Mass for Sir Guido. You are most welcome to attend. As for the rest, you are an honoured guest. However, we ask you to observe the courtesies. We are a monastic Order; certain parts of this building are our enclosure: outsiders are not permitted to enter.'

Corbett nodded and followed Legrave out into the corridor and back to the hallway where Ranulf and Maltote were sitting in a small recess just inside the front door. Legrave took them all out across the gravel path to the bottom floor of the east wing.

'They are just cells,' Legrave explained. He opened one door. 'Sir Hugh, your servants can share this.'

He then pushed open another chamber door and ushered Corbett into a large, cavernous cell with a single arrow-slit window. The walls were lime-washed. A large crucifix hung above the trestle bed; at the foot of this stood a large, leather chest with an iron-bound coffer on the table beside it. Beneath the window was a writing table and a throne-like chair, its back and arms intricately carved.

'You may join us in the refectory for meals,' Legrave told him. He looked over his shoulder at Maltote and Ranulf who were still standing in the corridor. He closed the door and leaned against it, his eyes crinkled into a smile.

'Sir Hugh, do not take offence at the reception given. Our Order is in turmoil. We are like a ship without a rudder, blown this way and that by different winds. The Holy Land is lost. The Infidels squat in our sacred places and what are we supposed to do now? Many of our companions left family, home and hearth to become Templars. This is their family, yet all they can see is their beloved Order being plundered by princes.'

'There is still no excuse for murder or treason,' Corbett retorted.

'No, no, there isn't, but that, Sir Hugh, is still to be proved. Anyway, you'll hear the bells ring for supper.' And with that Legrave slipped quietly out of the room.

Ranulf and Maltote entered, carrying Corbett's saddlebags.

'The horses are stabled,' Maltote said. 'Including that vicious brute of a sumpter pony: it gave the stable boys all the devil's bother.'

'What do you think, Master?' Ranulf asked, placing Corbett's saddlebags into the great trunk and pulling across a stool.

'Mysterious,' Corbett replied. 'The Templars are a closed book: hard-bitten, fighting men. They don't like us. They resent our interference, yet, beneath it all, there is something wrong.'

'You mean the death of the keeper? We heard all about it,' Ranulf declared. 'Oh, not from the Templars, they're all tight-lipped and soft-footed, but from the ordinary servants.'

'And did you learn anything?'

'No, they are just terrified. The usual mumblings about

strange lights at night, comings and goings. Apparently, all was peace and quiet until de Molay and the commanders arrived. Usually, the manor is left empty under its keeper and a few servants. Now everything has been turned topsy-turvy. They believe the keeper was murdered by black magic, consumed by flames sent up from hell. They are already deserting, refusing to work here.'

Corbett stared out of the window. The sky was scarred with the red-gold flashes of a setting sun. He wanted to lie down and compose his thoughts but he kept remembering that grisly burden lying on the table in the council chamber.

'Look, Ranulf, Maltote, unpack our belongings. Lock the door after me. I am going down to the maze. Meanwhile you two can try blundering about, acting the innocent.' Corbett winked at Maltote. 'For you, that won't be hard. Try and see where you can go. Ranulf, if you are turned away, don't argue. We'll meet back here within the hour.'

Corbett left the guesthouse and walked round the manor. He sauntered by the stables, smithies, outhouses and, going through a huge gate, entered a large garden, a place of silent peace, beautifully laid out. It contained a tunnelled arbour along one side, covered by white roses, lily of the valley and honeysuckle. Corbett sat down on a turf seat and stared round in admiration.

'Oh,' he whispered. 'If only Maeve could see this!'

His wife had a passion for gardens, yet this was better than any Corbett had seen even in Edward's palaces. There were chequerboard beds in one corner, and the sweet fragrance from the herbs growing there hung heavily in the evening air. After a while Corbett rose, walked across and stared down at the periwinkle, polypody, fennel, cowslip and white orris. Next to these were nerbers, small raised flower beds containing yarrow, daisy and Lady's bedstraw. Corbett walked on, into a small orchard with apple, pear and black mulberry trees, all providing cool shade against the brightness of the setting sun. He looked back towards the manor, its arrow-slit windows and small bays full of glass, and wondered if he was being watched.

He left the garden through a small postern gate built into the wall. This led to a meadow, which sloped down to a small copse at the edge of a broad, shimmering lake. From the nearby byres, Corbett heard the cattle lowing as they were brought in for the night. A man was singing and, on the breeze, he heard the crash of a blacksmith's hammer on the anvil. An idyllic scene which brought back bitter-sweet memories of his own manor at Leighton. Nevertheless, Corbett felt uneasy: he was sure someone was studying his every movement. He turned right and walked behind the manor house to a fringe of trees. Behind these stood the maze, a sea of high, green, prickly hedgerows which stretched out to the curtain wall of the manor. He walked along, staring into each entrance, then he found the long line of rope lying on the ground. Corbett made his way, following the rope as it twisted through the hedgerows.

'Lord save us!' Corbett whispered as he stared up at the thick green bushes on either side. 'Guido Reverchien must have been a glutton for punishment.'

He started as a bird flew out of the hedge and soared above him in a whirr or wings. The sound reminded Corbett of a crossbow bolt. He walked on: the maze became silent, as if he was lost in some magical, secret forest. He followed the rope along the path. The ominous silence seemed to intensify; he felt his heart skip a beat and sweat prickle the nape of his neck. Shadows were beginning to fall and, in some places, the high hedgerows blocked the rays of the dying sun. Corbett trudged on. He was regretting not waiting till the following morning when suddenly he heard a crunch on the gravel. Corbett whirled round. Was someone following him? Or did the sound come from some bird or animal on the other side of the hedgerow? He stood listening for any noise then, satisfied, walked on. At last the rope snaked round a corner and into the centre of the maze. A large stone crucifix stood here; in front of it were paved steps on which Reverchien must have knelt. Now the stonework and the heavy iron candelabra were cracked and scorched. Corbett stared up at the carved face of his Saviour.

'What happened?' he asked. 'How can an old soldier saying his prayers be consumed by a mysterious fire?'

Corbett studied the area where the fire had blazed: he could not detect how the inferno had been caused. The candles were gone, mere streaks of wax: these might spark or scorch but not turn a man into a living flame. Corbett sat on a turf seat and tried to visualise the scene: Reverchien would have come out along the same path he had, chanting his psalms, his beads in his hand. Dawn would be breaking, there would be enough light for Reverchien to notice anyone hiding in this small enclosure. Moreover, although Reverchien was old, he had been a soldier: his hearing would be sharp and sensitive. He would know if someone had followed him through the maze. Yet if the killer was a Templar commander, one of the five he had met in the council chamber, he could not have possibly been here when Reverchien had died. Corbett stared at the great scorch-mark.

'But what happens,' he murmured, 'if there was more than one killer? If there was a coven here at Framlingham? If someone entered the maze long before Sir Guido?'

But if that was the case, the killer would have to have got out again, and that would have been impossible without being detected.

Corbett looked up at the sky. As he did so, he heard the crunch of a boot on gravel from behind the wall of privet, then a creak, like a door opening. Corbett immediately threw himself to the right as a long yew arrow smashed into the cross. Corbett moved behind this, drawing his dagger. Again the crunch on the gravel and an arrow whipped by his head into the privet beyond. Corbett did not wait for a third but ran to the entrance where he could see the rope lying. He fled, keeping his eyes on that rope as it wound and snaked through the maze. Behind him Corbett heard the sounds of quiet pursuit. He turned a corner and suddenly the rope was no longer there. Corbett stopped, sobbing for breath. Should he go to the left or the right? He tried to climb the hedge but the branches were stubby, pointed, and cut his hands. He found it impossible to gain a foothold. Corbett crouched, fighting for breath, trying to calm the thudding of his heart. He remembered how far he had run and quickly gauged that he must be somewhere near the entrance. However, if he took the wrong path he could find himself lost, trapped, a clear target for the assassin. For a while Corbett waited, straining his ears, listening for any sound: all he could hear was the cawing of the crows and an occasional rustle as some bird nesting in the hedgerow burst up into the sky.

At last Corbett felt he was calm enough to move. He took off his cloak and began to cut strips of cloth from it, which he tied around twigs.

'At least,' he muttered, 'I will know if I am going round in circles.'

He crept forward, trying to recall how he had entered the maze.

'Turning left,' he whispered. 'I kept turning left.'

He chose the path to his right and began to work his way forward. Now and again he lost his way, coming round to find a strip of cloth hanging from the bush. He cursed and tried again, a mixture of trial and error. Only once did he hear the pursuer. A crunch of gravel and his heart skipped a beat, the assailant was now in front of him. Darkness was beginning to fall. Somewhere a dog howled mournfully as the daylight began to fade. After a while Corbett felt secure, no longer pursued or watched. He realised the rope had been removed, not to trap him, but as a means of delaying him, should he survive and the assailant had to flee. Corbett edged forward, then he heard Ranulf's voice.

'Master?'

'Here!' Corbett shouted and, doffing his cloak, waved it high above his head.

'I saw that!' Ranulf shouted back.

'Keep shouting!' Corbett ordered.

Ranulf happily obliged, bawling out encouragement as Corbett made his way, following the sound of Ranulf's voice. The hedgerows thinned and he was out on the path where Ranulf and Maltote stood, grinning from ear to ear.

'You should be more careful,' his manservant exclaimed.

'I was bloody careful,' Corbett grunted. 'Some bastard removed the rope and tried to kill me.'

Ranulf looked round. 'Then where is he? He must be still in the maze.'

'No, he's gone. Ranulf, did you see anyone?'

'Only a gardener pushing a wheelbarrow.'

'What did he look like?'

'He wore a cowl and cloak, Master. But the manor is full of servants.'

Corbett closed his eyes. He remembered seeing a wheelbarrow near the maze, covered by a dirty sheet.

'Why should they kill me?' he rasped. 'If this secret coven of Templars wants the destruction of the king, how can murdering me bring that about?'

'They don't want you to investigate.'

'But the king will send someone else. Why create more suspicion?' Corbett glanced up at the darkened sky. 'Well, they failed for the second time today. That's the last time I'm wandering round this benighted manor by myself. Well, what did you find?'

A bell began to toll, the sign for evening supper. They walked back to the main entrance, Ranulf explaining how they had wandered the galleries and passageways. He paused, clutching his master's arm.

'Framlingham is a mysterious place. There are chambers, stairways, cellars, even a dungeon. The place is well guarded: armed men everywhere. Never once did they try to stop us, except when we tried to climb to the garret at the top of the manor. The stairway is guarded by soldiers. They were polite and shook their heads. When I asked them why not, they just smiled and told me to mind my own business.'

'Oh, and tell him the other thing,' Maltote interrupted.

'Oh, yes, Master.' Ranulf leaned closer. 'On the second floor of the main building there are eight windows.'

'So?' Corbett asked.

'But, Master, on the gallery inside there are only seven chambers.'

Chapter 5

Corbett and his companions returned to the guesthouse and changed for supper.

'Make no mention about the attack on me,' Corbett warned them as they returned along the passageway to the refectory.

The Templars were already assembled, seated round a table down the centre of the hall, which was a small, comfortable room, brightly caparisoned by banners hanging from the hammer-beam rafters. De Molay quickly said grace, blessing the food on the table, but then, before they sat down, a servant came in bearing a tray with goblets and an equal number of dishes containing bread sprinkled with salt. Each Templar and their three guests were given a cup and a piece of the salted bread.

'Let us remember,' de Molay intoned, 'those of our brothers who have gone before us. Those of our comrades who have gone down into the dust.'

'Amen!' the Templars chorused.

Corbett glanced round the shadow-filled hall and suppressed a shiver, as if the ghosts of those on whom de Molay had called were now thronging all around them. He sipped from his cup and bit into the salted bread. Ranulf began to cough, but Corbett nudged him and Ranulf hurriedly ate the salted morsels.

'Let us remember,' de Molay continued, 'those fair cities and fortresses which have fallen to our foes.'

Again the wine and bread were tasted.

'Let us remember,' de Molay spoke for a third time, 'the

Holy Places where the Lord Jesus ate, drank, suffered, died and rose again.'

After this the cups and plates were cleared. De Molay gestured at them to sit and the supper began. Despite such a sombre toast, the meal proved to be delicious: spiced pheasant, jugged hare, dishes of fresh vegetables, cups of claret, and whilst the sweetmeats were served, iced wine from Alsace. Corbett sipped the wine and remembered the king's gift to de Molay as he listened to the conversation around him. Most of the talk was about matters abroad, as if the Templars wished to forget the recent occurrences. They talked of ships, corsairs in the Middle Sea, the recent Chapter in Paris and the great question of whether they should unite with the Hospitaller Order. Corbett and his two companions were not ignored, but never once were they drawn into the conversation. Only when Odo the librarian, a thin, bald-pated man with a flowing white beard joined them, did the conversation lighten. Odo was a carefree soul with a smiling mouth and laughter-filled eyes. Corbett immediately warmed to him.

'You are boring our guests,' Odo declared from the foot of the table. 'You are not knights and gentlemen but grizzled old soldiers who don't know any better.' He bowed to de Molay. 'Grand Master, I apologise for being late.'

'Nonsense.' De Molay smiled back. 'We know you and your books, Brother Odo, and what you say is right. We should improve our manners.'

A scullion came from the kitchen and laid a fresh trancher in front of the librarian. Odo rested his elbows on the table and Corbett gaped: Odo had no left hand, nothing but a polished, wooden stump. Legrave, sitting opposite, leaned across.

'We put up with Brother Odo,' he whispered loudly, smiling down at the librarian who stared back in mock anger. 'He will not like us telling you this, but Odo is a hero, a veritable paladin.'

'It's true!' Branquier trumpeted. 'Why do you think we put

up with his speeches and bad manners?'

Corbett felt the deep admiration, even love for the old Templar.

'In his time,' Symmes declared, 'Brother Odo was a knight of whom even Arthur or Roland and Oliver would have been proud.'

'Oh, stop it!' The librarian gestured with his good hand, though he openly revelled in this warm-hearted badinage.

'He was at Acre,' Legrave continued, 'as we all were, but he defended the breach when the walls were broken. He was the last to leave. Tell us, Brother, tell our guests what happened.'

Corbett realised this was a ritual time-honoured, only this time with a difference. These men were desperate to show Corbett that, despite the rumours and whispered allegations, once, in a different age, they had been defenders of Christendom: heroes, saints in armour. The other Templars joined in, so Odo took a deep swig of wine and raised the polished stump.

'I lost my hand in Acre,' he began. 'Yes, I was there when the city fell in March 1291.' He stared round at the four Templar commanders. 'You were there too.'

'We broke and ran.' Legrave did not lift his eyes. 'We fled the city, our shields on our backs, our faces towards the sea.'

'No you didn't,' Odo replied gently. 'You had to retreat. I have told you hundreds of times: there's no glory in dying. There's no honour in a bloody corpse. There's no pride in captivity.'

'You didn't flee,' Branquier remarked.

'Brother,' de Molay tapped the hilt of his knife on the tablecloth. 'In truth, you all have the advantage of me, I wasn't even there. I have never known the scorching heat of the deserts of Outremer. I have never heard the blood-curdling cry of the Mamelukes nor felt the savage fury of battle. Acre did not fall because of us. But, because . . .' He caught Corbett's gaze and his voice trailed off. Then the grand master looked up, eyes brimming with tears. 'Tell us once again, Odo,' he whispered. 'Tell us how the city fell.'

'The siege began in March.' Odo's voice was deep and mellow. He leaned back, closing his eyes, painting pictures with his words. 'As you all know, Acre was a doomed city, yet the streets were full of life and the taverns thronged, feasting far into the night. Syrian and Greek girls filled the upper rooms of wine shops. A feverish excitement seized Acre as the Turks began to ring the city.' He opened his eyes. 'Why is it?' he asked, 'that when people are about to die, they dance even faster? Sir Hugh, have you ever been in battle?'

'Ambuscades in Wales and in the wet heather on the Scottish march, but nothing like you, Brother Odo.' Corbett glanced round at the Templars. 'I cannot condemn any man for what he did in battle. I am not too sure how I would behave.'

Odo toasted him silently before continuing. 'The final attack came in May. The thudding of the siege engines, the cracking of boulders against the crumbling walls of the city, the crash and roar of exploding fire – and those drums. Do you remember them, Brothers, the Mameluke drums constantly rattling?'

'Even now,' Branquier declared. 'Sometimes at night, when I lie down to sleep in my cell, I can still hear that drumming.' He stared round sheepishly. 'I get up and stare through the window into the shadows amongst the trees. I wonder if Satan and all his army have come to taunt me.'

Odo nodded. 'I was on the western wall,' he continued. 'A breach was caused and oil poured in, blackening the ground, creating a curtain of smoke. The Mamelukes filled in the ditches by stampeding columns of beasts of burden. These fell into the moat, were slaughtered, and so formed a bridge over which they could pour across. There were not many of us left. I was weary, blinded by smoke, my arms heavy.' He paused. 'Behind the smoke we could hear the songs of the dervishes, the rattle of their drums drawing closer. In the half-light, just before dawn, the first attack came: dark masses, as if hell was spitting out legions of demons. We fought them off but then armoured regiments of Mamelukes followed and the walls were taken. We fell back. We passed a group of monks, Dominicans. They had gathered together to sing the "Salve Regina". We could do nothing to save them. All around us men were dying, burning in their towers, in the entrances to houses, or on the barricades across the alleyways.'

'But you stopped them,' Branquier intervened. 'For a while, Brother Odo, you stopped them.'

'Aye. There was a street leading down to the docks; everyone was fleeing there. All command had collapsed and the ships were filling up as fast as they could. I and about two dozen other Templars – chosen men – manned the last barricade.' Odo straightened up. His face became youthful, his eyes bright with excitement. 'We fought all afternoon,' he declared. 'And, as we did, we sang the "*Paschale Laudes*", the Easter hymn, until even the Infidels pulled back and promised us our lives. We laughed at them. They closed again. Balls of fire rained down on the barricades; then there was blackness.' His shoulders slumped. 'When I woke up I was in one of the transports fleeing out to the open sea. My left hand was gone; Acre had fallen. I later learnt one man had survived; he'd dragged me down to the quayside steps. He found a boat.' Odo's voice trembled. 'Sometimes, I wish to God I had died there with my brothers.'

'Nonsense.' William Symmes, his scarred face now softer, rose and went to kneel beside the old librarian. 'If you had died,' he said softly, 'we would never have heard the story and Framlingham would not have its favourite librarian.'

'So,' Corbett asked, 'apart from the grand master, you were all in Acre?'

'We came back with the rest,' Legrave replied. 'Each of us is now a principal commander. I at Beverley, Baddlesmere in London, Symmes at Templecombe in Dorset, Branquier in Chester.'

'And at your Grand Chapter,' Corbett insisted, hoping to

lighten the atmosphere, 'were fresh plans laid? Will the Order attempt to regain what it has lost?'

'In time,' de Molay replied. 'But where are your questions leading, Sir Hugh?' He flicked his fingers and a servant came out of the shadows to fill their wine goblets.

'Perhaps this is not the time nor occasion.' Corbett glanced quickly at Ranulf and Maltote who, having filled their stomachs, were now staring, round-eyed, at these strange men who had witnessed scenes they could never imagine.

'Nonsense,' de Molay replied. 'What is it you want to know, Corbett?'

'You all went to France for the Grand Chapter? Grand Master, why did you come back to England? And why did you all stay together instead of returning to your different posts?'

'It is my duty to visit every province,' de Molay replied. 'And when I do, I am to be attended by the senior commanders.'

'When did you return?'

'Seven days before the warning was pinned to the doors of St Paul's Cathedral,' de Molay replied sardonically, 'and a few days after the attack on Philip of France in the Bois de Boulogne.'

'Do continue.' Legrave put his elbows on the table, licking his fingers.

'And you came to Framlingham?' Corbett asked.

'Yes,' Legrave replied, taunting him. 'We were here at Framlingham when that terrible murder occurred outside Botham Bar.'

'And we were in York,' Branquier spoke up. 'When your king was attacked and you were so nearly assassinated.'

'But all this,' Baddlesmere declared, 'is coincidence, not proof of any treason.'

'And remember,' Brother Odo intervened, 'none of my comrades was here when Sir Guido died at the centre of that maze. They had all left Framlingham the previous evening for their meeting with the king at St Leonard's Priory.'

'Sir Guido was your friend?' Corbett asked.

'Yes and, before you ask, the reason why I am not grieving is that I am glad Sir Guido is dead. He was a man who constantly tortured himself. Now he's at peace in the arms of Christ. No more pain, no more doubt.' The old librarian's eyes blinked quickly. 'Tomorrow we bury him and he'll be at rest.'

'You were there,' Corbett said. 'You went to the mouth of the maze with him?'

'Yes, I did, just before dawn. It was a beautiful morning. The sky was turning a deep blue. Sir Guido said it reminded him of Outremer. He knelt down, his rosary in his hand, and began his pilgrimage. I just sat there, as I always did, revelling in the sweet smells of the morning breeze and wishing Sir Guido would not torture himself. I was dozing when I heard his terrible screams. I stood up and saw a black pall of smoke rising above the maze. The rest you know.'

'And you are sure no one else was there?' Corbett asked.

'God be my witness, Sir Hugh, there was no one.'

Corbett now looked at the Templars. 'And then you all came back, late in the afternoon?'

'As we have said,' de Molay replied. 'We were in the city. We had business to do. Brother Odo could see no point in sending a message to us. Sir Guido was dead, no hustle or bustle would bring him back.'

'Except Branquier,' Odo declared. 'He came back early. He had asked to meet me at one o'clock.' He smiled and picked at his food. 'I was asleep, Branquier had to wake me.' He grinned. 'Sometimes I feel my age,' he added. 'But what hour was it?'

'The hour candle had scarcely reached the thirteenth ring,' Branquier replied. 'You saw that yourself.' He glanced across at Corbett. 'I wanted Brother Odo to find me a book. However, when I arrived at Framlingham, a servant told me about Sir Guido, so I went to my cell, left my belongings, then visited Brother Odo.'

'And this is the information I need,' Corbett declared. 'Grand

Master, I apologise, but I must interrogate all of you about your precise movements.' He lifted his hand in a gesture of peace. 'I am sure these questions will clarify matters. Neither I, nor His Grace the King intend insult. Indeed, Grand Master, I have brought a tun of wine from the Greenmantle tavern, the best wine Gascony has ever produced, as a gift from His Grace.'

'Ah.' De Molay smiled his thanks. 'From the king's own vintner, Hubert Seagrave. He has applied to purchase certain lands from us. A waste area . . .'

He broke off at the terrible screaming from the kitchen. Ranulf was the first to react: throwing back his chair, he hastened into the kitchen. Corbett and the rest followed into a large, cavernous room, its walls lined with hooks from which skillets, pots and pans hung. Now it was transformed into a scene from hell: near the oven one of the cooks stood screaming, watched by his horror-struck companions, as flames roared about him. The fire had run along the man's apron, which was fully alight, whilst tongues of flame caught his hose and the cloth around his neck. He staggered forward then crumpled to his knees. Ranulf poured a large bucket of water over him and, helped by Maltote, seized a piece of heavy sacking lying near a bread basket and threw it over the tortured man to damp down the flames. Corbett quickly glanced at the Templars. De Molay had turned away, his face to the wall. Brother Odo and the four commanders just stared, a look of horror on their faces as the cook's screams faded to a whimper then died completely. At last, the writhing figure lay still. Ranulf, his hands and face black with smoke, pulled back the sacking. The cook lay dead, his entire body terribly burnt. A horrid sight. Maltote retched and headed straight for the door leading to the yard.

The other servants, spit boys, scullions and cooks, edged away from the Templars. One knocked a pewter pot, which fell with a resounding crash.

'He was laughing,' one of the cooks whispered. 'He was just

laughing, then he was on fire. You saw it? Flames all over him.' The man's eyes rolled in panic. 'We were just having a joke. He was laughing.' The fellow's hand flew to his nose as he became aware of the terrible stench.

'Who was he?' Corbett asked quietly.

'Peterkin. He lived with his mother in Coppergate. Had grand ambitions, he did, to open his own cookshop.'

'Take him away.' De Molay turned to the Templar serjeants now thronging in at the door of the refectory. 'Cover him with a sheet and take him to the Infirmary.'

The servants continued to edge to the door. The principal cook, with massive shoulders and balding head, stepped forward. He took off his leather apron and threw it on the floor.

'That's it!' he snorted. 'We are leaving. Try and stop us, but in the morning we'll be gone.' He pushed his hand towards the Templars. 'We want payment and then we'll be gone.'

Corbett saw the red, angry abscess on the palm of the man's hand, and his stomach churned a little at what he had eaten. The cook's demands were echoed by the rest. The mood in the kitchen perceptibly changed. One of the scullions picked up a fleshing knife, another a cleaver still red with the blood of the meat it had cut. Behind him Corbett heard the Templar serjeants drawing their swords.

'This is ridiculous,' Corbett exclaimed. 'I am the king's commissioner here. Grand Master, pay these men, and, once they've answered certain questions, let them go. But not here. God save the poor wretch but the place stinks with his burning.'

De Molay turned to his commanders. 'Make sure the manor's secure.' He declared, 'Our supper is ended. Sir Hugh and I will question these good people,' adding diplomatically, 'and don't worry.' De Molay smiled faintly. 'I am sure Master Ranulf here will protect us all.'

At first all four commanders seemed about to refuse. Hands on dagger hilts, they glared at the cooks and then at Corbett.

'Go on,' de Molay urged quietly.

The group broke up. Corbett led the cooks back into the refectory towards the dais. He stood on this, the cooks thronging together. Out of their kitchen they became more anxious, frightened, shifting their feet, eager to be away.

'What happened?' Corbett asked.

'It's as they say,' the principal cook spoke up. 'The meal was finished. We were clearing up the kitchen. Peterkin was pastry cook. He was raking the coals out of the oven, laughing and talking. The next minute I heard him scream. I turned round and there was fire all along his front.'

He turned and snapped his fingers. One of the scullions took off a thin, leather apron and handed it to Corbett.

'He was wearing one of these.'

Corbett examined it curiously. The leather was very thin, a loop at the neck so it could go over the head and a cord to fasten it around the middle. It would protect a man against stains and the occasional spark but not the angry fire Corbett had seen.

'What was he wearing on his hands?'

'Thick woollen mittens,' the cook replied. 'They covered his arms up to the elbow.'

'Show me what he was doing,' Corbett urged. 'Come, just you and me.'

The cook was about to protest, but Corbett stepped off the dais and held a silver coin in front of the cook's face.

'I'll be with you all the time,' Corbett assured him.

The silver coin disappeared and the two went into the kitchen. The cook led Corbett to the great fire-grate: on either side of this was a large oven built into the wall.

'He was here,' the cook explained, pulling open the iron door.

Corbett gingerly peered in, only to flinch at the blast of heat from the burning charcoal piled high beneath a steel wire netting. The cook picked up a pole with a wooden board at the end. He pointed into the oven.

'You see, Master, Peterkin would put the pies on to the netting, shut the door and allow them to bake. He knew exactly how long to leave them.' The man's greasy face broke into a sad smile. 'He was a good cook. The crusts of his pies were always golden and light, the meat fresh and savoury. He leaves a mother,' he continued. 'And she is a widow.'

Corbett put a silver piece into the man's blackened hand. 'Then give her that,' he said. 'Now the king is in York,' he added, 'tell her to petition him for mercy.'

'Much good that will do,' the fellow grunted.

'No, it won't,' Corbett replied. 'The petition will come to me. Now, what was Peterkin doing?'

The cook pointed to an iron tray full of dust which lay on the floor.

'Once the baking's done, the ovens have to be doused. Peterkin always insisted on doing it himself in preparation for the next day. He knew exactly how clean the oven must be, how to spread the charcoal. Well, he was raking it all out into the tray when I heard him scream.'

'What do you think happened?' Corbett asked, walking away from the oven.

The cook followed. 'I don't know, sir. Oh, I have seen men burnt in kitchens, especially when they mix oil with fire – bad burns to hands and faces. Now and again we scald our legs or feet.' The man took a rag from beneath his leather apron and wiped the sweat from his face. 'But, Master,' he edged so close that Corbett could smell his stale odour. 'But, Master,' he repeated, 'I have seen nothing like that. A good man turned into a sheet of flame within seconds.'

Corbett walked to the back door of the kitchen which had been flung open. The acrid smell of burning flesh still hung heavily in the air. From the hall he could hear the faint murmur of voices, as well as the clink of mailed men outside in the darkness. He stood, just within the kitchen, watching the moonlight reflected in the puddles in the cobbled yard.

'What did you see?' Corbett asked. 'I mean, the first time you saw Peterkin burn?'

'The flames.' The man brushed his apron. 'Along his front, chest, stomach and his hands. Yes, even the woollen mittens were ablaze.'

'And did you notice anything untoward during the evening?'

'No, sir!'

'Nothing?' Corbett asked.

'We were busy, sir.'

'And no one came in? Either before the meal or during the day?'

'Not that I saw, sir!'

'Then what have you seen?'

The cook pulled a face. 'There's the horseman . . .'

'What horseman?'

'Masked and cowled, a great two-handed sword hanging from his saddlebag.' The man shifted uncomfortably. 'I've only seen him once. I was, er, hunting for rabbits in the woods nearby. He was sitting like the shadow of death amongst the trees, staring at the manor. He never moved – I just fled.'

Corbett's heart skipped a beat. Was there, he wondered, a secret assassin lurking in the woods between Framlingham and York?

'Do you think this masked horseman was from Framlingham?' he asked.

'I don't know, but this place is accursed,' the cook continued in a rush. 'Some of us live here. Others, like Peterkin, live in the city. We heard about the strange murder outside Botham Bar. This was a quiet manor, sir, before those commanders arrived with their soldiers. Now they are singing strange hymns at night, up all hours. You can't go here and you can't go there! Then there's the death of Sir Guido. He was a good man. A little forbidding, but kind – that's what Peterkin was laughing about.'

Corbett turned abruptly. 'What do you mean?'

'He said the fire which killed Guido came from hell: Satan's fire.'

'Why should it?' Corbett asked.

The man glanced back at the door to the refectory, then at another silver coin held between Corbett's fingers.

'Well,' he said, 'there are rumours.'

'Rumours about what?' Corbett insisted. 'Come on, man, you have nothing to fear.'

'Well, a scullion saw one of the Templars.' The cook paused.

'You mean one of the commanders?'

'Yes. I don't know which one but, well, he saw him kissing a man. You know, sir, like you would a woman. And before you ask, he couldn't make out who it was.'

'You are sure?' Corbett asked.

'Certain. He was coming down a passageway. He glimpsed the commander who had his back to him. He knew it was one of the visitors from the cloak he wore. I think the other was one of the Templar serjeants, a youngish man. You've seen how dark this place is, sir. They were in the shadows. The scullion was frightened so he turned and fled. Anyway, Peterkin was laughing about that. He made a joke of everything. He said the place smelt of Satan's sulphur and then it happened.' The man plucked the coin from Corbett's fingers. 'And now I am going, sir.'

He strode out of the kitchen in the hall. Corbett heard raised voices and, by the time he returned, the cook was marching the rest down towards the door.

'I couldn't stop them,' de Molay murmured. 'They can visit the almoner, collect their wages and go. What do you think, Sir Hugh?' The grand master stepped into the pool of light from the candles on the table and wearily sat down, face in hands. Ranulf and Maltote also took their seats. Both had drunk deeply and were now feeling its effect.

'I have seen similar accidents,' Ranulf declared. 'Men

getting burnt, in cookshops in London.'

'Not like that,' Corbett replied, sitting down opposite de Molay.

The grand master looked up. He seemed to have aged years; his iron-grey hair was tousled, dark shadows ringed his eyes. His face had lost that serene, rather imperious look. 'Satan attacks us on every side,' he murmured.

'Why do you say that?' Corbett asked. 'What happened in the kitchen could have been an accident.'

De Molay leaned back in his chair. 'That was no accident, Corbett. The murder outside Botham Bar, the attack on the king, the death of Sir Guido. Now this!'

'So why should Satan attack you?'

'I don't know,' the grand master snarled, rising to his feet, 'but when you meet him, Corbett, ask him the same question!' De Molay strode out of the refectory, slamming the door behind him.

Corbett, too, rose, beckoning Ranulf and Maltote to follow.

'Listen! From now on, we sleep in the same chamber. Each does a watch. Be careful what you eat and drink. No one travels round the manor by themselves.' Corbett sighed. 'As far as I am concerned, we're back on the Scottish march. The only difference being that there we knew our enemy, here we don't!'

They walked back towards the guesthouse: Corbett stopped, heart in his throat, as a figure came rushing out of the darkness but it was only a servant, belongings packed into a fardel, scurrying towards the gates.

'By morning they'll all be gone,' Ranulf muttered. 'If I had my way, Master, we'd follow!'

'Where to?' Corbett asked. 'Edward in York or Leighton Manor?'

Ranulf refused to answer. Once they were back in the guesthouse, a sleepy-eyed Maltote stood guard outside whilst Corbett told Ranulf to join him. The servant sat down on a stool. Corbett studied him curiously: Ranulf's usual cheeky face was now pallid, his attitude no longer devil-may-care.

'What's wrong?' Corbett asked.

'Oh, nothing.' Ranulf kicked at the rushes. 'I am so happy I am thinking of becoming a Templar.' He glared at Corbett. 'I hate this bloody place. I don't like the Templars. I can't make them out, monks or soldiers. The librarian may be a grand old man but the rest make my skin crawl.'

'You are frightened, aren't you?' Corbett sat down on the edge of the bed.

Ranulf scratched his head. 'No, Master, I'm not frightened. I am terrified. All Maltote thinks about is horses, that's all he talks about. What's happening here hasn't yet sunk into his thick skull.' Ranulf plucked at the dagger in his belt. 'I can deal with enemies, Master: the footpad in the alleyway, the assassin in the darkened chamber. But this? Men mysteriously bursting into flames, Reverchien at the centre of a maze, that poor bastard in the kitchen . . .'

'For every natural phenomenon,' Corbett replied, 'Aristotle said there must be a natural cause.'

'Bugger that!' Ranulf snarled. 'Bloody Aristotle's not here. If he was, the silly bastard would soon change his mind!'

Corbett began to laugh.

'Oh, you're amused, Master,' Ranulf snapped. 'We have only been here a few hours and we've been threatened, shot at and hunted in a maze.'

Corbett grasped Ranulf's hand. 'Yes, I am frightened, Ranulf.'

He got to his feet, stretched and stared at the black carved crucifix on the wall. 'In all my years of pursuing murderers I have never seen the like. Yes, I was hunted in the maze.' He turned, his face set hard. 'I don't like being hunted, Ranulf. I don't like being threatened. I don't like nightmares about a royal messenger telling Maeve and Baby Eleanor that I am gone but my corpse will soon arrive for burial.' He sat down. 'I am a clerk. I deal with wax and parchment. I resolve problems.

I protect the king and hunt down his enemies. Sometimes I am frightened; so terrified that I wake up sweating from head to toe.' Corbett paused. 'This morning I was frightened. If it hadn't been for you, I would have fled. But that's what the assassin wants, everything to be in chaos. But we *will* impose order and, once we do, we wait!'

'If we live long enough.'

'We'll live. I'll make my mistakes, but in the end I'm going to see the cruel bastard behind all this arrested and pay the price. So, let's impose order. We have the Templars. They have houses in England and throughout Western Europe. They have been driven from the Holy Land. They have lost their purpose and have provoked the hostility and, because of their wealth, the envy of men. They, too, are frightened: that's why they have offered our king the princely sum of fifty thousand pounds. That cunning old fox knew he could get it. So come on Ranulf, Clerk of the Green Wax, what has happened so far?'

'It began with the Grand Chapter in Paris.'

'De Molay presided over that meeting,' Corbett continued. 'The four English Commanders were present. They left for England just after the attack on Philip IV was launched. Whilst they are in London, the Assassins' warning is pinned to the doors of St Paul's Cathedral. They come to York; there is unease about their stay here at Framlingham. The manor house is heavily defended, certain places carefully guarded. Then we have the deaths: the strange murder outside Botham Bar, the attack on the king and on me. The slaying of Reverchien and now the death of Peterkin the pastry cook. Well, Ranulf, what logic is there to all this?'

Ranulf scratched his head. 'Only one: where de Molay and his four commanders are, trouble occurs. There is neither rhyme nor reason for what happens. Most assassins have a motive. True, there could be divisions in the Templar Order, a secret coven dabbling in black magic. One or all of the Commanders, even de Molay, could be intent on wrecking vengeance against the kings of France and England.'

'But that does not explain,' Corbett added, 'the strange deaths outside Botham Bar and the slaying of Peterkin. Why should a poor pastry cook be consumed by fire? And, more importantly, how do these strange fires occur?'

Ranulf got up and paced restlessly up and down the chamber. 'Master, you said that for every natural phenomenon there's a natural cause. But what happens if this is not natural? People don't just break into flames?'

Corbett shook his head. 'I hear what you say, Ranulf. Yet, I suspect, that's what we are supposed to think.'

'But how can it happen?' Ranulf persisted. 'True, the Templars were in the city when the attack was launched on the king. But they weren't here when Reverchien was killed. We know that for a fact.'

'Brother Odo was,' Corbett replied. 'He was here. He may be old but, by his own confession, he is a fighting man. He could have killed Sir Guido, left the manor, joined Murston, then prowled the streets of York waiting for us. After that he could have hastened back to Framlingham before the others arrived. Legrave did say he found him asleep.'

'He's missing one hand.'

'So? I have heard of men with greater handicaps committing murder. How do we know he didn't follow Reverchien into the maze and kill him? Or somehow arrange for Peterkin's death?'

'And outside Botham Bar?' Ranulf asked. 'Swinging a two-handed sword?'

Corbett spread his hands. 'Concedo, that would be difficult – but not impossible. There again, the cook told me of a masked horseman lurking in the woods near the manor.'

'An assassin?' Ranulf asked.

'Possibly, though the cook could be lying. Finally one other matter remains. The counterfeit coins. Or perhaps they are not counterfeit . . .' Corbett continued, 'Anyway, these appeared in York just after the Templars arrived.'

'Then we are back to alchemy or magic,' Ranulf snapped. 'Master, when I ran wild in the streets of London, I knew some counterfeiters. What they do is take a good coin and make two bad ones out of it. I have never heard of anyone producing solid gold coins.'

Corbett sat down on the bed and rubbed his face with his hands. '"If you analyse everything,"' he quoted, '"And you can only reach one conclusion, then that conclusion must be the truth."' he glanced over at Ranulf. 'Perhaps it is magic.' He added slowly, 'Perhaps Satan's fire is burning amongst us.'

Chapter 6

The two knights took up position at either end of the tilt-yard. Down the dusty yard which separated them ran the tilt barrier, a long wooden fence covered with a leather sheet. The knights were fully armoured, great jousting helmets on their heads. Squires passed up shields and then the long wooden tourney lances. Corbett watched as each rider, guiding his horse with his legs, balanced his lance expertly. A trumpet shrilled. The knights began to move slowly. Another trumpet call and the horses burst into a gallop, their iron-shod hooves kicking up the dust, heads straining as each knight, keeping to the tilt barrier on his left, headed straight for his opponent. Shields came up, lances lowered. They met with a resounding crash in the centre. Lances shattered. Both knights swayed in the saddle but both kept their seats and passed to the other end of the tilt-yard.

'Well done!' Brother Odo cried, leaning against the wall and banging his stick on the ground. 'Good lance, Legrave. Symmes!' the old librarian bawled, 'bring your lance down sooner or you'll land on your arse!'

This sally provoked laughter from the watching knights and serjeants. Corbett and his two companions kept to the shadows of the wall. The sun was strong and the dust from the tilt-yard caught at their eyes and throats. Again the knights prepared. Fresh lances, shields in position and, with another trumpet call, the great destriers, caparisoned in gaily coloured harnesses, lunged forward, breaking into a gallop as each rider bore down on his opponent. The two jousters met, but this time Symmes was too slow: his lance missed Legrave whilst at the same time his shield slipped, making him vulnerable to his opponent's lance. There was a terrible crash. Symmes's horse went down on its hind legs and Symmes toppled from the saddle.

'Oh, well done!' de Molay cried, sitting on his throne-like chair under a silken canopy. He beckoned Corbett forward.

'Did you see Legrave? He changed his lance, held it in his left! Such expertise! Come, Sir Hugh, have you seen that amongst the king's knights?'

'No, Grand Master, I have not.'

Corbett spoke the truth. Ever since they had broken their fast after the morning Requiem Mass, the Templars had jousted. Corbett, though tired and suffering rather badly from the heat and dust, had been quick to admire the consummate skill of the Knights Templars. He looked across the tilt-yard where squires were now helping Symmes to his feet, taking off his helmet, offering him ladles of water to slake the dust from his throat and the sweat from his face. Legrave also dismounted and took off his helmet. He walked over to his fallen opponent. Symmes was a little dazed and shaken, but he met his former adversary: they embraced, exchanging the kiss of peace on each other's cheeks.

'If only all such differences were settled so peacefully,' de Molay murmured. He passed a cup of chilled white wine to Corbett, indicating to a servitor that the same be given to Ranulf and Maltote. 'Sir Hugh, I would like to thank you.' De Molay leaned forward so only Corbett could hear. 'It was chivalrous of you to let us bury our dead and salute his memory in a passage of arms.' He sighed. 'Now it's all finished. You wish to speak to us?'

'Yes, Grand Master.'

De Molay shrugged. 'I have instructed my comrades. You can question us in the refectory.'

Corbett drained his cup and handed it back to the servitor, motioning to Ranulf and Maltote to follow him. They walked across the tilt-yard, which lay at the opposite side of the manor to their quarters, and returned to the guesthouse.

'Thank God,' Ranulf groaned, easing himself down on a stool, 'I am not a Templar. They attack with such vehemence.'

'They are superb horsemen,' Maltote declared. 'Did you see how they guide their war-horses with the inside of their knees?'

'We are wasting time,' Ranulf replied crossly. 'I thought that Requiem Mass would never end!'

Corbett, standing at the window to catch the cool breeze, thought differently but kept his own counsel. The Requiem had been beautiful. Reverchien's body, in a wooden casket draped with the flags and banners of the Order, had been placed in front of the high altar of the beautifully decorated Templar chapel. The small church had been packed and the deep voiced singing of the Templars intoning the 'Requiem Dona Ei' had possessed its own solemn majesty. Corbett had sat in one of the side aisles, moved by de Molay's elegant panegyric on Sir Guido Reverchien. True, now and again, the clerk had carefully studied the congregation. The four Templar commanders had sat with their grand master in the sanctuary, whilst the serjeants, squires and other retainers had stood in the nave of the church just beyond the wooden rood-screen.

Corbett had tried to concentrate on the Mass but the cook's story was still fresh in his mind, and he wondered which of the Templar commanders and other members of this congregation were enjoying a homosexual relationship. Time and again the clerk had tried to dismiss this as a distraction for himself and a terrible danger to those concerned: in the eyes of the Church, homosexuality was a great sin. If the culprits were found they would face the cruellest of deaths. Yet his curiosity got the better of him. At the 'osculum pacis', the kiss of peace just before communion, he'd watched Baddlesmere and a young Templar serjeant meet at the entrance to the rood-screen. Now the kiss of peace was exchanged by all, but Corbett glimpsed something different between the grizzled Templar knight and the youthful, fair-haired serjeant. Ranulf, of course, found it very difficult to keep his eyes open in church but, alerted by his master's tenseness, followed his gaze. He leaned forward.

'God forgive me, but, are you thinking what I am?'

Corbett had grabbed Ranulf by the shoulders and kissed him lightly on his cheek.

'*Pax frater*,' he whispered. 'Peace brother.'

'*Et cum spirituo tuo*,' Ranulf whispered back.

'Keep your thoughts to yourself,' Corbett had hissed, and returned to concentrate on the Mass.

After Reverchien's body had been buried in the vaults below the chapel, Corbett and Ranulf had attended a light collation in the refectory, followed by the tournament held in memory of the dead knight.

'Do you think they'll come?' Ranulf broke into his reverie.

Corbett turned away from the window. 'If de Molay has ordered them to, they will.'

'Do they like women?' Ranulf abruptly blurted out.

Corbett shrugged. 'They are supposed to. The only difference between them and us, Ranulf, is they take vows of celibacy and chastity. Their bride is Christ's Church.'

Ranulf whistled under his breath. 'But they must have feelings,' he added teasingly.

Corbett sat down at the small table and undid the saddle panniers containing his writing equipment. 'Why not be more blunt, Ranulf? Every member of the Templar Order is dedicated to a life of celibacy and chastity. It's part of their sacrifice. However, like all such male communities, there are men attracted to each other.'

'But that's a sin,' Maltote declared. 'And if they are caught?'

'God help them: the Templar Order has been known to put such men into a cell, brick the doors and windows up and leave them to starve.'

'Will you question de Molay about the secret chamber?' Ranulf asked. 'On the second floor where there's one window extra. I checked it again this morning after Mass. Between two of the chambers there's fresh wooden panelling. I think a door was once there.'

'The grand master has many questions to answer,' Corbett answered. 'I'm eager to learn what they keep hidden here.'

'Could that be the cause of the fire? Some secret weapon or even powerful relic!' Maltote exclaimed. 'I met a man in London who claimed to have travelled deep into Egypt, beyond Alexandria, to a tribe who possessed the Ark of the Covenant. They say that, if you touched it, strange fire burst out and consumed you. It's true!' Maltote's voice rose as Ranulf began to laugh behind his hand. 'I paid him tuppence for a piece of the wood!'

'I'll wager, the fellow never got further than Southampton,' Ranulf chortled. 'Have you seen Maltote's collection of relics, Master? It includes a rusty sword which Herod's soldiers are supposed to have used when killing the Holy Innocents . . .'

A sudden rap on the door ended the banter. Corbett answered it, expecting to find a messenger from the grand master. Instead the young Templar serjeant he had glimpsed during Mass stood there. Beside him was a squat, thickset man with the features of a fighting mastiff. He had a jutting jaw, firmly clenched mouth, eyes which never blinked, and ridiculously cropped black hair shaved high on all sides, leaving the rest to stand up like some unruly bush.

'Well?' Corbett asked.

'A visitor for you, Sir Hugh.'

'Didn't you expect me?' the stranger barked and, without further ado, walked into the chamber. He almost knocked Corbett aside, slamming the door behind him in the young Templar's face. He stood, his squat legs apart, his fingers jammed into his swordbelt. He took off his dark-maroon cloak and slung it over a chair.

'Devil's tits!' He smacked his lips. 'I'm as dry as a whore's armpit!'

'You'll be drier still if you don't explain yourself!'

Ranulf got to his feet. 'Who in God's name are you?'

'Roger Claverley, Under-sheriff of York.' Their visitor unbuckled his pouch, took out a warrant and thrust a piece of parchment at Corbett. 'This is my warrant from the mayor and sheriff. I'm here to help you.'

Corbett chewed his lip to stop himself smiling: the more he watched Claverley's confrontation with Ranulf, the more his visitor reminded him of the small fighting mastiff that Uncle Morgan, Maeve's kinsman, always had trotting behind him. The mastiff didn't like Ranulf and the feeling was warmly reciprocated.

'Get our visitor some wine, Ranulf,' Corbett said, studying the letter closely. 'He's a very important official and, if this letter is correct, he can provide us with valuable information about the gold coins as well as other matters.' Corbett put the parchment down on the table and came forward, extending a hand.

Claverley clasped it in a bone-crushing grip.

'You are very welcome, Roger,' Corbett said, trying to hide his wince.

The under-sheriff relaxed, his ugly face breaking into a warm smile.

'I am really the city thief-taker,' he declared grandly. 'I know all the villains of the city and they know me. A bit like the good shepherd, only in reverse: where they go, I follow.'

Corbett waved him to a seat, warning Ranulf with his eyes to stand off. Claverley looked first at Maltote who, as usual, was staring open-mouthed, and then at Ranulf.

'I'll wager a month's provisions you have seen the inside of a gaol, my lad. Even across a crowded room, I know a felon when I see one.'

'Yes, I have been inside Newgate.' Ranulf replied tartly. 'I ran wild with the rufflers, the foists, the palliards, the upright men. But tell me, Claverley, were you just born this discourteous? Or does it come with the office you hold?'

Claverley suddenly leaned forward, hands extended, that charming smile back on his face. Ranulf clasped his hand.

'I didn't mean to give offence. I have been there as well,' Claverley remarked. 'After all, the best gamekeepers were once poachers. Now, Sir Hugh, I have been told to assist you, so that's what I'll do. I'll be honest: if I help, would you mention my name to the king?'

Corbett grinned at this ambitious little man's blunt honesty.

'Master Claverley, I will not forget you.'

'Good,' the under-sheriff replied. 'First, we've found the remains, the decomposing bottom half of that man's corpse. Do you remember, the good sisters' guide, Thurston, glimpsed it as the horse careered by them. Some of our young merchants went hunting and their dogs unearthed it.'

'And the horse?'

'Neither hide nor hair has been seen.'

'Anything else?' Corbett asked.

'Well, the Templar crossbowman: I was responsible for having him gibbeted on the pavement. Hung him up in a nice metal cage I did. With a placard, proclaiming this to be the fate of traitors and regicides, tied to it.'

'And?'

'Well, this morning the placard was removed. This was attached by a piece of wire to the gibbet cage.' Claverley handed over a piece of parchment.

'Oh Lord!' Corbett groaned as he read it.

'KNOWEST THOU, THAT WHAT THOU POSSESSES SHALL ESCAPE THEE IN THE END AND RETURN TO US.
'KNOWEST THOU, THAT WE GO FORTH AND RETURN AS BEFORE AND BY NO MEANS CAN YOU HINDER US.
'KNOWEST THOU, THAT WE HOLD YOU AND

WILL KEEP THEE UNTIL THE ACCOUNT BE CLOSED.'

Corbett held the parchment up. 'The verses are slightly changed but it is the Assassins' warning.'

'But the Templars could not have done that,' Ranulf exclaimed. 'They are confined here at Framlingham on the king's orders.'

'They can climb a wall as easily as anyone,' Maltote declared.

'I doubt it,' Claverley intervened. 'We have our orders in the city. No Templar is allowed in.'

'He might have gone disguised,' Maltote added.

Claverley shrugged. 'The guards at the gates have been doubled. Strangers have been stopped and searched but, I suppose, it's possible.'

'There might be an assassin in York,' Corbett replied, and described the masked horseman the cook had seen.

Claverley scratched his chin. 'An assassin hiding along the Botham Bar road?' He pulled a face. 'I've heard nothing about that. Anyway,' Claverley indicated with his head, 'what's happening here? There are no servants, just Templar soldiers and squires.'

'They have all fled,' Corbett retorted. 'There was a death here last night.'

He paused at a knock on the door and Legrave came in. 'Sir Hugh, we are ready in the refectory. The grand master . . .' He paused and glared at Claverley. 'Your visitor from the king?'

'Yes,' Corbett replied. 'Ranulf, you stay here and tell our guest what we know. Sir Ralph, I'll join you now.'

Corbett followed the Templar out of the guesthouse and across into the refectory. De Molay was seated at the head of the table, his companions on either side. De Molay indicated for Corbett to sit at the far end facing him. He noticed the leather bag of writing implements which Corbett laid out on the table, together with parchment, pen and ink-horn.

'Sir Hugh, this is a formal occasion.'

Corbett agreed.

'You will interrogate us on behalf of the king. So you will not object if we, too, keep a fair record of what is said. Sir Richard Branquier will be our clerk.'

'Grand Master, do what you wish, but time is short, so I'll be blunt. If I give offence then I apologise. And you'll forgive me if I repeat what I have asked before?'

De Molay nodded.

'Grand Master, are there divisions in your Order?'

'Yes.'

'Are there those, amongst your principal commanders, who are bitter at the lack of support from the Western Princes?'

'Of course, but that does not mean we are traitors!'

'Have you ever heard,' Corbett continued remorselessly, 'of a high-ranking officer in the Templars who carries the nickname of Sagittarius, the Archer?' He watched the rest but they remained inscrutable.

'Never!' de Molay snapped. 'Though some of the knights, indeed all, are accomplished archers, with the arbalest, the Welsh longbow and even with Saracen weapons.'

'Have you heard any news about the Templar interrogated by the Inquisition?'

'No, but we expect news daily. We do not even know his name.'

'But you knew Murston?'

Corbett watched as Branquier, holding his pen in his left hand, conscientiously scribbled what was being said.

'Murston was my retainer. A weak man, not liked by his colleagues. He drank a lot. He had become bitter.'

'But not a traitor?'

'No, Sir Hugh, I think not.'

'Wasn't he missed from his quarters? After all, he hired the garret in that tavern the night before the attack on the king?'

'You must remember, Sir Hugh, all of us had met the king at

St Leonard's Priory the previous day. My companions and I then went into York. It could have been some days before Murston was missed.'

Corbett paused to write down what he had learnt. His quill skimmed across the soft parchment, writing in a cipher known only to himself.

'And on the day the king entered York?' he asked, placing the quill down.

'We left the priory of St Leonard,' de Molay replied, 'and entered York. Legrave and I visited our bankers, goldsmiths in Stonegate.'

'What are their names?'

'Coningsby,' Legrave replied. 'William Coningsby and Peter Lamode.'

'And you stayed there all the morning?'

'There is no need for this,' Branquier broke in. 'We are knights of the Cross, not felons seized by the Crown!'

'Hush!' De Molay raised his hand. 'All we are telling, Brother, is the truth. Legrave and myself were in Stonegate well into the afternoon. I inspected our accounts, then journeyed up Petergate and through Botham Bar. The king's procession was in the grounds of York Minster. I would have liked to have visited the place.' The grand master smiled thinly. 'But I let it wait for another day.'

'And you, Sir William?' Corbett asked.

Not a muscle moved in Symmes's scarred face, though his good eye looked threateningly at Corbett.

'For a while I was with the grand master, but then I visited merchants in Goodramgate and journeyed to see a friend, a priest who serves the church of St Mary. I arranged to meet the grand master just outside the parchmenters' house within sight of Botham bar. I journeyed back with him.'

'And Sir Bartholomew?' Corbett made a few notes on the parchment.

'I went to Jubbergate where the armourers and fletchers

keep their shops. I was to buy arms.'

'And you were alone?' Corbett asked innocently.

'No, I was with a serjeant.'

'And his name?' Corbett asked.

The Templar swallowed hard. 'John Scoudas. He's here in the manor.'

'You needn't ask me!' Branquier almost shouted down the table. 'I left St Leonard's Priory after the rest. When I reached York, its streets were thronged because of the royal procession. I lingered for a while but the city grew hot and packed. I came back here, as Brother Odo will tell you.'

Corbett quickly studied what he'd written: de Molay and Legrave, he reasoned swiftly, could vouch for each other, Brother Odo for Branquier. But Baddlesmere? Corbett suspected he was lying. And the same went for Symmes, who sat stroking his pet weasel which he kept under the rim of the table. Corbett stared at the parchment. He was aware that the Templars were becoming impatient: chairs were scraped back with loud sighs of exasperation.

'Where do you think we were?' Legrave abruptly asked. 'Helping Murston to try and kill the king? Or sending you messages on Ouse Bridge?'

'Or setting an ambush for you?' Baddlesmere scoffed.

'Grand Master.' Branquier threw his quill down, splashing the table with ink. 'This is the last time I will answer such questions. Just because an idiot of a serjeant, with addled wits, attempts to kill the king, and silly pretentious warnings are sent hither and thither, does that make us all guilty?'

His words provoked a murmur of assent. De Molay looked distinctly uncomfortable, his dark, aristocratic face betrayed an unease. Corbett glanced to the left and right. Baddlesmere sat scratching his grizzled, weather-beaten face. Was he the murderer, Corbett wondered, with his secret sin? Or Legrave, with his neatly combed brown hair and olive-skinned, boyish face? A consummate soldier. Or one-eyed Symmes? Or

Branquier, tall and stooping over the table? Yet Corbett was certain that one of these men, or perhaps all, were assassins, and that other murders could soon occur.

'We have sent Peterkin's body into the city,' de Molay spoke up, 'suitably coffined.' He raised a hand. 'Don't worry. No Templars accompanied it, only one of our stewards with a letter of commiseration and a purse of silver for the man's mother. Sir Hugh, why should anyone kill a poor cook? What profit lay in his death?'

'Or even poor Reverchien?' Baddlesmere snapped.

'I don't know,' Corbett replied. 'But, Grand Master, why have you come to York?'

'I have told you: it is the duty of every grand master to visit each province.'

'And, before you came,' Corbett continued easily, 'Framlingham Manor was supervised by Sir Guido Reverchien, its bailiff and steward?'

'Yes.'

'So why are certain stairwells now guarded? What other secrets does this manor hold?'

'Such as?'

'A masked horseman has been seen hiding in the woods near Framlingham.'

De Molay looked at his companions then shook his head. 'We know nothing of that. What else?'

'A sealed room on the second floor of the manor?'

'Silence!' de Molay ordered as his companions began to accuse Corbett of snooping. 'Have you finished your questioning, Sir Hugh?'

'Yes.'

'Then let me show you our secret room.'

De Molay rose. Corbett put away his writing implements as quickly as possible and followed him out of the room.

'Sir Richard Branquier,' de Molay called over his shoulder. 'You may follow us.'

The grand master, fighting hard to control his temper, led Corbett up the stairs and along the second gallery, a wooden-floored passageway with carved panelling on the walls on either side. De Molay walked half-way down and stopped.

'Branquier, open this room for Sir Hugh!'

The Templar shouldered by Corbett roughly, almost knocking him aside. He pulled open a panelling and pressed a lever. There was a click and part of the wooden wainscoting came away to reveal a door. De Molay took a key from his pouch, inserted this into the lock and a door opened. Inside was a small, narrow cell, the floor bare, the walls whitewashed. A small casement window provided light.

Corbett, slightly embarrassed, stared round at the trunks and coffers stored there.

'It's our treasure house,' Branquier explained. 'Many of our houses and manors have such a room. Doesn't the king have the same?' Branquier pushed his face near Corbett's. 'Perhaps even you, Keeper of His Secret Seal. Are all your rooms and chambers, Sir Hugh, open to the curious and inquisitive?'

'I simply asked,' Corbett replied.

'And you have your answer.'

Corbett stared at a tapestry on the wall: a beautifully embroidered piece of cloth held in place by a thin wooden frame. The tapestry depicted the taking of Christ down from the cross by Nicodemus and St John. Mary knelt, arms outstretched, waiting to receive him. The artist had executed a brilliant scene: the gold, blue, red, green and purple colours seemed more like a picture than a tapestry.

'It's very costly,' de Molay explained. 'Done by an Italian artist. The goldwork alone is worth the profits of this manor. But come, Sir Hugh, we have more to show you.'

Corbett left the chamber. De Molay made the door secure and Branquier closed the wooden partition before leading him along the gallery and up some steps. In the stairwell at the top, two soldiers guarded a flight of stairs to what must be the garret. De Molay told them to stand aside. He unlocked the door, ushering Corbett inside. The room was long, rather musty, a small oval window at the far end just above a makeshift dais on which stood a wooden altar with candlesticks at either end.

'Look around,' Branquier taunted Corbett.

'There's no need to,' Corbett retorted. 'It's as bare as a hay-loft.'

He glanced up at the slanted ceiling and, through chinks in the tiles, glimpsed the sky beyond. He walked towards the altar, noticing the two cushions on the floor before it. He picked at the wax on top of the table.

'There's nothing here!' Branquier snapped, but he looked uneasy, as if frightened to be here.

'So why is it guarded so securely?' Corbett asked.

Branquier, startled, opened his mouth to reply. De Molay, however, was quicker.

'Sir Hugh, you are so suspicious. We are the Templar Order. We have our own rites and rituals.'

'You have a fair enough chapel downstairs.'

'True. True,' the grand master replied. 'But go to any religious house in York: Cistercians, Carthusians, the Crutched Friars, Friars of the Sack. They all have their own private chanceries and chapels well away from the public gaze. This is what happens here.'

'For everyone?' Corbett asked.

'No, no,' de Molay replied. 'Only Sir Richard and myself. We have reached that stage of development in our Order.'

De Molay kept in the shadows, his face turned away. Corbett intuitively knew he was hiding something, but what else could he say? He'd asked his questions and de Molay had replied.

'Grand Master.' He walked to the door. 'I thank you for your courtesy. This morning my servant left the king's gift of wine in your kitchens.' He smiled over his shoulder. 'A poor token compared to the trouble I have caused.'

Chapter 7

Corbett left the garret but turned half-way down the stairs.

'Oh, by the way, Grand Master, did anyone leave Framlingham Manor last night?'

'Apart from the servants who fled, no. The rest of our community are under strict orders: they are not to leave Framlingham.'

Corbett thanked him and returned to his quarters. Ranulf and Maltote were deep in conversation with Claverley over the intricacies of spoilt dice and how easy it was to cheat at shuffle penny.

'We are leaving,' Corbett announced briskly. 'Maltote, get our horses ready. Ranulf, collect my cloak and swordbelt, I'll meet you down at the stables.'

'And you, Master?'

'I want to see Brother Odo. Oh, by the way, Claverley,' Corbett called out as he left. 'Whatever you do, don't play dice with Ranulf or buy any of his potions!'

A Templar serjeant showed him to the library: a long, high-vaulted room at the back of the manor house overlooking the garden. It was pleasant and cool. Books filled the shelves along all the walls; some were chained and padlocked, others stood open on lecterns. At the far end were the study carrels each built into a small portico containing a table, chair, a tray of writing implements and a large, metal-capped beeswax candle. At first Corbett thought the library was deserted. He walked slowly down, his footsteps echoing through the cavernous room.

'Who's there?'

Corbett's heart skipped a beat. Brother Odo emerged from the shadows where he had been poring over a manuscript: his one good hand was covered in ink.

'Sir Hugh, I did not know you were a bibliophile.'

'I wish I was, Brother.'

Corbett shook his hand and the librarian led him into one of the study carrels.

'All these books and manuscripts belong to the Templars,' Odo explained. 'Well, at least to its province north of the Trent.' He fingered his ink-stained lips and looked round wistfully. 'We lost so many libraries in the East. We even had an original of Jerome's commentary . . . but you haven't come to ask me about that, have you?'

He jabbed a finger at a stool next to his chair. Corbett sat down self-consciously and stared at the manuscripts littered across the desk.

'I am writing a chronicle,' Odo announced proudly. 'A history of the siege of Acre and its fall.'

He pulled across a piece of vellum and Corbett stared at the drawing: Templar knights, distinctive by the crosses on their cloaks, were defending a tower; they were throwing spears and boulders down at evil-looking Turks. The drawing was not accurate, it lacked proportion – yet it possessed a vigour and vibrancy all of its own. Underneath, written in a cramped hand, was a Latin commentary.

'I have done seventy-three pieces,' Odo announced. 'But I hope that the chronicle will include two hundred; a lasting testament to the valour of our Order.'

A piece of parchment fell off the table. Corbett picked it up. There was writing on this but it was strange and twisted. Corbett, fluent in Latin and the Norman French of the Royal Chancery, thought it might be Greek.

'What language is that, Corbett?' Odo teased.

'Greek?'

Odo grinned and seized the parchment.

'No. They are runes, Anglo-Saxon runes. My mother's name was Tharlestone. She claimed descent from Leofric, Harold's brother, who died at the Battle of Hastings. She owned lands in Norfolk. Have you ever been there, Corbett?'

The clerk recalled his recent, and most dangerous, stay outside Mortlake Manor the previous November.

'Yes,' he replied. 'But perhaps it was not the happiest of visits.'

'Well, I was raised there. My mother died young.' The old librarian's eyes misted over. 'Gentle as a fawn she was. No other woman like her: that's probably the reason I entered the Order. Ah well,' he continued briskly, 'my grandfather raised me. He would take me fishing on the marshes. I still do that now, you know: I have a little boat down near the lake. I call it *The Ghost of the Tower*. Anyway, whilst Grandfather and I were waiting for the fish to bite, he'd scratch out the runes on a piece of bark and make me learn them. See that letter there like our "P"? That's "W". The arrow is a "T" and the sign like a gate is "V". I make my own notes.' He plucked the parchment from Corbett's hand. 'So no one really knows what I am doing.' He smiled. 'Ah well, how can I help you?'

'On the day Reverchien died,' Corbett asked, 'did you notice anything amiss, anything wrong?'

'No. Both Sir Guido and I were pleased when the grand master and his commanders left. Framlingham went back to its usual serene ways. We went round checking stores, I spent most of the time here in the library. We met in church to sing the Divine Office. He had a good voice, Reverchien, slightly higher than mine. We thundered out the verses then supped in the refectory. The next morning, just after Matins, Sir Guido went on what he called his little Crusade.' He shrugged. 'The rest you know.'

'And then what?'

'Well, when I smelt the smoke and heard the screams, some

115

of the servants and I went into the maze. It looks difficult to thread so you must keep moving in a certain direction.' The old man's face became sad. 'But, by the time we reached the centre . . .' His voice faltered. 'Oh, don't misunderstand me. I have seen men burning alive at Acre but, in the centre of an English maze on a warm spring morning, to see a comrade's body smouldering, blackened ash from head to toe. The flames must have been intense. The ground and the great iron candelabra were all burnt black. We sheeted the corpse and took it to the death-house. I went into the buttery. Perhaps I drank more than I should have. I felt sleepy so I went back to my cell. I was snoring my head off when Branquier woke me.'

'What do you think caused the fire?' Corbett asked.

'I don't know. The whispers say the fire of hell.' The old librarian leaned closer. 'But Sir Guido was a good man, kind and generous: a little addled in his wits but he loved God, Holy Mother Church and his Order. Why should such a good man be burnt, whilst the wicked swagger around boasting of their evil?' The librarian blinked; he ran his good hand across the parchment, stroking it gently like a mother would a child.

'I don't believe it was the fire of hell,' Corbett remarked. 'Sir Guido was a good man. He was murdered. But how, and why, God only knows.'

'The flames had died but it smelt so bad.' Odo murmured. 'I could smell the sulphur and brimstone in the air. Just like . . .'

'Like what?' Corbett asked.

The old librarian scratched his unshaven cheek. 'I can't remember,' he whispered. 'God forgive me, Corbett, but I can't.' He looked at the clerk. 'Is there anything else?'

Corbett shook his head and got to his feet. He gently pressed Odo's thin shoulder.

'They'll talk of you in years to come,' Corbett declared kindly. 'They'll talk of Odo Tharlestone, soldier and scholar. Your chronicle will be copied in monasteries, libraries and abbeys throughout the land. The halls of Oxford and Cambridge will bid for it.'

Odo looked up, his eyes sparkling. 'Do you really think so?'

'Oh, yes, the king has a great library at Westminster. He'll want a copy as well but, Brother,' Corbett added, 'reflect on what you saw the morning Sir Guido died.'

And with the librarian's assurance that he would do so ringing in his ears, Corbett went to the stables to join his companions.

A few minutes later, accompanied by Claverley and Ranulf, who were arguing noisily about which was the fairest, York or London, Corbett left Framlingham. They rode down the lonely pathway, past the guards and through the gate, turning left on to the Botham Bar road. The day was drawing on but the sun was still strong. The hedgerows on either side were alive with the rustling of birds and the buzzing of bees searching for honey amongst the wild flowers.

'I have beehives,' Claverley announced. 'At least a dozen steppes in my garden. The best honey in York, Sir Hugh.'

Corbett smiled absentmindedly. His mind was back in that library. Odo had remembered something. Corbett just hoped the old man's long memory would produce a key to unlock all these mysteries. They rode on under the shadow of the towering trees. At last Claverley reined in.

'We have to leave the road here.' The under-sheriff pointed to a small, beaten trackway on the edge of the forest. 'The remains were found deeper in.'

'What happened to them?' Ranulf asked.

'They had been unearthed by some animal. They were rotting, rather mangled, then tossed about by the hunting dogs. They were put into a leather sack; a verderer took them into the city for burial in a pauper's grave. Look, I'll show you.'

They left the trackway and entered the forest. The sunlight began to fade as the path wound along between holm, oak, elm, larch, black poplar, sycamore, beech and copper beech. The

117

sky became shut off, the sunlight blocked out by the thick canopy of leaves and entwining branches. Their horses became uneasy at the rustling amongst the bracken and the sudden, startling song of some bird. Now and again there would be a break in the trees, and they'd cross a clearing where the grass grew long and lush and wild flowers filled the air with their heady scent. Then back into the green darkness, as if entering some strange cathedral where the walls were wooded, the roof green and the distant bird-song the chanting of some choir. Ranulf, frightened of nothing, stopped his banter with Claverley and peered nervously about. Corbett rode ahead, guiding his horse carefully, ears straining for the snap of the twig or a footfall which could mean danger. Now and again his horse would toss its head, snorting angrily. Corbett tightened his reins, stroking his horse's neck, talking to it gently.

'Of course, I've already been here,' Claverley declared in a voice which seemed to boom amongst the trees. 'It's not far now.'

He pushed his horse forward and they entered a small glade. Claverley pointed to an outcrop of rock in the centre where the soil had been dug up and piled on either side of a hole. Corbett nudged his horse forward and carefully examined where the grisly remains of that mysterious victim had been buried. He stared at the rough cross carved on the rock.

'Is there any settlement round here? A village or hamlet?'

Claverley shrugged and scratched his cropped hair. 'Not that I know of.'

'Well, there's nothing behind us.' Corbett remarked. 'And there's no trace of any settlement to the left or right, so let's keep to the path we are following.'

They rode deeper into the forest. Corbett closed his eyes and prayed that the assassin from Framlingham had not followed them; he reined in, his horse whinnying at the acrid tang of the woodsmoke.

'There's something ahead,' he called back.

'Possibly a verderer,' Claverley replied. 'Or a woodcutter.'

At last the trees thinned and they rode into a clearing. At the far end, just in front of the line of trees, was a large, thatched cottage, its roof heavy and sloping. On either side of it were wooden sheds or byres and stacks of logs, around which scrawny-necked chickens pecked at the earth. A gaggle of geese, alarmed at their approach, turned from their feeding and fled screeching towards the house. The door opened and a mongrel dog came yapping at them, followed by two children dressed in ragged tunics, their hands and faces covered in soot, their thick hair greasy and matted. They showed no fear but stared up at these unexpected visitors, chattering in a dialect Corbett couldn't understand.

'What do you want?'

A man stood in the doorway. He was dressed in a dark-brown tunic, a piece of rope around his protuberant belly, leggings of the same colour pushed into black, battered boots. Over his shoulder a woman peered nervously at Corbett and his companions. The clerk raised his hand in peace. The man put down the axe he carried, called off the dog and walked towards them.

'Are you lost?' he asked.

'No. We are from the city.' Claverley edged his horse forward. 'We are investigating the remains found in the clearing.'

The man glanced away. 'Aye, I heard about the excitement,' he muttered. He shuffled his feet nervously and turned to shout something at the children.

'Can we come in?' Corbett asked. He pointed across at the well. 'Perhaps a stoup of water and something to eat? We are hungry.'

'Master,' Maltote spoke up, 'we have just—' He shut up as Ranulf glared at him.

Corbett dismounted and held his hand out. 'I am Sir Hugh Corbett, King's Clerk – and you?'

The woodcutter lifted his windburnt face, though he refused

to meet Corbett's gaze. 'Osbert,' he muttered. 'Verderer and woodcutter.' He glanced back at his wife. 'You'd best come in!' he declared grudgingly.

Corbett told Maltote to guard the horses and they followed the woodcutter and his family into their long, shed-like house. A fire burnt on the stone hearth in the centre, the smoke escaping through a hole in the room. At the far end was a loft reached by a ladder where the family slept: there were a few sticks of furniture and shelves with some cooking pots on them.

'You'd best sit where you can.' The woodcutter pointed to the beaten earth floor.

Corbett, Ranulf and Claverley sat near the hearth. Corbett chatted to Osbert's wife, putting her at her ease whilst her husband filled pewter cups with water. The woman smiled, pushing back her hair, and leaned over to stir the pot which hung above the hearth.

'It smells delicious,' Corbett remarked, though the odour was less than savoury.

'What do you want?' Osbert asked. He served the water and sat down opposite them. 'You are a king's clerk. You are used to eating better than this. Your servants carry water-bottles so you don't need a drink.'

'No, I don't,' Corbett replied. 'And you, Master Osbert, have very sharp eyes. As do I. You buried those remains, didn't you?'

The woodcutter's wife scuttled away to look after the children who sat near the wall, thumbs in mouths, watching their visitors.

'You found the remains,' Corbett continued. 'And, because you are an upright man, you buried them. You dug a hole beneath the boulder, hoping that would keep wild animals out and, with your axe, scratched a faint cross on it.'

'Tell him,' Osbert's wife pointed at Corbett. 'He knows!' she shouted. 'Or we'll all hang!'

'Nonsense,' Corbett exclaimed. 'Just tell me, Osbert.'

'It was just before dawn,' the woodcutter replied. 'I was out hunting a fox, one of the chickens had been taken. I heard a whinny and found the horse just off the road: its leg was damaged. The horse limped towards me. I thought I'd died and gone to hell: the mangled legs of its rider were still in the stirrups. Blood and gore drenched the saddle. The horse was blown: I took the remains and buried them beneath the rock. I said a prayer, then I brought the horse home. I threw the saddle down a pit. I couldn't sell it, it was too soaked in blood.'

'And the horse itself?'

Osbert swallowed hard and pointed to the pot. 'We are eating it.'

Ranulf coughed and spluttered.

'We are hungry,' Osbert continued. 'Hungry for meat. All the deer have gone. They've got more sense than to stay near the city.' He spread his dirty hands. 'What could I do, Master? If I took the horse to market, I'd hang for a thief. If I'd kept it, the same might happen. The animal was sick, its leg was damaged and I know little physic. I killed it: gutted its belly, salted and pickled the rest and hid it away in a little hut deep in the forest, hung over some charcoal to smoke it and stop the putrefaction.'

'And what else did you find?' Corbett asked. He took two silver coins out of his purse. 'Tell me the truth and these will be yours; there'll be no recriminations over what you did.'

Osbert wetted his lips and pondered but his wife acted for him. She went to the far end of the hut, climbed the ladder to the bed-loft and returned carrying a set of battered saddle panniers over her arm. She slung these at Corbett's feet.

'There was a little money,' Osbert grumbled. 'Now it's all gone. I bought the geese with it. What's left is there.'

Corbett emptied the contents out: a jerkin, two pairs of hose neatly darned, a belt, a collection of small metal pilgrim badges and statues of saints, cheap geegaws to be bought outside any church. Finally a few scraps of parchment. Corbett studied the faded ink on these.

'Wulfstan of Beverley,' he announced. 'A seller of religious objects and petty relics.' He glanced at Claverley and Ranulf. 'Why on earth would someone kill poor Wulfstan? Cut his body in two, send his horse galloping madly into the darkness and burn the top half?' Corbett threw the saddlebag at Claverley. He got to his feet and pressed the two coins into Osbert's hands. 'Next time you go to Mass,' Corbett added, 'pray for the soul of poor Wulfstan.'

'I did what I could,' Osbert muttered. 'God assoil him. Is there anything else, Master?'

Corbett asked, 'In the forest, have you ever glimpsed a rider, masked and cowled?'

'Once,' Osbert replied. 'Only once, Master, just after I found the horse. I was out cutting firewood on the edge of Botham Bar road. I heard a sound so I hid in the bracken. A rider passed, dressed like a monk. His horse was a nag and the cloak was tattered but I glimpsed a great two-handed sword hanging from the saddlehorn. I thought he was an outlaw so I stayed hidden until he passed.' The woodcutter pulled a face. 'That's all I've seen.'

Corbett thanked him. They left the woodcutter's, collected their horses and rode back on to the Botham Bar road. Ranulf and Claverley immediately became involved in a fierce argument over the eating of horseflesh. Maltote, pale-faced, could only feebly protest.

'To eat a horse!' he kept exclaiming. 'To eat a horse!'

'You would,' Claverley called back. 'My father told me how, in the great famine outside Carlisle, they caught rats and sold them as a delicacy.'

Corbett urged his horse on, only stopping when he came to the place where Wulfstan's burnt remains had been found.

'What are you looking for?' Claverley called out as Corbett dismounted and walked into the line of trees.

'I'll tell you when I find it,' Corbett replied.

He walked further in and crouched down to examine the great scorch-marks on the earth. He then drew his sword and began cutting the brambles and long grass. As he did so, Corbett glimpsed more, though much smaller, scorch-marks. And on the trees which fringed the undergrowth, Corbett noticed scratch-marks, as if some great cat had clawed the back, gouging and scarring it.

'What on earth caused this?' Claverley exclaimed, coming up behind him.

Corbett looked back towards the road where Maltote sat on his horse staring soulfully at them.

'This is what I think happened,' Corbett explained. 'Someone came here to practise with the fire which burnt Wulfstan and the others.'

'It looks as if the devil himself has swept up from hell,' Claverley intervened. 'His tail scorched the earth and his claws gouged the trees.'

'Yes, you could sell such a story in York marketplace,' Corbett replied. 'But I am sure the Lord Satan has better things to do than journey up from hell to burn grass and brambles on the Botham Bar road. No. Somebody was practising with that fire, whilst the marks on the trees are made by arrows.'

'So, the killer was firing arrows?'

'Possibly,' Corbett explained. 'He created small fires, for God knows what reason, and practised shooting arrows using the trees as targets. Now I think he was so busy, so confident under the cover of dusk, that he failed to notice Wulfstan. Our poor relic-seller came trotting along the Botham Bar road, journeying to some village or market town to sell his geegaws. Now anyone else would have gone hastily by or even turned back. Wulfstan, however, was a pedlar, a man who loved to travel and collect stories as he did. He stopped where Maltote now is, probably calling out through the dusk. The assassin turns. He has been recognised. His horse stands nearby. He hurries up, draws his great two-handed sword hanging from the saddlehorn and rushes towards Wulfstan. The relic-seller would sit startled, frightened, immobile as a rabbit. He'd raise his hands to his face as the assassin swings that terrible sword, slicing his body in two with one savage cut.'

'And the horse bolts?' Ranulf asked.

'Yes, the violent stench of blood sends the poor nag stampeding down the road. Our killer then sets the top half of the corpse alight. In doing so, he not only prevents any identification but finds out, for his own devilish curiosity, the effect of this strange fire on human flesh.'

'And, of course,' Claverley intervened, 'Wulfstan being a pedlar, a stranger to these parts, no one came forward to declare he is missing.'

'Master.' Ranulf pointed to the scorch-marks on the ground. 'How can a man control fire? We have a tinder which can be clumsy to strike, especially in the open air. Or you can kindle a fire and take a burning stick or piece of charcoal, but this killer seems to be able to summon it out of the air.' Ranulf stared into the green darkness of the trees. 'Isn't that magic? The use of the black arts?'

'No,' Corbett retorted. 'I could call up Satan from hell but, whether he comes or not is another matter. This killer wants us to believe he has magical powers, the key to all sorcery.'

'And this mysterious rider,' Claverley asked. 'He might be the killer; he did carry a great two-handed sword.'

Corbett kicked at the scorched path. 'Perhaps. But, Master Under-sheriff, we must go: other matters, just as pressing, await us.'

They remounted their horses and rode down Botham Bar road. As they approached York, the road became busier: traders and pedlars making their way out of the city, packs and fardels on their backs: a dusty-gowned Franciscan of the Order of the Sack leading an even more tired mule. A beggar pushed a wheelbarrow in which an old man sprawled, his legs shorn from the knees down: both looked happy enough after a day's begging and, drunk as sots, raucously bawled out filthy songs as the barrow staggered along the road. Peasants huddled in their carts, their produce sold, and a woman and two children walked wearily, leading a cow. A royal messenger galloped by, his white wand of office tucked into his belt; the soldier riding behind him wore the resplendent livery of the king's chamber. Everyone drew aside to let them pass and, shortly afterwards, had to do the same again as a Templar soldier urged his foam-flecked horse along the road.

'I thought all Templars were confined to Framlingham?' Claverley asked.

'Probably a messenger,' Corbett replied. 'I wonder what's so urgent?'

They pressed on. Botham Bar came into sight, the great iron portcullis raised like jagged teeth over the people passing through. On top of the gatehouse were poles bearing the severed heads of malefactors and, on either side of the gateway, makeshift gallows had been set up. Each bore its own grisly corpse twirling in the late afternoon breeze, placards slung round the necks proclaiming their crimes.

'The king's justices have been busy,' Claverley declared. 'There's been sessions of gaol delivery all of yesterday.'

'Where are you taking us?' Corbett asked.

'To see the Limner.'

'The what?'

'The Greyhound: my nickname for the best counterfeiter in York.'

They continued under Botham Bar, along Petersgate, past the foul-smelling public latrines built next to St Michael the Belfry Church, and into the busiest part of the city. The market stalls were still open. The narrow streets thronged. The taverns were doing a roaring trade. One man lay in the middle of the street in a drunken stupor whilst a friend lying alongside tried to beat off marauding hogs, much to the delight of passers-by.

The stocks were also full. Some malefactors were fastened by the neck, others by the arms and legs. One apprentice had his thumbs only clasped into a finger press for helping himself to his master's food. Two whores stood in the pillory, heads shaven, shouting abuse at the crowd whilst a drunken bagpipe player tried to drown their cries as a bailiff birched their bare bottoms. On the corner of a street Corbett and his party had to stay for a while: a group of officials from the alderman's court had raided a tavern to search out old wine, long past its freshness. They'd seized three barrels and were trying to stave these in whilst, from the windows above, the landlord, his wife and family pelted the bailiffs and everyone else with the smelly contents of their chamberpots.

At last the bailiffs restored order and Claverley led them on along Patrick Pool and into the Shambles. The smells and dust caught at their noses and mouths: the butchers' and fletchers' narrow street, which ran between the overhanging houses, was covered in offal and black blood. Flies massed there, dogs and cats fought over scraps. The crowd, eager to buy fresh meat, thronged around the stalls from which gutted pigs, decapitated geese, chickens and other fowl hung. At last Claverley lost his temper. He drew his sword and, shouting, '*Le roi, le roi!*' forced a passage out on to the Pavement, the great open area fronting All Saints Church.

Here the crowds thronged before the grim city prison. Outside its main door stood a line of scaffolds, each three-branched, on which executions were being carried out. The condemned felons were led out from the prison, taken on to a platform, pushed up a ladder, where a noose was fixed round their neck. The ladder was then turned and the felon would dance and kick as the hempen cord tightened round his throat, choking his life out. Corbett had seen such sights before in many of the king's great cities. The royal justices would arrive, the gaols would be emptied, courts held and swift sentence passed. Most of the felons didn't even have time to protest. Dominicans, dressed in their black and white robes, moved from one scaffold to another whispering the final absolution. The crowd thronging there sometimes greeted the appearance of a prisoner with curses and yells. Now and again a friend or relative would shout their farewells and lift a tankard in salute. Claverley waited until the prison door opened, then pushed his way through into the sombre gatehouse. The doorkeeper recognised him.

'We are nearly finished, Claverley!' he shouted. 'And by dusk York will be a safer place.'

'I've come for the Limner!' Claverley snapped, leaning down from his horse. 'Where is he?'

The porter's beer-sodden face stared up. 'What do you want him for?'

'I need to talk to him.'

'Well, only if you know the path to hell.'

Claverley groaned and beat his saddlehorn.

'The bugger's dead,' the porter laughed. 'Hanged not an hour since.'

Claverley, conscious of his companions, their horses growing restless in the enclosed space, cursed colourfully.

'What now?' Corbett asked.

Claverley turned, spat in the direction of the porter, then tapped the side of his nose.

'There's nothing for it,' he whispered. 'Let me introduce you to one of my great secrets!'

On the other side of York, another man was dying. The Unknown lay on a pallet bed in a small, stark chamber of the Lazar hospital, his sweat-soaked hair fanned out against the white bolster.

'It's all over,' he whispered. 'I shall not leave here alive.'

The Franciscan, crouching by the bed, grasped his hand and did not disagree.

'I can feel no life in my legs,' the Unknown muttered. He

127

forced a smile. 'In my youth, Father, I was a superb horseman. I could ride like the wind.' He moved his head slightly. 'What happens after death, Father?'

'Only God knows,' the Franciscan replied. 'But I think it's like a journey, like being born all over again. A baby struggles against leaving the womb, we struggle against leaving life but, as we do after we're born, we forget and journey on. What is important,' the Franciscan added, 'is how prepared we are for that journey.'

'I have sinned,' the Unknown whispered. 'I have sinned against Heaven and earth. I, a knight of the Temple, a defender of the city of Acre, have committed dreadful sins of hate and a desire for vengeance.'

'Tell me,' the Franciscan replied. 'Make your confession now. Receive absolution.'

The Unknown needed no further prompting but, staring up at the ceiling, began to recite his life: his youth on a farm in Barnsleydale; his admission to the Temple; those final, bloody days at Acre followed by the long years of pent-up bitterness in the dungeons of the Old Man of the Mountain. The Franciscan listened quietly; only now and again did he interrupt and softly ask a question. The knight always answered. At the end the Franciscan lifted his hand, carefully enunciating the words of absolution. He promised that, the following morning, he'd bring the Viaticum after Mass. The Unknown grasped the friar's hand.

'Father, in all truth, I must tell what I know to someone else.'

'A Templar?' the Franciscan asked. 'The commanders are gathered at Framlingham.'

The Unknown closed his eyes and sighed. 'No, the traitor may be there.' He opened his cracked lips, gasping for air. 'The King's Council is in York, yes?'

The Franciscan nodded. The Unknown squeezed his hand tightly.

'For the love of God, Father, I must speak to one of the King's Council. A man I can trust. Please, Father.' The eyes in that thin, disfigured face burned with life. 'Please, before I die!'

Chapter 8

Claverley led Corbett and his companions from the Pavement up towards the Minster, and into a more refined, serene quarter of the city. The streets were broad and clean, the houses on either side had their plaster painted pink and white, the upright beams a polished or a dark mahogany, sometimes gilt-edged around windows and doors. Each stood, four or five storeys high, in its own little garden. The windows on the bottom floors were filled with glass and on the top storey with horn or oiled linen. Claverley stopped in front of one which stood on a corner of an alleyway, across from the Jackanapes tavern. He brought up the iron clanger carved in the shape of a monk's face, and rapped loudly. At first there was no sound, though Corbett could see the glow of candlelight through the windows.

'Don't worry.' Claverley grinned over his shoulder. 'She'll be at home.'

At last the door swung open. A maid poked her head out. Claverley whispered to her and the door closed. Corbett heard chains being removed, then it swung open and a small, grey-haired lady, dressed in a white, gold-edged veil and a gown of dark burgundy, came out. She smiled and kissed Claverley on his cheek; bright button eyes in a swarthy face studied Corbett and his companions.

'Well, you'd best come in,' she said huskily. 'You can leave your horses in the stable at the Jackanapes.'

Whilst Maltote led their mounts off, the woman took them

into what she called 'her downstairs parlour', a long, comfortable chamber which must have stretched the length of the house. Through the open window at the far end, Corbett glimpsed flowerbeds and a small orchard of apple trees. The room was luxurious. There had been rushes in the passageway outside, but in here carpets lay on the floor and broad strips of bright cloth hung against the wall. A tapestry was fixed above the hearth, and on a long beam which spanned the ceiling stood row upon row of flickering candles.

'Sir Hugh Corbett,' Claverley made the introductions. 'May I introduce Jocasta Kitcher, gentlewoman, merchant, the maker of fine cloth, owner of the Jackanapes tavern and, in her time, a much travelled lady.'

'Once a flatterer always a flatterer,' Jocasta retorted.

She ushered her visitors towards the hearth as a maid, hurrying from the kitchens, pulled up chairs around the weak fire. At first there was confusion: Ranulf knocked a stool over and then Dame Jocasta insisted that they 'partake of her hospitality', telling the maid to bring goblets of wine and a tray of marzipan biscuits.

Corbett's stomach was still unsettled after the executions, but the effusive bonhomie of this little lady and the air of mystery around her soon distracted him. He sat on his chair and sipped the wine, surprised at its sweet coolness.

Dame Jocasta leaned forward. 'My cellars are always flooded,' she declared. 'Oh, not with sewer muck. York has underground rivers and the water is icy cold, it keeps the white wine chilled.'

'Are there many such rivers?' Corbett asked.

'Oh, Lord above.' Jocasta twirled her cup, inlaid with mother-of-pearl, between her hands. 'York is two cities, Sir Hugh. There's what you see in the streets, but – ' her voice dropped to a deep whisper – 'underneath the lanes there's another city built by the Romans: it has sewers and paths, long forgotten.' She grinned. 'I know, my husband and I used those sewers a great deal. Oh, don't look so puzzled,' she rattled on. 'Hasn't Claverley told you?'

'That's the reason I brought him here!' Claverley declared. 'I haven't yet told him our secrets, Dame Jocasta, but I thought you could help. There's a counterfeiter in York,' he continued hurriedly.

'Then trap and hang him!'

'This is different,' Corbett replied. He took a gold coin and handed it over.

Jocasta's hand was warm and soft, her fingers covered with expensive rings. She grasped the coin and examined it with a sigh of admiration, letting it drop from hand to hand, weighing it carefully, studying the rim and the cross carved on either side.

'This is pure gold.'

'Whatever they are,' Corbett intervened, 'they are not from the king's Mint and are issued without royal licence. Now, I agree, Dame Jocasta, counterfeiters usually take one good coin and make two bad, adulterating the silver with base alloys and metals. However, I've never heard of anyone using the finest gold to counterfeit coins.'

Dame Jocasta lifted her head. 'Sir Hugh, you need not tell me about counterfeiting. Forty years ago – aye I look younger than I am,' she added merrily, her small eyes bright with laughter. '. . . forty years ago I ran wild in this city. My parents could not control me. On a hot midsummer's day I went to a fair outside Micklegate Bar. I met the merriest rogue on God's own earth, my husband, Robard. Now he was a clerk, fallen on hard times. He couldn't abide the stuffy Chanceries and the long, miserable-faced clerks.'

She paused as Ranulf choked on the biscuit he was eating. Corbett's glare soon made him clear his throat. Ranulf hid his face, staring into the wine cup as if something very precious lay there.

'Robard was a knave born and bred,' Jocasta continued.

'He could sing like a robin and dance the maypole into the ground. He was attracted to mischief like a cat to cream. I loved him immediately. I still do, even though he's ten years dead.'

Claverley stretched over and touched her hand. 'Finish your story,' he murmured.

'Well, well, well.' Jocasta held up the gold piece, she turned it so it caught the candlelight. 'Robard would have loved this. He wanted to be rich, amass silver and go to foreign parts to be a great merchant or warrior. I became part of his knavery. I'd steal out of my house at night and join him in the moonlight. We'd lie on the tombstones of St Peter's Church and he would tell me tales of what we could do. We became handfast, betrothed, then Robard's desire to become rich led him into counterfeiting. He became known amongst the cunning and upright men of the city, the cranks, the palliards, the foists, pickpockets, all the scum of the earth.' She shrugged. 'We hired a small forge just off Coney Street and began to counterfeit coins. This was in the old king's time, when the governance of the city was not what it should be . . . Then we were caught. At the assizes Robard was given two choices: either hang from the gallows on the Pavement or join Prince Edward's Crusade. Of course, he chose the latter. The levies massed outside in the meadows in Bishop's Fields just across the river. Robard, however, was a pressed man: he was kept in chains until he boarded the king's ships. I went with him.'

'You went to Outremer!' Corbett exclaimed.

'Oh, yes. Three years in all. But we came back rich. We bought the tavern across the alleyway: Robard became a landlord, an ale-master and a taverner. My parents were dead. I became his wife, but old habits die hard, Sir Hugh. Once the rogues of the city knew he was home, we were never left alone. Robard would receive visitors at the dead of night but he always kept within the law.' She laughed self-consciously. 'Or nearly so. Once again we were drawn into counterfeiting but, this time, I swear to God, I was not party to it. Now pride always goes before a fall. The king's justices returned to York, a grand jury was convened, and allegations were laid against my husband.'

Claverley interrupted. 'Twice convicted, Robard would have hanged. Moreover, his first crimes were still remembered. Dame Jocasta came before the sheriffs and a secret pact was made. Robard would receive a pardon but Jocasta swore a great oath that in future she would let the sheriffs and thief-takers know of crimes and felonies being planned in the city.'

'I turned king's evidence,' Dame Jocasta quietly added. 'And my husband never knew. Oh, I was selective. I still am. The little foists, the petty criminals, I ignore, but not those who kill and maim, the rapists and violators of churches. As any tavern-keeper does, I hear the whispers and I pass them on . . .'

'But your husband never knew?'

'Never,' Jocasta declared. 'And nor does anyone else except Claverley.' Her face became hard. 'I don't dress in widow's weeds.' She tapped her chest. 'Robard's still here. I close my eyes and I can hear him singing. At night, if I turn on the bolster, I see his face smiling at me. He wasn't a bad man, Sir Hugh, but oh, Lord save us, he loved mischief.'

'And yet you tell us now?' Corbett asked.

'Before I left York to meet you, Sir Hugh,' Claverley interrupted, 'I came here. If Limner refused to help you, Dame Jocasta promised she would.' He shrugged and turned to the woman. 'But Limner's hanged,' he announced flatly.

'God grant him safe passage.'

'Dame Jocasta and I have known each other for years,' Claverley explained. 'True,' he wagged a finger, 'the art of counterfeiting may well be a subtle one but, in this city, Dame Jocasta knows everything about it.'

Corbett stared through the window at the far end of the room and watched the sunshine die. A wild thought occurred to him: what if Jocasta was the master counterfeiter?

'I couldn't do it,' she declared, as if reading his thoughts. 'I don't have a forge or the precious metal. More importantly, I know all the secret whispers. Yet, I've heard nothing.' She held the coin up. 'And, believe me, tongues would certainly clack about this.'

Corbett cleared his throat and glanced away in embarrassment.

'So, how is it done?' Ranulf asked. 'Who's responsible?'

Jocasta put her cup down. 'Sir Hugh, I have never seen a coin like this before. Most counterfeiters debase the king's coin, yes?'

Corbett agreed.

'So, why should someone produce gold coins except . . .' She paused.

'Except what?'

'Well, let us say, Sir Hugh, you found a pot of gold. No, not at the end of a rainbow, but a treasure trove: cups, mazers, ewers, crosses. What would you do?'

'I'd take it to the sheriffs or the royal justices.'

Dame Jocasta laughed: Claverley and Ranulf joined in. The old woman shook her head.

'I am not mocking you, Sir Hugh; you are an honest man.' Her face became serious. 'But what would happen then?'

Now Corbett smiled. 'Well, the royal clerks would seize the gold. They'd examine it then come back and interrogate me.'

'And how long would that last?'

'A year, maybe even two: until I'd proved both my innocence and that the gold was truly treasure trove.'

'So!' Jocasta exclaimed. 'You found some treasure. You are honest but the king's clerks take it and all you get is a sea of troubles.'

'Aye,' Corbett added. 'And at the end of it all, half of what I found, though, knowing the Exchequer officials as I do, I'd be lucky if I got a quarter.'

'So,' Ranulf spoke up. 'Dame Jocasta, this gold.' He paused.

'By the way, Master, Maltote has not returned.'

'Oh, he's probably in the tavern,' Corbett replied. 'You know Maltote: he'll be talking horses with the stable boy and grooms and downing tankards as if his life depended on it. What were you going to say?'

'Someone in York,' Ranulf continued, 'has found a treasure trove, melted it down and made coins. He has then used those coins to buy comforts and luxuries for himself.'

'Precisely,' Dame Jocasta agreed. 'It's the only way. If you take gold and silver objects to a goldsmith, you immediately become suspect, either as a felon or someone who's found treasure trove and is flouting the king's rights in the matter. Now, such treasure is easy to trace. No goldsmith would be party to that.' She played with the coin in her hand. 'Whoever made this has a very good forge and the means to buy all the coining tools.'

'But wouldn't anyone become suspicious?' Claverley asked. 'If gold vessels can be traced back to their original owner, so can gold coins.'

'Not if fifty or sixty appeared at the same time,' Jocasta replied. 'And that's what Robard used to do with his counterfeit coins. The more you distribute, the safer you are. The man who counterfeited these coins did the same. He must have the means to move round York and bring these coins into circulation without raising suspicion.' She rubbed the coin between her fingers. 'And that's the whole beauty of it. All a goldsmith and a banker will do is weigh coins on a scale. After all, its not their fault if these coins end up in their possession. They have become party to the crime but can act the innocent. They have sold foodstuffs or cloths, wines or whatever. They have a right to be paid: the coins are accepted and people become forgetful.'

Corbett leaned back in the chair. 'Brilliant,' he whispered. 'You find gold. You melt it down into coins, you distribute them and, by doing so, bring everyone else into your game. At

the same time you evade the law and become very, very rich.'
He looked at Dame Jocasta. 'And you have no idea . . .?'

'Don't stare at me like that, Clerk,' she teased back. 'This
counterfeiter is no ruffian or miscreant clipping coins or melting
them down over a charcoal fire. This cunning man is very
wealthy: he has the means and the wherewithal.'

'But couldn't the coins be traced?' Ranulf asked insistently.
'Someone, somewhere, would remember?'

Dame Jocasta pointed to Corbett's purse. 'Master Clerk,
you have good silver there? Can you remember exactly which
coin was given to you by what person?'

'But I'd remember a gold coin,' Ranulf replied.

'Would you?' Jocasta retorted. 'If you thought it might be
seized and taken away from you? However,' she handed the
coin back to Corbett, 'you have a point. This counterfeiter
probably doesn't use coins to buy anything from city merchants.
After all, anyone paying gold here and there would eventually
be recognised.'

'So?' Corbett asked.

Dame Jocasta looked into the flames of the fire. She watched
the small, sweet-smelling pine logs crackle and snap on their
charcoal bed.

'I wish Robard was here,' she whispered. 'He'd know.' She
glanced up quickly. 'You are staying at Framlingham, the
Templar manor?'

Corbett nodded.

'Why not start there?' Jocasta murmured. 'The Templars
have the means: woods and copses to hide a secret forge. They
import foodstuffs and goods from abroad. They have connections
with bankers and goldsmiths. And, unless I am mistaken, this
gold appeared at the time the Templars arrived in York.'

'Yes, it did,' Corbett replied. 'The king and Court moved
down from the Scottish march and stayed outside York. Shortly
after the Templar commanders arrived, these coins began to
appear.'

'But where would they get the gold from?' Claverley asked.

Corbett toyed with his Chancery ring which bore the insignia of the Secret Seal.

'They did grant the king a huge gift,' Ranulf remarked. 'And they have treasures not known to anyone.'

Corbett recalled the secret room at Framlingham. Was there a connection between this gold and the murders?

'Sir Hugh?'

Corbett shook himself from his reverie. 'I am sorry, Dame Jocasta.' He rose to his feet, took her hand and pressed it with his lips. 'I thank you for your help.'

'You are not just hunting a counterfeiter, are you?' she asked shrewdly. 'Not the king's principal clerk!'

Corbett stroked her cheek gently with his finger. 'No, Domina, I am not. As usual,' he added bitterly, 'I am hunting demons: men who kill for the-devil-knows-what reason.'

'Then you should be careful, Clerk,' she replied softly. 'For those who hunt demons either become hunted, or demons themselves.'

Ranulf, standing in the shadows of the doorway, saw his master start, as if Jocasta's words had struck home, but then the old lady smiled and the tension eased. Corbett and Claverley made their farewells and followed Ranulf out and across into the yard of the Jackanapes tavern: here, a guilty-faced Maltote, brimming tankard to his lips, was declaiming to the round-eyed ostlers and slatterns what an important man he was. Ranulf, ever with an eye for mischief, joined the group and began to tease Maltote, whilst Corbett and Claverley went into the taproom. They took a table overlooking the small garden. For a while Corbett stared out, watching the sun set in a glorious explosion of colours. Claverley ordered some ale. Corbett sipped his, thinking of Dame Jocasta's warning as he fought the waves of homesickness. The flowers and the garden reminded him of home and, in his heart, Corbett knew that he would not stay here much longer. He wanted Maeve and Eleanor. He'd even sit for hours and listen to Uncle Morgan's fabulous boasting about the great Welsh heroes. He wanted to sleep in a bed with no dagger by his side and walk without a warbelt strapped round his waist.

'Was that helpful?' Claverley interrupted.

'Oh, yes, it was.' Corbett smiled an apology. 'We at least know the counterfeiter is powerful, wealthy, has access to gold and knows how to distribute these coins.'

'Could it be the Templars?' Claverley asked. 'At the Guildhall we've heard rumours . . .'

'I don't know,' Corbett replied. He leaned across the table and clapped the man on his shoulder. 'I am not the best of companions: Roger, are you a family man?'

'Twice married,' the under-sheriff replied with a grin. 'My first wife died but my second has given me lovely children.'

'Do you ever tire of hunting demons?' Corbett asked.

Claverley shook his head. 'I heard what Dame Jocasta said, Sir Hugh.' He sipped from his tankard and continued. 'We all bear the mark of Cain. Like you, Sir Hugh, I've seen the breakdown of law and order, when the demons come out of the shadows. So no, I don't ever tire of fighting them. If we don't hunt them, as God is my witness, they'll eventually come hunting us.'

Across the rim of his tankard, Corbett stared at Claverley. A good man, Corbett thought, just and upright. He promised himself to mention Claverley's name to the king. Ranulf and Maltote joined him: they would have continued their banter but one look at Corbett's face made Ranulf change his mind.

'Where now, Master?'

Corbett leaned back against the wall. 'We are not going back to Framlingham,' he declared. 'Not tonight. The Botham Bar road is dark and dangerous. Master Claverley, one favour, or rather four.'

'My orders are to give you every assistance.'

'First, I'd like rooms here.'

'That can be arranged.'

'Secondly,' Corbett said, 'our counterfeiter must have a forge. Now the city has tax rolls, forges are always part of an assessment.'

'Unless it's a secret one,' Claverley added.

'I also want a list,' Corbett persisted, 'of all those who have a licence to import goods into the city. Finally, if this gold is treasure trove, it must have been found during some building work. No burgess can do that without a licence from the aldermen.'

'Agreed,' Claverley said. 'So, you want a list of blacksmiths or anyone owning a forge: those with a licence to import and any citizen who has received a writ permitting him to build?'

'Yes, as soon as possible!'

'The Templars,' Claverley continued, 'will be on all three lists.'

'That's an extra favour,' Corbett replied. 'On the morning of the attack on the king, the grand master, Jacques de Molay, and four of his principal commanders, Legrave, Branquier, Baddlesmere and Symmes, came into the city. Now Branquier left early, or so he said. Baddlesmere and Symmes were by themselves for a long period of time whilst Legrave accompanied the grand master to a goldsmith's in Stonegate. Now York is a great city, but people know each other. The Templars would stand out. I want you to find just exactly what they did that morning.'

Claverley whistled under his breath. 'And where do I start?'

Corbett grinned and gestured around him. 'Ask the tavernmasters and landlords. Whatever you find, I'll be grateful.'

Claverley finished his drink and made his farewells. He promised that, if he discovered any information, he would personally travel out to Framlingham. Then he went across to talk to the landlord, standing behind a counter made out of wine barrels. Corbett saw the fellow nod. Claverley lifted his hand, shouted that all would be well and went out into the street.

'I am tired,' Corbett declared. 'Ranulf, Maltote, you can do what you want, provided you are back in our chamber within the hour.'

And, leaving his companions to grumble about 'Master Long Face', Corbett followed the landlord up to the second floor to what was grandly described as the tavern's principal guest-chamber. The room had only two beds but the landlord promised to provide a third. Whilst servants brought up straw-filled mattresses, new bolsters, fresh jugs of water and a tray containing bread and wine, Corbett went and lay down on a bed. This time he did not think of Leighton Manor and Maeve but tried to marshal his thoughts. He heard a noise in the passage outside, then Ranulf and Maltote burst into the room.

'For the love of God!' Corbett groaned, swinging his legs off the bed.

Ranulf, his face a picture of innocence, pulled across a stool and sat opposite Corbett.

'That old woman frightened you, didn't she?' he demanded.

'No, she did not frighten me, Ranulf,' Corbett replied. 'I am already frightened.' He pointed to his writing implements laid out on the table. 'Think of the murderers we have hunted, Ranulf. There's always been a motive: greed, lechery, treason. There's always a pattern to the killings, as the assassin removes those who block his way or may have guessed his identity. Yet this is different: here we have a man killing without purpose.'

'But you said the Templars were divided? They want revenge on the king.'

'In which case,' Corbett retorted, 'why kill Reverchien? Why attack me? And what threat in God's name did poor Peterkin pose? Moreover, there's no connection between the three.' Corbett continued. 'Oh, yes, if the king was injured or killed: if his principal clerk suffered some dreadful mishap, I suppose there's a logic to that. But why Reverchien and Peterkin?'

'Perhaps they knew something,' Ranulf retorted.

'Perhaps,' Corbett replied. 'But then we come to the second problem. How? Murston may have shot an arrow at the king but how did he die so quickly? How was that fire caused? Reverchien died in the centre of a maze early on a spring morning, Peterkin burst into flames in the middle of a busy kitchen.'

Corbett paused, chewing the corner of his lip. 'And what progress have we made? We know the Templar Order is demoralised, possibly splitting into factions: I'm sure that is why de Molay has come to England. These factions may be manifesting themselves through the attacks against Philip of France as well as our own king. We also have these warnings, sent by that strange sect "the Assassins". We know there's some mystery in the Order, hence those secret rooms at Framlingham. We've learnt Murston was eaten up with revenge and bitterness, yet he must have been managed by someone else.'

Corbett paused. 'The killer,' he continued after a while, 'is using some form of secret fire. He was practising with it amongst the trees along the Botham Bar road: that poor pedlar paid for his curiosity with his life. We think it's a Templar commander but, if all the Templars are confined to Framlingham and the city gates are so closely guarded, who attached that notice to Murston's gibbeted corpse? And who could have sent a similar warning to me? Whatever the Templars did in York, we have established that by the time these arrows were fired at me, they were on the road back to Framlingham Manor.'

'That masked rider, maybe he's the assassin?' Maltote asked hopefully. 'Or one of the commanders in disguise?'

'The counterfeit coins,' Ranulf interjected, 'may also be Templar villainy.'

'Possibly,' Corbett said. 'But whatever, Ranulf . . .' He lay back on his bed. 'If there's no method in this madness, if the assassin is killing for the sake of it, then he'll strike again and again.'

'And what will we do?' Ranulf asked.

'In the end,' Corbett replied, 'we will go back to the king and report what we have found: a divided, demoralised Order, bereft of its original purpose.' He half sat up, leaning on one arm. 'And if I report that,' he concluded, 'it will only be a matter of time before the Exchequer officials begin to ask why such a wealthy Order should exist when it lacks purpose and, moreover, is riddled with treason, sorcery, murder and other scandals?'

The serjeant patrolling the great meadow at Framlingham Manor stared down at the boat bobbing on the lake. 'It's time the old man came in,' he grumbled.

Hitching his swordbelt higher, he began the long walk down to the lakeside. Nevertheless, the sunset was glorious, and a cool evening breeze soothed the serjeant's sweat-soaked brow.

'Oh, let the old one fish,' he muttered to himself.

He sat down on the grass, took off his helmet and pulled back the mail coif beneath. He studied Odo: the old librarian had taken his boat *The Ghost of the Tower*, and had been fishing for some time.

'More bloody use than what I've been doing,' the serjeant grumbled as he grabbed a clump of grass to cool his sweaty cheeks.

The garrison at Framlingham had relaxed after that snooping royal clerk and his companions had left: that is, until the messenger had arrived and de Molay and the other great ones had gathered in the hall for a secret council. Orders had gone out, reinforcing the grand master's edict that no one was to leave Framlingham, whilst any stranger found wandering on the estate was to be arrested immediately. The Templar serjeant chewed on a piece of grass, narrowing his eyes against the setting sun as he watched Brother Odo's black cloak flap and curl in the evening breeze. The old librarian was apparently fighting to hold the long rod and line he was wielding. The

Templar serjeant envied the serenity of the scene after the turbulence of the last few days. The news of the attack upon the king, the killing of Reverchien and Peterkin the cook were known to all. Very few mentioned Murston's death, though many felt guilty at what he had done. Nevertheless, Murston had always been a hothead: just because he had served in Outremer, he'd set himself up as an authority on what was right and what was wrong.

The Templar lay back in the grass and stared up at the fleecy clouds.

'I wish I was away from here,' he whispered. 'But where?'

The fall of Acre had put a stop to service abroad. No more dark-skinned girls, no more wandering around the bazaars. There was now little excitement about battle or talk of guarding the holy sepulchre. The best one could expect was lonely garrison duty in a God-forsaken manor house or, if you were lucky, some expedition into the Middle Sea to fight the corsairs. The serjeant rubbed his eyes; it wasn't his duty to wonder or to speculate. Murston's fate had put an end to all that. And who was he to question the masters of his Order? They knew best. They had the secret knowledge which they discussed behind closed doors. The serjeant remembered that lonely garret at the top of Framlingham Manor. What *did* go on there, he wondered? Why were only de Molay and Branquier allowed to go in? Why the purple wax candles and the chanting? He'd once been on guard outside, when his superiors had come out, he'd noticed how both were covered in dust from head to toe. What was so special in that room, the serjeant wondered, that such important men should lie face down in the dust? He heard a sound and struggled to his feet. Odo was moving as if straining at the rod, but then the Templar serjeant glimpsed the fire burning in the prow of the boat. He dropped his helmet and began to run.

'Brother Odo! Brother Odo!' He shouted, but still that black cowled figure sat as if impervious to the leaping flames. The serjeant undid his swordbelt, running until his lungs were fit to burst. He watched as the boat and Brother Odo suddenly erupted into a sheet of fire. The Templar fell to his knees, shaking with fright. He watched the fire consuming the boat and its occupant from prow to stern; even the water of the lake seemed to provide no protection.

'Oh, Lord save us,' he gasped, 'from Satan's fire!'

Chapter 9

Corbett and his companions arrived back at Framlingham to find the manor in complete uproar. As soon as they dismounted in the stable yard, Baddlesmere, whiskers bristling, hurried out to greet them.

'Sir Hugh!' He swallowed hard. 'You'd best come to see the grand master!'

Despite the warm sun and blue skies, Corbett felt his feeling of oppression return. He glanced round the stables: Templar soldiers, now doing the tasks of the ostlers and grooms, stared blankly at him.

'There's been another death, hasn't there?' Corbett asked.

Baddlesmere nodded, indicating with his hand for Corbett to follow him.

The clerk told Maltote to take care of the horses and, with Ranulf striding beside him, walked into the manor. Baddlesmere took them across a small cloister-garth and into the grand master's chamber: a stark, unfurnished cell, much bigger than Corbett's but just as austere with its whitewashed walls, black crucifix, and its stone floor covered with rushes. De Molay sat behind a small table, a metal crucifix in the centre. The other Templar commanders were already assembled, their agitation apparent from their grave faces and red-rimmed eyes.

De Molay rose as Corbett came in, snapping at Baddlesmere to bring in extra chairs. Once they were seated, the grand master tapped the top of the table.

'Sir Hugh, whilst you were gone yesterday, Brother Odo

died. Or rather, he was killed. Late in the afternoon he went fishing, as he often did, in his small boat, *The Ghost of the Tower*. He stayed on the lake some time: this was not out of the ordinary. A Templar serjeant watched him and was about to go down to tell him it was time for Vespers and the evening meal, when he saw flames in the prow. He was too late: Brother Odo and the boat were consumed in a sheet of fire.'

Corbett put his face into his hands and said softly, 'I spoke to him just before I left for York, I visited him in the library. He showed me his chronicle; I could see how proud he was of it.' Corbett gazed at the others. 'Why?' he asked. 'How could it happen?'

'We don't know,' Branquier retorted. 'We don't bloody know, Corbett: that's why we're waiting for you. You are the king's clerk.' He jabbed a finger at him. 'You were sent here to find out. So, find out!'

'It's not as easy as that.' Legrave leaned forward. 'How can Sir Hugh deal with this? Brother Odo went fishing, everything was calm and serene. For the love of God, the boat was in the centre of the lake! Nobody swam out. Nobody else was with him. Yet both he and the craft were consumed by a fire which not even the water of the lake could extinguish.'

'What remains have been found?' Ranulf asked abruptly.

The Templars looked at him with disdain.

Corbett spoke up. 'My friend's question is an important one.'

'Very little,' De Molay replied. 'Brother Odo's corpse was charred beyond recognition. A few burnt planks of the boat but that's all.'

'Nothing else?' Corbett asked.

'Nothing,' de Molay replied. 'Just floating, charred remains. It was difficult to tell one thing from the other.'

'And who pulled these out?' Corbett asked.

'Well,' Branquier replied, 'the Templar serjeant could do

nothing. He raised the alarm and we all hurried down to the lakeside. Another boat, moored some distance away, was used: by then the flames were beginning to die down. Brother Odo's remains have already been sheeted and coffined, he'll be buried tonight. What we want to know, Sir Hugh, is why this happened? And how can it be stopped?'

Corbett gazed across the room: the tun of wine he'd brought as a gift from the king stood broached on a side-table, the red wax seal of the vintner now hanging down like a huge blob of blood. He sighed and pushed back his chair.

'I don't know,' he replied. 'Though I tell you this: forget the tittle-tattle and gossip about fires from hell.'

Corbett then told them what he had found on the Botham Bar road. De Molay sat up, his eyes bright with excitement.

'So you know the name of the victim and how he died?'

'Yes. I also believe someone was in that wood, using a strange form of fire. Now, when I listened to Brother Odo's account of the fall of Acre the evening before last, he talked of the Turks throwing fire into the city.'

'But that was nothing,' Branquier intervened. 'Just bundles of wood faggots, soaked in tar, lit, then thrown as a fire ball by a catapult or mangonel.'

'Are you saying the same thing is happening here?' Symmes asked.

Corbett saw movement beneath the knight's gown and realised the Templar still had his pet weasel with him.

'But that's impossible,' Baddlesmere scoffed before Corbett could reply. 'Such fires are clumsy. Nothing more than heaps of burning material. How can that explain the death of Reverchien at the centre of a maze? Nobody else was there. Or Peterkin in the kitchen? And, as for Brother Odo . . .'

'What about a fire arrow?' Corbett interrupted. 'Covered in tar and pitch.' He shrugged. 'I know, before you answer, if a fire arrow had been loosed into Brother Odo's craft, he would have tried to put it out and, if that failed, just jumped into the water and swam for shore.' He paused. 'Grand Master, may I ask one favour?'

De Molay spread his hands.

'Permission,' Corbett continued, 'to go round this manor, to question whom I like, to poke my long nose – as others put it – into your affairs.'

'Granted,' de Molay replied. 'On one condition, Sir Hugh. The chambers I showed you yesterday? You must stay well away from those. As for the rest, we are in your hands.'

Corbett thanked him and left.

'Did you really believe that?' Ranulf hissed as they walked back to the guesthouse.

'Corbett stopped. 'Believe what, Ranulf?'

'Fire arrows!'

'What else could I say? Here we have a man fishing in the centre of a lake. Within minutes, nay, seconds even, both he and the boat are consumed by fire. What else could have caused it?' Corbett shrugged. 'It's a wild guess but the best I can do.' He plucked Ranulf by the sleeve and drew him into a window embrasure. 'Whatever we discover,' he whispered, 'we keep silent about it. I believe the assassin was in that room.'

'What about the masked rider in the woods?' Ranulf asked.

'I don't know, but he wasn't in that kitchen when Peterkin died. Now the assassin, this Sagittarius, could be de Molay, or one of the other four, or any combination of them working together. I don't know why the assassin strikes and I don't know how but, whoever it is, he now realises, thanks to our discovery on the Botham Bar road, that we have glimpsed some of the truth.'

'In which case he may try to shut our mouths.'

'He's tried that already,' Corbett retorted, 'but yes, he may try it again. In doing so, though, he might make a mistake.'

Corbett poked his head out and looked down the empty passageway. 'I said that we would stay together, but now we'll have to work separately. You and Maltote are to scour this manor. Examine the smithy, go out into the fields and copses. Look for any trace of fire or scorch-marks and, if possible, some secret forge.'

'And you, Master?'

'I am going to the library. Brother Odo may have died not because he lived in this manor but also because he discovered something. The assassin must have seen me visit him. I believe the truth, or some of it, lies amongst Brother Odo's papers.'

Ranulf went back to the guesthouse to collect Maltote whilst Corbett, taking directions from one of the guards, traced his steps back to the library. The door was open. He went inside and stared round the long, shadow-filled room.

'God rest you, Brother Odo,' he whispered. 'And God forgive me if I was responsible for your death.'

He walked down the library to Brother Odo's carrel; the table was littered with scraps of paper and the great roll of vellum containing Odo's chronicle. Corbett laid this out flat: he turned over the squares of vellum, following the dramatic history of the fall of Acre. Corbett searched this carefully, wondering if the manuscript contained some reference to the secret fire. However, although Odo's drawings contained mangonels throwing flaming bundles of tar, there was nothing significant. Corbett closed it with a sigh and picked up the scraps of parchment. Some were old scribblings but one caught Corbett's eye. Apparently done on the day he died, Odo had drawn the picture of a long-nosed clerk and beside it a rough drawing of a crow. Corbett smiled at the pun on his own name, '*le Corbeil*', the French word for 'crow'. The rest of the jottings, however, were in some form of shorthand. Corbett remembered Brother Odo's description of Anglo-Saxon runes. There were the same markings, done time and time again, all with question marks beside them. A few he could decipher, though he found it impossible to make sense of them all. He went back along the library, searching amongst the shelves until he found what he was looking for: a thick, yellow-leaved *'Codex Grammaticus'*, bound in calf-skin and kept together by a huge clasp. Corbett pulled this from the shelf and took it back to the carrel. He opened it and began to leaf through: the codex contained references to Greek and Hebrew and, in a well-thumbed appendix at the end, all the letters of the alphabet with the Anglo-Saxon runes beside them. Corbett seized a quill, took Odo's scrap of paper and tried to decipher the dead librarian's scrawls. At first he could make no sense, the runes formed words which did not exist, then Corbett remembered that Odo had used Latin in his chronicle. He tried again and the words were deciphered: *'Ignis Diaboli'*, 'Devil Fire'; *'Liber Ignium'*, 'The Book of Fires', and, finally a phrase repeated time and again, 'Bacon's Mystery'.

'Sweet God in heaven!' Corbett whispered. 'What on earth can that refer to?'

The Devil's fire, he thought: that's how Odo described the flames which consumed poor Peterkin and his colleague Reverchien. The 'Book of Fires'? Was that some sort of grimoire? A book of spells? And 'Bacon's Mystery'? What had that got to do with the terrible fires? Corbett, mystified, got to his feet: for a while he searched for an index to what the library contained but, when he found it, he could discover no reference to a 'Book of Fires', or anything which would clarify the phrase 'Bacon's Mystery'. He was just clearing the desk, rolling up the notes he had made, when he heard a sound at the back of the library, the creak of a door followed by the bolts being driven home. Corbett rose. Drawing the dagger from his belt, he stared down the library, but all he could see were the dustmotes dancing in the sunbeams above the highly polished floor.

'Who's there?' he called. Corbett moved to one side. 'Who's there?' he repeated.

'Knowest thou that we go forth and return.' The voice was low and unrecognisable, though the words rang hollow round the library, like the sombre tolling of a death knell.

Corbett heard another sound, a metallic click. He threw himself sideways even as the crossbow bolt whipped by his head and smacked into the wall behind him.

'Knowest thou,' the voice grew louder, 'that what thou possesses shall escape thee in the end and return to us.'

Again the click. Corbett, now hiding behind the shelves, heard the thud as another barbed quarrel sank into the woodwork above his head. Corbett fought hard to control his breathing. He stared wildly around: the windows were too small, no escape there.

'Knowest thou,' the voice again intoned, 'that we hold you and will keep thee until the account be closed!'

Corbett, lying flat, peered round the shelves. His heart skipped a beat. At the far end of the library stood a figure, a tilting helm on his head, a jet black robe covering him from head to toe, an arbalest in his hand. Corbett watched the winch being pulled back, he heard the catch click and a third bolt speed to where his head had been. Another sound, a footfall, the assassin was slowly drawing closer. If Corbett rose and ran towards him, he'd never be fast enough: a crossbow bolt would take him before he reached his mysterious assailant. Corbett's mouth went dry. He fought hard to curb his fear. For some strange reason he kept thinking of a royal messenger riding up the pathway to Leighton Manor, Maeve hurrying down to greet him . . .

Corbett wiped the sweat from his face and gripped his Welsh dagger even more firmly. He looked across the library and glimpsed a small postern door behind one of the carrels. 'Oh, Christ Jesus,' he prayed, 'let it be unlocked.'

He pushed his head out but drew back quickly as another crossbow bolt whirred like a hawk through the air. Then he was up before the mysterious archer could fit another bolt. Swearing and cursing, Corbett pulled the carrel aside and raised the latch, but the door wouldn't move. Corbett blindly crashed against it even as the footfalls behind him drew closer. Then he glimpsed the bolts on the top. He drew these back, the door opened, creaking on its leather hinges. Corbett was through it, slamming it shut even as the crossbow bolt thudded into the other side. The door led into a passageway and Corbett ran blindly round a corner, so quickly he knocked a Templar serjeant flying. Ignoring his shouts, Corbett continued running until he was through an open door which led into a small disused garden behind the tilt-yard.

For a while Corbett crouched to catch his breath then, resheathing his dagger, he made his way back to the guesthouse. He slammed and locked the door behind him, checked the chamber carefully and sprawled on the bed. Eventually relief gave way to anger, a terrible fury at how he had been so nearly trapped. It was tempting to sweep through the manor demanding to see de Molay and seek an investigation, but what would that prove? Nothing except his own fear. The assassin would have slipped out of the library and be impossible to trace. Corbett got up and splashed water over his face. He dried himself slowly, recalling the cloaked figure, the arbalest and the bolts whistling through the air all around him.

'At least,' Corbett whispered, 'I know you are not from Hell.'

He paused: the attack in the library had been a desperate move. Was that why Odo had been killed? To prevent him discovering the cause of that dreadful fire? The assassin would have checked the carrel but, unaware of the runes, he would have overlooked the piece of parchment Corbett now kept in his wallet. There was a knock on the door.

'Master!'

Corbett went and unlocked it. Ranulf and Maltote swept excitedly into the room.

'They are here!' Maltote exclaimed.

'Shut up!' Ranulf shouted. 'I found them, Master, scorch-marks, the same as we found on the Botham Bar road. You remember the trees which ring the curtain wall around the manor? Well, Maltote and I discovered them there.' He peered at his master's face. 'Don't you want to come? Master, what has happened?'

Corbett told them.

'In the library!' Ranulf exclaimed. 'Why there, Master?'

'First, because the assassin knew I was there. Secondly, he wanted to stop me from finding anything.' Corbett withdrew the scrap of parchment from his wallet. 'Forget the scorch-marks. Maltote, I want you to go back into York.' Corbett crossed to the table and, seizing a quill, wrote a short note listing the phrases he had found in Odo's carrel. 'Go to the king, he's staying in the archbishop's palace at York Minster!' He handed over the message. 'Give this to him. If he interrogates you about what has happened here, tell him–' Corbett pulled a face – 'well, tell him the truth. But I need an answer to that as soon as possible.'

'Can I go with him?' Ranulf asked expectantly.

'No, you can't. A few more days away from the fleshpots of York will do your soul, not to mention your body, the world of good.'

Maltote hurriedly went to fill the saddlebag. He came back to make his farewells and almost ran down the passageway.

'Well, there goes a happy man,' Ranulf remarked. 'But what do we do?'

'Let's go for a walk, Ranulf. The sunshine and fresh air will do us good.'

They sauntered out into the grounds. Corbett did his best to relax. They first went back to the library. The door was now open but when Corbett returned to the carrel, he found the crossbow bolts had been pulled from the woodwork. Apart from a few scratches on the carrel and postern door, there was little sign of any disturbance. They walked back to the stables. After making a few inquiries, Corbett found the serjeant who had seen Odo and his boat burst into flames.

'Come,' Corbett said, 'let's walk to the edge of the lake. Tell us what you saw.'

The serjeant shrugged, threw down the belt he had been mending and walked with them, describing what he'd seen.

'How long had Brother Odo been fishing?' Corbett interrupted.

'Oh, it must have been some time, two or three hours.'

'And you were on guard?'

'Yes, I was patrolling the meadow, bored out of my mind. Every so often I would look down at the lake. I was hot, I grew tired.' He paused as they entered the cool shade of the trees which fringed the edge of the lake. 'When I looked up, I saw the flame; it was as if the fire had sprung from the lake itself.'

Corbett pointed to the wooden causeway which stretched out into the lake.

'Odo's boat, *The Ghost of the Tower*, was moored here?'

'Oh yes. Odo would climb in, row himself out, then sit for hours with his rod and line.'

Corbett walked on to the causeway. It felt strange to have the lake moving and shimmering on either side. At the end of the platform, he peered down at fire-blackened fragments being washed to and fro.

'And you came down here?'

'Well, by the time I reached where you stand there was nothing left, just fire.'

Corbett looked over his shoulder. 'What do you mean?'

'Well, the fire burnt out the bottom of the boat but the lake seemed to make little difference to it.' The Templar looked worried. 'That's what made me think it was Devil's fire.'

'And when the flames did die?' Corbett asked.

'It took some time. Afterwards all that remained was wood, a few scraps of cloth and Brother Odo's mangled remains.'

'Is the lake well stocked with fish?' Ranulf asked.

'Of course,' the serjeant replied. 'Especially with trout. The kitchen often serve it, nice and fresh, covered in a cream sauce.'

'But you saw no fish?' Ranulf asked. 'I mean, if Brother Odo had been fishing for hours and the lake's well stocked, he must have made a considerable catch.'

'I didn't see any fish but they may have burnt.'

Corbett thanked him and the serjeant walked back into the line of trees.

'You think Odo was already dead when the fire broke out, don't you?' Corbett asked.

'Yes, Master, I do.' Ranulf walked carefully backwards along the wooden causeway. 'Have you noticed, Master, how the trees on either side of the lake grow out and conceal this platform from view? Odo wouldn't be seen until he was in the centre of the lake. I think he was killed before he ever got into that boat. His body was lashed upright. He wore his cloak and cowl so nobody from the shore would notice. And why should an old Templar wear a cloak and cowl on a warm spring day? Moreover, if he was fishing, where is his catch, burnt or not?'

Corbett nodded. 'Very good, Ranulf, but the question still remains: how did the fire start?'

'Well, that's why I think he was dead,' Ranulf continued. 'Remember, Master, the serjeant said he saw flames licking the boat but Odo never moved to douse them, nor did he spring up in alarm or attempt to escape.' He blew his breath out. 'But that's all I can say. How the fire was started is a mystery.'

They walked back up the meadow. Half-way up, Corbett sat down, stretching his legs in the long grass. He leaned back on his hands, stared up at the blue sky, then closed his eyes. He savoured the warmth, the sweet smell of crushed grass and wild flowers, the chattering of birds in the trees and the melodious bee hum.

'If I keep my eyes closed,' he murmured, 'I'd say this was paradise.'

Ranulf moaned. 'If I was in a tavern in Cheapside with a

blackjack of ale in my right hand and the other on the knee of a pretty doxy, I'd agree, Master.' He tore at the grass. 'Master, these warnings from the sect of Assassins. Why has the killer chosen them?'

Corbett opened his eyes. 'The Assassins are an Islamic sect,' he replied. 'Garbed in white, with blood-red girdles and slippers. They live under the command of their leader, the Old Man of the Mountain, in their castle, the Eagle's Nest near the Dead Sea. I have heard the king speak of them. Their fortress stands on the summit of an unclimbable mountain. Inside it are walled gardens filled with exotic trees, marble fountains, beautiful flowerbeds and silk-carpeted pavilions. The members of this sect, the 'Devoted Ones', are fed saffron cakes and wine drugged with opiates. They dream of Paradise: every so often the Old Man sends them out to kill those he has marked down for death.

'Now the Assassins did terrible work amongst the Crusaders.' Corbett sat up and stared down at the lake. 'They are a nightmare, phantoms from hell, who stir up black terrors, particularly in our king's soul. Edward still dreams about the attack on him some thirty years ago.'

'Could there be Assassins in the Templar Order?' Ranulf asked, 'apostates who have renounced their vows? Or better still,' he hurried on, 'what if the Assassins are using this Templar coven to weaken the Western Kingdoms?'

Corbett got to his feet, brushing the grass from his hose.

'I can't answer, Ranulf, but I do think it's time we spoke to the grand master.'

They returned to the manor house and, after a while, secured an audience with de Molay. The grand master sat at his desk littered with manuscripts. He gestured for them to sit.

'Sir Hugh.' De Molay rubbed his face. 'This cannot go on for ever. I have to travel back to France. The king's ban must be lifted.'

'Why?' Corbett asked, recalling the messenger he had seen

pounding along the Botham Bar road. 'Is there a fresh crisis in Paris?'

De Molay sifted amongst the documents. 'Yes, of course there is. The attack on Philip of France was carried out by a Templar. The serjeant in question was one of those hotheads. He was handed over to the Inquisition and, yes, he did confess.'

'But I told you that.'

'What you don't know,' de Molay replied, 'is that a few days ago Philip of France was crossing the Grand Ponte, returning to the Louvre Palace after visiting the tombs at St Denis. Apparently,' de Molay threw the piece of parchment back on the desk, 'another attempt was made on his life. Paris is swept by rumours and scandals, the Chapter demands my return.'

'And is there any truth in the rumours?'

De Molay refused to meet his gaze.

'Grand Master,' Corbett insisted, 'I am not your enemy. I admire your Order. Men like Brother Odo and Sir Guido were true knights of the Cross but, for God's sake, open your eyes, there's something rotten here. Did you know,' Corbett continued, 'about the rumours and allegations of sodomy amongst your company?'

De Molay glanced up angrily. 'Don't preach to me, Corbett! I can list bishops and their mistresses, priests who visit whores, noble lords with a penchant for page-boys. Of course there are brethren here who are subject to the frailties of the flesh, as you or I!' he snapped.

'And these murders?' Corbett asked. 'Grand Master, can you explain them? Or why a Templar should send the same warnings as those of the Old Man of the Mountain? Could one of your Order, or more, be apostates, Assassins? What is your relationship with that sect?'

De Molay leaned back in his chair, playing with a thin-bladed parchment knife. 'For centuries,' he replied, 'the Templar Order guarded the Holy Places. We built our castles. We put down roots. We made peace with those around us. Just because a man worships Allah and meets you in battle does not mean that in peace you can't sit down at the same table to exchange ideas, gifts and presents.'

'But the Assassins?' Corbett asked.

'Aye, even with the Assassins. They control some trade routes: certain territories are under their jurisdiction. They are as amenable to bribes as any other.'

'So, your Order did business with them?'

'Yes and, before you ask, Sir Bartholomew Baddlesmere and William Symmes once served an embassy to the Eagle's Nest. They were entertained by the Old Man of the Mountain.'

'Why didn't you tell us this before?'

'I didn't think it was relevant,' de Molay snapped. 'Baddlesmere and Symmes have seen the beautiful gardens, drunk the iced sherbert, listened to the Old Man's speeches. Yes, they've been his guests, but that does not make them apostates. The Assassins are not our enemies.'

'Then who are?' Corbett asked.

'The Western princes,' de Molay replied. 'They see our manors, our granges, our barns, our well-stocked herds and fertile fields. The treasures of the Temple in Paris, London, Cologne, Rome and Avignon make their fingers itch. What do the Templars do, they ask? Why do they need such power and wealth? Should it not be better used for other purposes?'

'So you have no idea who the assassin could be?' Corbett insisted.

'No more than you do, Sir Hugh!' De Molay pushed the parchment aside and picked up a letter. 'I am sending a messenger to the king.'

Corbett nodded.

'I am going to beg him,' de Molay continued, 'for licence to return to France.' He leaned on the table and glared across at Corbett. 'Now there's a thought, Sir Hugh: here am I, Grand Master of Christendom's premier fighting Order, yet I have to beg to travel home, offer money as a surety for my good conduct.' De Molay's face became suffused with rage. 'Now, God forgive me Sir Hugh for saying so, but such humiliation would make a saint plot revenge!'

A few hours later, in the woods overlooking the lake, Sagittarius sat on the trunk of a fallen tree. He picked at the lichen and moss and stared at the cross-hilt of his sword buried in the ground before him. He looked at the cross engraved on the hilt and his face became hard. He rocked himself backwards and forwards. His master, or at least his new one, was right, the Order was finished. And what good would it do then? He stared out across the lake and thought of Brother Odo.

'I am sorry,' he whispered.

Yes, he was truly sorry the old one had to die but, with his long memory and meddling ways, the librarian could have proved a danger. Sagittarius licked his lips as he remembered the wine tun Corbett had brought. He had seen it broached, noticing the red seal with the vintner's mark stamped on it, round as a coin, boldly displaying the year 1292. The wine had tasted rich and mellow on his tongue. Perhaps one day he would have such riches and be able to call up what he wanted. And who could oppose him? The Templars? Stupid, brawny men, frightened by their own secrets and mysterious rituals, scampering about like chickens without their heads. He grasped the hilt of his sword, pulled it out of the soil and lay it over his lap, cleaning the dirt from its point. Corbett was his only danger. The first time the clerk should have been frightened but, in the library, if it hadn't been for that bloody door, he'd have caught and killed him. What a storm that would have provoked! He dared not creep out of the manor and try to enter York, that would be dangerous. So what next? He recalled the gossip and rumours he had heard, the hints and the sniggers. The assassin sat down on the log and coolly planned other murders.

Chapter 10

The tolling of the bell woke Corbett. Ranulf was already up, searching for his swordbelt. Outside the corridors echoed with the running of feet and shouted orders. Other bells in the Templar manor began to toll. Corbett dressed hurriedly. He wrapped his swordbelt around him and peered through the window: the darkened sky was brightening under the first light of dawn.

'Are we under attack?' Ranulf exclaimed, hopping around, putting his boots on.

'I doubt it,' Corbett gasped.

There was a hammering at the door. Ranulf drew back the bolts. A Templar serjeant, his face blackened, hair awry, his surcoat and hose scorched and filthy, almost fell into the room.

'Sir Hugh!' he gasped. 'The grand master's compliments but you are to come. There's a fire in the main building!'

Once outside the guesthouse, Corbett saw the smoke billowing out of the far wing of the manor. The courtyard was now filling with Templars: half-dressed, coughing and spluttering, they were forming a chain so buckets could be passed along. Corbett pushed his way through the door. Inside the passage was full of smoke and, as it parted in a breeze, Corbett saw the orange glow of fire at the far end. Now and again a Templar would dash in, a slopping pail of water in his hand. Branquier, followed by de Molay, came out of the smoke coughing and spluttering. They pushed by Corbett, staggering into the morning air.

'It's Baddlesmere's cell!' de Molay gasped. 'It's a lighted torch from one end to another.' He squatted on the cobbles and greedily drank from the water stoup a servant brought, then threw the rest over his face. 'The water's having no effect,' he muttered.

Corbett crouched beside him. Branquier stumbled off into the darkness, unable to speak, his eyes streaming because of the acrid smoke. Other Templars were now staggering out of the building, shouting that they could do nothing.

'The cell's burning!' de Molay exclaimed. 'If the flames are not brought under control, it will engulf the entire manor house.'

His frustration soon spread to the rest: the chain of buckets faltered. Legrave, a wet cloak covering his nose and mouth, dashed into the passageway. A few minutes later he re-emerged, the top part of his face a mask of ash. Corbett recalled Murston's smouldering corpse.

'Forget the water!' the clerk exclaimed. He pointed across the cobbles where a huge mound of sand, probably used in some building work, lay heaped against the wall. 'Use that!' he said. 'Sand, dirt, soil. Smother the flames rather than drown them!'

At first everything was confusion but then Symmes arrived, his pet weasel popping his little head out of the top of his tunic. He forced the retainers into one long line. Soldiers were sent in, wet cloths over their nostrils and mouths: each carried buckets of sand whilst another was armed with a heavy blanket. An hour passed, eventually the flames died and the fire was brought under control.

'Thank God!' de Molay murmured. 'Thank God, Sir Hugh, the walls are of stone, as is the floor: the whole manor could have been turned into a blazing pyre.'

'It's bad enough,' Legrave remarked, coming up. 'The cell on the other side is damaged, as are the two rooms above. The beams and floor joists are burnt away.' He stared around. 'Where's Baddlesmere?' he exclaimed. 'I'm sure I saw . . .' His voice faltered.

Branquier hastened away, calling Baddlesmere's name. He came back, shaking his head.

'That was Baddlesmere's chamber?' Corbett asked.

Symmes nodded.

'What happened?' Corbett asked.

Symmes turned away and shouted out names. Two Templars hurried up, stripped to the waist, their bodies covered in soot. They looked like two demons from hell.

'You raised the alarm?' Branquier asked one of them.

'Yes, Domine. I was on patrol. I turned the corridor and saw the smoke coming out beneath the door. I hurried down and banged with all my might.' He extended his bloody, scorched fist. 'The door was boiling hot so I called for help. Waldo and Gibner came. Gibner ran off to ring the bell and raise the alarm, whilst Waldo and I tried to force the door, which was locked and barred. We took a bench from the corridor and smashed it on the left so as to snap the hinges. We were successful,' he gasped, 'but the flames and the smoke seemed to leap out at us. Inside it was terrible, fire and smoke. It was like the heart of hell, an inferno.'

'Did you see Sir Bartholomew?' Legrave snapped. 'Speak the truth!'

'Yes, he was lying on the bed. The flames had already reached it. I only saw him for a few seconds.' He stammered. 'Him and . . .'

'And?' Corbett asked.

'There was another,' the Templar mumbled. 'They were sprawled on the bed: the flames were already taking hold of the tester and counterpane. I shouted once, then we ran. Honestly, Master, we could do nothing.'

'Who was the other?' Branquier cried. 'Oh, for God's sake, man! We have lost two of our Order!'

'One was Sir Bartholomew,' the serjeant replied. 'I think the other was Scoudas.'

De Molay cursed under his breath and walked away. Corbett stood aside, watching the dirty and blackened Templars wash themselves in buckets of water from the well. Above him the sun was rising fast and strong whilst, a short distance away, de Molay and his commanders waited for it to be safe before re-entering the building. Eventually a serjeant reported the fire was extinguished. De Molay ordered his companions to stay where they were and, beckoning Corbett and Ranulf, entered the charred, stinking corridor. The walls and woodwork were all scorched; when they reached Baddlesmere's chamber, Corbett was surprised at the intensity of the fire. It had reduced the chamber to nothing but a blackened charnel-house. The floor was ankle-deep in ash. The bedding, furniture and ornaments had been turned to cinder. Above them, the ceiling had been gutted; they stared into the upper chamber where the hungry flames had roared, consuming all in its path.

'Are the beams safe?' Corbett asked.

'We always build well,' de Molay replied. 'Fire is our great enemy. Three, possibly four, chambers will have to be gutted and repaired.'

He walked across and stopped where the bed had been. Very little remained of the two dead Templars: charred skeletons lying next to each other made unrecognisable by the horror which had occurred. Despite the ash and dirt, de Molay, tears streaming down his face, knelt down and crossed himself.

'Requiem aeternam dona eis Domine,' he intoned. 'Eternal rest give unto them oh Lord and let perpetual light shine upon them.' He blessed the remains with his hand. 'Turn not your face away from them,' he prayed. 'And, in your infinite mercy, forgive their offence.'

He rose to his feet, stumbled, and would have fallen if Corbett had not grasped his arm. De Molay lifted his face. Corbett was shocked: the grand master had aged, his face grey, mouth slack, eyes like a lost child.

'What is happening, Corbett?' he whispered hoarsely. 'For the love of God, what is happening? The fire is terrible enough but Bartholomew? A good soldier, to die in his bed with another man beside him. How will that be seen by the Judge of us all? What terrible damage to the name of our Order!'

He pulled his hand away and stumbled towards the door. Corbett indicated Ranulf to help him. The grand master hobbled like an old man into the passageway. He leaned against the wall and closed his eyes.

'I have heard the rumours,' he whispered. 'Friendships are formed. Sometimes we, who can have no sons, look for someone we would have liked to have had as one. Perhaps that was the case with Bartholomew. Now God's judgement has caught up with him and the power of the Evil One has made itself felt.'

Corbett wiped the soot and ash away from his face. 'Nonsense!' he snapped. 'Baddlesmere and his companion were murdered. Their deaths were planned.'

'But rumours will go out amongst the wicked.' De Molay looked glassy-eyed at him. 'He cast his lot.'

'Shut up!' Corbett shouted.

The grand master bowed his head. For a while he stood sobbing quietly, then, wiping his eyes on his sleeve, he grasped Corbett's arm like a man who had lost his sight. He stumbled down the passageway towards the door. Outside he ignored his companions but, accompanied by Corbett and Ranulf, walked slowly back to his own chamber. Once there, the grand master relaxed a little, bathing his face in a bowl of water, washing the grime and sweat from his face and hands. He then poured three goblets of wine, serving Ranulf and Corbett. He apologised deeply for the early hour, but quoted St Paul that they should take a little wine for their stomach's sake. Then he sat for a while, staring out of the window, mouth open, now and again sipping from the wine goblet. Ranulf looked at Corbett but he shook his head, bringing his finger to his lips. The door opened.

Branquier, Symmes and Legrave crept into the room and sat down. At last de Molay sighed and, turning, looked squarely at Corbett.

'It was no accident, was it?'

'No,' Corbett replied. 'It was murder.'

'But how?' Symmes exclaimed. 'Grand Master, I have just studied what remains of the lock and bolts. The key was welded into the lock on the inside. The bolts at top and bottom were secure.'

'What about the window?' Ranulf asked. 'If that was open, a firebrand could have been tossed through.'

'I have checked that,' Symmes retorted. 'The serjeants on duty outside say that the shutters of Bartholomew's window were firmly closed.'

Everyone concentrated on the fire: no one dared to mention the circumstances in which Baddlesmere had died.

'The flames were so intense,' de Molay exclaimed, 'burning savagely. What on God's earth would cause such a fire?' He waved his hand. 'Oh, accidents happen. Candles fall on to the rushes or an oil-lamp is tipped over, but the speed of that fire!' He shook his head. 'It can't have been anything like that.'

'And if such an accident had occurred?' Corbett remarked. 'Why didn't Baddlesmere and his companion raise the alarm, douse the flames themselves?'

'According to the serjeant,' Legrave said. 'Baddlesmere and Scoudas were either unconscious or dead.'

'They were sodomites.' Symmes's face twisted in revulsion. 'They died in their sin.' His voice had risen.

'That's for God to decide,' Corbett retorted. 'What concerns me is how they died. The windows and doors were barred, so how could someone get into a room and start such an inferno?' He stared round. 'Did anything untoward happen yesterday evening?'

His question was answered by headshakes and murmurs of dissent.

'Was Baddlesmere . . .' Corbett paused to marshal his words more carefully. 'Was his liaison with Scoudas well known?'

'There were rumours,' Symmes replied. 'You know, the sort of gossip which runs like a river through any enclosed community . . .'

He paused at a knock on the door. A serjeant hurried in. He whispered in Branquier's ear, laid a pair of saddlebags at his feet and left. Branquier undid the straps carefully. He shook the contents into his lap whilst the rest watched curiously.

'The bag belongs to Scoudas,' Branquier explained. 'I told the serjeant to collect anything he might find in his quarters.'

He held up a small steel ring by its stem. Corbett recognised a sighting which skilled arbalesters used on their crossbows. The rest were a few paltry objects: a knife, a sheath and small squares of parchment. Branquier undid these, cursed and handed them over to Corbett.

The first was a diagram: Corbett recognised it as a street plan of York: Trinity, the road the king had ridden up, its line of houses, the place where Murston had lurked, was marked with a cross.

'It's in Baddlesmere's hand,' Branquier explained. 'As are the rest.'

Corbett stared down at the cramped writing and the fatal message it bore.

KNOWEST THOU, THAT WE GO FORTH AND RETURN AS BEFORE AND BY NO MEANS CAN YOU HINDER US.
KNOWEST THOU, THAT WHAT THOU POSSESSES SHALL ESCAPE THEE IN THE END AND RETURN TO US.
KNOWEST THOU, THAT WE HOLD YOU AND WILL KEEP THEE UNTIL THE ACCOUNT BE CLOSED.

'It's the Assassin's warning.' Corbett put the parchment on the table in front of the grand master. De Molay studied it.

'Sir Hugh?' he asked. 'Could the assassin have been Baddlesmere? Remember the morning we entered York, Baddlesmere was with Scoudas.'

'But he returned to Framlingham with us,' Symmes intervened. 'He couldn't possibly have been in York when Corbett received his warning or narrowly missed the assailant's arrows.'

'True,' de Molay replied, 'but Scoudas was. He came back much later in the afternoon . . . He was Genoese by birth, a professional crossbowman.'

'And this,' Branquier held up a yellowing stub of parchment he'd taken from the saddlebag, 'is a billa with Murston's mark on it, acknowledging the receipt of certain monies.'

'Are you saying,' Corbett looked at the billa and passed it over to de Molay, 'that Baddlesmere and his lover Scoudas were the assassins?'

'It stands to reason,' Branquier retorted.

'Yes, it does,' de Molay declared. 'Baddlesmere was discontented. He had knowledge of the Assassins and their secrets. He attended the Chapter in Paris after which Philip of France was attacked. He was in London when the Assassins' message was pinned to the door of St Paul's Cathedral. He knew when the king was entering York and what route he would take. Scoudas, his lover, paid Murston, the most harebrained of men, a large amount of money. Copies of the Assassins' message are found in Scoudas's saddlebag together with a map of York. Finally, Scoudas was a professional crossbowman.'

'But why?' Corbett asked. 'Why did the fire break out in Baddlesmere's room? And, when it did, surely he and Scoudas would have tried to escape?'

'I can't answer that,' the grand master replied. 'Perhaps they held some secret which went wrong and they were overcome by the smoke.'

'Did any of you see Baddlesmere last night?' Corbett asked.

'Yes, yes, I did,' Branquier replied. 'We dined together.' He smiled weakly. 'We finished up the excellent wine you brought. Baddlesmere did like his wine. He always took a small jug into his chamber.'

'And Scoudas?' Ranulf asked.

'Sir Hugh,' Legrave exclaimed, 'we are a fighting community, bound by vows and a rule of discipline. Nevertheless, we are free men. Our Order is our family; friendships are formed. We do not poke our fingers into every man's pie. We have enough troubles without checking on every man, where he goes and what he does.'

'May I have those pieces of parchment?' Corbett asked, getting to his feet.

De Molay handed them over. Corbett abruptly made his farewells and returned to the guesthouse.

'Do you believe all that?' Ranulf asked, hurrying beside him.

'It's possible,' Corbett replied. 'It would make sense: Scoudas was in York when I was threatened and later attacked. I believe the grand master; this map of York and the Assassins' warning is written in Baddlesmere's hand. But why was it found in Scoudas's possession? Why wasn't it better hidden?'

'Perhaps Scoudas was his messenger boy?'

'In which case we face three possibilities,' Corbett retorted as they entered his chamber.

'First, Scoudas and Bartholomew were the assassins and, due to some dreadful accident, they were killed: that seems a strong possibility. We have documentary evidence and there is no valid explanation of how the fire could begin.' Corbett went over to the table and laid the scraps of parchment out. 'Secondly, Bartholomew and Scoudas were part of a coven, so others in this manor and elsewhere could be implicated in their treason.'

'And thirdly?' Ranulf asked.

'That Baddlesmere and Scoudas were victims and the real assassin, the Sagittarius, still walks free. Now,' Corbett sat down at the table, 'we are still awaiting Claverley and Maltote's return.' He grinned over his shoulder at Ranulf. 'You are free to play dice whenever you wish. I am going to be busy.'

For a while Ranulf stayed, kicking his heels, pacing up and down the chamber, peering through the window, muttering about Maltote's good luck at getting away. At last Corbett told him to shut up and go for a walk. Ranulf needed no second bidding and sped off like a greyhound. Corbett returned to drafting the letter he was writing, then threw his quill down in exasperation. Murder, treason, attempted regicide, sodomy, perhaps black magic! He got up and went to the door and bolted it. Corbett knew how Edward would react. He would rant and rave, but others in the Council would urge more pragmatic steps: the closing of all ports to the Templars as well as the possible seizure of their lands and chattels.

Corbett abandoned the letter and, for the next two hours, began to write down everything that had happened, everything he had heard and seen since this business began: conversations and conclusions. These, however, led nowhere, so he went back to the scraps of parchment he had found in Brother Odo's desk, as well as the ones taken from Scoudas's saddlebags. Corbett scrutinised the Assassins' warning again. The first pinned on the doors of St Paul's; the second given to him in York; the third handed over by Claverley, and the fourth plucked from Scoudas's saddlebag. Corbett rose and stretched. And the fifth? Ah yes, the assassin in the library. Corbett seized his quill and wrote this down. He looked at all five, particularly the last, then, his curiosity aroused, he studied them again. There was a difference: he had noticed it before, but was it significant? Corbett bit his lips in excitement. The one delivered by Claverley and the one given to him in York were different. In the other three the message had stated:

KNOWEST THOU, THAT WE GO FORTH AND
RETURN AS BEFORE AND BY NO MEANS CAN
YOU HINDER US.
KNOWEST THOU, THAT WHAT THOU POSSESSES
SHALL ESCAPE THEE IN THE END AND RETURN
TO US.
KNOWEST THOU, THAT WE HOLD YOU AND WILL
KEEP THEE UNTIL THE ACCOUNT BE CLOSED.

Now the scribbled notice mysteriously attached to Murston's
gibbet and the one given to him in York had read as follows:

KNOWEST THOU, THAT WHAT THOU POSSESSES
SHALL ESCAPE THEE IN THE END AND RETURN
TO US.
KNOWEST THOU, THAT WE GO FORTH AND
RETURN AS BEFORE AND BY NO MEANS CAN
YOU HINDER US.
KNOWEST THOU, THAT WE HOLD YOU AND WILL
KEEP THEE UNTIL THE ACCOUNT BE CLOSED.

Why the difference, Corbett wondered? A simple error? He
went to the window and stared down into the yard, watching the
Templar soldiers hurry backwards and forwards as they began
to clear up the debris from the burnt chambers. Was it a simple
mistake? But, if it wasn't, what was the significance?

'Let us say,' Corbett murmured, 'that there were three
conspirators: Murston, Baddlesmere and Scoudas. Each
delivered warnings at certain times. Would that explain why
the message was written out wrongly?'

Corbett went across to the lavarium and splashed water over
his face. He looked down at the grimy water and realised that
he had been so absorbed that he still bore traces of the smoke
and fire, so he went into the corridor and asked a serjeant to
bring fresh water. The man agreed and, once he'd returned,

Corbett stripped, washed and shaved himself in a small steel mirror, then changed into fresh clothes. Still thinking of the problem, he went down to the kitchen where he begged some bread, cheese and a jug of ale. Everyone else ignored him. The murders, the secret scandals and the hard work in dousing the flames had all wrought their effect on the Templar community. Ranulf joined him, his grimy face now furrowed by streaks of sweat.

'A good game?' Corbett asked.

His manservant grinned.

'You look more like an imp from hell than ever. Be careful, Ranulf,' Corbett added. 'People might want to examine the dice you are using.'

'I always throw honest,' Ranulf replied.

'Aye, and pigs fly,' Corbett replied.

Ranulf left to change and wash, Corbett finished his food and went and sat on a stone bench outside the front door of the manor. He revelled in the sun's warmth, his mind still concentrating on those warnings; he was trying to remember something which was out of place, but he couldn't for his life remember it. He closed his eyes, letting himself relax, and thought of Maeve's last letter.

'You must come home,' she had written. 'Eleanor misses you. Uncle Morgan swears you have some pretty doxy in every city. I lie awake every night hoping that the next morning I'll hear the servants' excited cries and you will be back.'

'Sir Hugh?'

Corbett's eyes flew open. Claverley was standing staring anxiously down at him.

'Roger!'

The under-sheriff's ugly face broke into a smile.

'How long have you been here?' Corbett asked.

'Oh, I left my horse in the stables and went up to your chamber. Ranulf was there.' Claverley's face grew serious. 'He told me the news.' The under-sheriff sat on the bench beside Corbett. 'This place is like a morgue,' he murmured. 'And when the news gets out . . .'

'What has happened?' Corbett asked.

'Well, we have already received our orders. Any Templar seen in the city of York is to be arrested on sight. In the Guildhall there are whispers and rumours that the king has sent messengers ordering the keepers of all the ports and the harbourmasters to seize any Templar coming into the country, as well as all letters and writs bearing their seal. Finally, under pain of forfeiture of life and limb, no Templar is allowed to leave the kingdom.'

Corbett got to his feet. 'I just hope,' he declared, 'that His Grace knows what he is doing. The Templars are under the direct control of the Pope. Any attack on them,' he added drily, 'is seen as an attack upon Christ's Vicar himself.' Corbett linked his arm through Claverley's and they walked back into the manor. 'The king doesn't give a damn about the Templars,' Corbett continued. 'He and his great lords would love to get their fingers on their possessions. Anyway, Claverley, what else do you have for me?'

Claverley handed him a small scroll of parchment.

'Bad news going to worse,' he replied. 'I have had my clerks list all those who have access to forges, all those who have licences to import into York, as well as all those who've applied for licence to build.'

'And?' Corbett asked, ushering Claverley into his chamber.

'See for yourself.'

Corbett unrolled the small parchment. Each of the three lists were very short. Corbett recognised the names of some of the leading aldermen and merchants of York, including Hubert Seagrave, vintner and owner of the Greenmantle tavern. However, the only name which appeared in each of the three small columns was that of the Templars. They owned smithies and forges in York. They had the right to import foodstuffs and other goods into the city. They also owned tenements and dwelling houses under the care of their steward, the now deceased Sir Guido Reverchien; he had apparently sought permission from the mayor and aldermen to build or renovate some of those places. Corbett groaned and tossed the parchment on to the bed.

'There's nothing new here!' he exclaimed.

Claverley handed him a gold coin. 'I went to see Mistress Jocasta. She thanks you for your gift but, in view of her past history, she thought it best to send it back. She asked you to examine the coin carefully, especially the rim.'

Corbett did so and saw the faint red marks.

'What are they?' Corbett asked, scraping at one and noticing how it came away under his nail.

'Mistress Jocasta thinks it's wax. She also said the gold is very old.' Claverley sat down on the stool, undoing his swordbelt. 'Apparently gold is like cloth, of different textures and makes: this is soft, precious and very rarely seen nowadays.'

'But why should the Templars be minting their own coins?' Corbett asked.

'I don't know, Sir Hugh. They may be bankrupt and beginning to melt down their bullion, or they may have simply found treasure trove which they do not wish to hand over to the king. Sir Hugh, I travelled fast, the road was dusty . . .'

Corbett apologised and poured out a goblet of wine. He'd hardly finished when Ranulf burst into the room, loudly protesting at how he had been searching high and low. He forgot his moans when Corbett handed him a cup of wine.

'Thank God you've come, Claverley!' Ranulf exclaimed between sips from his cup. 'As I said, this is a morgue, a death-house.'

'Did you make inquiries about the Templars in York, the morning the king was attacked?' Corbett asked.

'Yes, and I didn't find much. Apparently one of them left the city early.'

'Yes, that would be Branquier.'

'And one of the guards near Botham Bar definitely saw the grand master and the others meet and ride off.'

'But what were they doing before?'

Claverley explained. 'Well, the one-eyed one, Symmes, he apparently spent a great deal of his time in the tavern watching the doxies, though he wandered about and was seen in different locations throughout the morning.'

'And the dead one, Baddlesmere?'

'Well, some of the market bailiffs remember him, walking amongst the stalls near the Pavement. They definitely saw him and a young serjeant standing there when Murston's corpse was gibbeted.'

'And the grand master and Legrave?'

'De Molay did visit the goldsmith's but, Legrave spent a great deal of time in the streets outside. It's the glovers' quarter, and some of the shopkeepers recall him making purchases. They thought he was guarding the entrance whilst de Molay was inside.'

'So any of them could have slipped down to that tavern near Trinity where Murston was lurking?'

'Yes they could have done so,' Claverley replied. 'Oh, and one final thing.' Claverley sipped from the goblet. 'Much later in the afternoon, the guards at Botham Bar remember a Templar serjeant, the same young, blond-haired one glimpsed with Baddlesmere, leaving the city. He was riding fast, shouting at people to get out of his way.'

Corbett sighed. 'That would be Scoudas, who's also died. So we know all the Templars, including Baddlesmere, were in York when the attack was launched on the king. We know they separated, but that they met before Botham Bar and left the city before I received that threatening message on Ouse Bridge. They were certainly gone by the time that hidden archer tried to kill me. The only Templar in York when that happened was Scoudas.'

Corbett sat down on the edge of his bed. Was it possible, he thought, that the men behind these attacks – Baddlesmere and Scoudas – were already dead? Is that why Baddlesmere had left the city with de Molay, to put himself beyond suspicion whilst his friend and lover, Scoudas, carried out the attack? If that was the case, Corbett hid the tingle of excitement in his stomach, there would be no more deaths and he could report as much to the king. He glanced at his two companions.

'Can you leave me alone for a while?' he murmured.

Claverley drained his cup. 'I have another message.'

'Yes?'

'A lazar, an unknown knight, is dying in the Franciscan hospital. He claims he was a Templar and wishes to speak to you.'

'A Templar, a lazar!' Ranulf exclaimed. 'Could he be the mysterious hooded rider glimpsed in the woods near the Botham Bar road?'

Claverley shrugged.

'Look,' Corbett smiled faintly, 'Ranulf will look after you. But don't go far. We may have to leave quickly.'

Once they had gone, Corbett tried to marshal his thoughts. All the evidence pointed to Baddlesmere's guilt, yet there was something amiss. Only he was too absorbed to catch and hold it in his mind. He'd certainly go to York and visit the Lazar hospital. He picked up the list which Claverley had brought and fished the gold coin out of his purse. He stared at the red wax on the rim of the coin, then absentmindedly felt for his wine cup. He paused, recalling the tun of wine he'd brought to Framlingham, and stared at the list again.

'Of course!' he breathed. '*In vino veritas*: in wine there is always truth!'

Chapter 11

Hubert Seagrave, tavern master and vintner to the King, mopped his sweaty face, now turned a dull pasty hue. He stared in terror across his counting-room at Sir Hugh Corbett. Roger Claverley, under-sheriff, sat on the clerk's left, whilst that cat-eyed servant stood just behind him. Seagrave's gaze shifted to the gold coin lying on the table.

'Naturally, naturally,' he stuttered, 'I have seen such coins. They are good gold.' He stared piteously at the door where his ashen-faced wife and young sons stared fearfully at him.

'Close the door, Ranulf,' Corbett murmured. 'Now, Master Seagrave.' The clerk pulled his chair to the edge of the counting table, admiring the black and white squares laid out on top. 'I shall begin again. This coin and others like it are not the work of some petty counterfeiter but a wealthy, powerful man. This person discovered a treasure trove which should rightly belong to the Crown but, instead, he decided to melt that gold down in the furnace of his forge and recast it into coins. He used the same moulds he has for forming the red wax discs with which he seals his goods. Now, no one but a fool would go out into the market place with such coins and start buying goods from foreign merchants. He used those coins to purchase his merchandise, and these foreign merchants would then enter the markets of York with the same gold to buy their own purchases. The subtlety of this trick is apparent: the Crown does not get its treasure trove; the merchant keeps it to amass further wealth, whilst four or five foreign merchants use these gold coins to buy goods to import into their own countries. So, who can trace them back? Indeed, who will ask questions? The traders of York are only too pleased to see good gold pouring into their coffers, their memories would soon grow dim.'

Corbett paused and sipped from the excellent wine Seagrave had served when he mistakenly thought the clerk had just arrived on a courtesy visit.

'Now,' Corbett struck his breast, 'I made a mistake. I thought it might be the Templars. They are always applying for licences to refurbish their tenements in York. They have the licence to import goods from abroad and, of course, they have their own forges and ironsmiths. But why should the Templars incur royal anger?'

Corbett paused. He felt truly sorry for this fat merchant whose greed had got the better of him. 'However, the same applies to you, Master Seagrave. You have at least two forges at the Greenmantle. You have also applied for a licence to build on an adjoining piece of waste land. Before I left Framlingham I scrutinised the steward's accounts. You offer a price well above the market value for the wasteland on the other side of your tavern.'

Seagrave opened his mouth but then put his face in his hands.

'The mistake I made,' Corbett continued remorselessly, 'was assuming that the guilty party must have applied for a licence to import from abroad. But, as the King's own vintner in his royal city of York, you need no such licence. Foreign ships bring the wine down the Ouse, they unload their barrels, and you paid them with these gold coins.'

'You don't want that field for more buildings,' Ranulf intervened, 'but because it might contain more treasure trove.'

'You made one mistake,' Corbett added. 'The die casts you used to make your wax seals, you also used to mint the gold. On a few of the coins some of the red wax is still embedded, very deeply in the rim.'

'There are other merchants,' Seagrave mumbled, not raising his head. He dragged his hands across the table and Corbett saw the sweat-marks left by his fingers.

'Master Seagrave,' Claverley spoke up, 'you are an important burgess. A merchant prince. Your tavern is famous, not only in York but well beyond the city walls. You were born and bred here. You have heard the stories: how once the Romans had a great city here and, in the time before Alfred, the Vikings turned the city into a great fortress where they piled their plunder. Such treasure trove is common – the odd cup, a few coins. But what did you find?'

'We can go away,' Corbett added. 'And come back with the king's soldiers. They will tear this tavern apart, dig up every inch of soil.' He leaned against the table. 'Master Seagrave, look at me.'

The merchant glanced up fearfully. 'It was so easy,' he muttered. 'Different merchants at different times. I knew they'd keep their mouths shut. After all, Sir Hugh, who objects to being paid in gold? But you found wax engrained in the rim?'

Corbett nodded.

'Well, God knows how that got there.' Seagrave got to his feet, pushing his chair back. He smiled sourly as Claverley's hand went to his dagger. 'Don't worry, Under-sheriff, I am not going to flee or do anything stupid. I want to show you what I found.'

The merchant left the counting-house. A few minutes later he came staggering back with a small chest about two feet long and a foot high. He dropped this on the table with a crash and threw back the lid.

'Sweet God and all his angels!' Ranulf exclaimed, staring at the gold coins which lay heaped there.

'There's more,' Seagrave added.

He went out and returned with a leather sack. He undid the cord at the neck and spilled the precious objects on to the table: a gold, jewel-encrusted pyx, a drinking horn inlaid with mother-of-pearl. Two small goblets, the cups thick with silver. An agnus dei of pure jade, a pectoral cross, amethysts gleaming in each of the four stems.

'Riches in abundance,' Seagrave murmured. 'I found it all about three months ago when the builders were digging in the garden. They paused because of the snow and frost. I went out to inspect. My children were playing in the trench: they'd pulled a piece of paving stone away from the side of the hole which had strange markings on it. I got down and investigated.' Seagrave paused. 'I don't know whether it was a sewer or a pipe made of elm. I put my hand inside.' He shook his head. 'I thought I was dreaming. I pulled out one bag after another, all full of coins.' He slumped down. 'For God's sake, Sir Hugh, I couldn't mint coins like that.'

'But they look so new!' Corbett exclaimed. 'The cross on each side, the red wax on the rim.'

'I made my own inquiries amongst the chronicles and histories of the city,' Seagrave replied. 'Once York was called Jorvik; the Viking war gangs set up camp here.' He pointed to the precious objects which lay gleaming on the table. 'Perhaps some chieftain took church gold and melted it down and, being superstitious, carved a cross on either side.'

'Candlesticks,' Claverley explained. 'Sir Hugh, they must have been candlesticks, which explains the red wax.'

Corbett lifted up the gold and let the coins run through his fingers.

'Strange,' he murmured. 'In my cleverness I thought the coins were newly minted.'

'They are,' Seagrave replied. 'Whoever made those coins, Sir Hugh, never used them but hid them away with the rest of the treasure. They must have brought him the same ill luck as they did me. The wooden pipes were scorched, as was the earth around it. I didn't know what to do,' he continued. 'I was tired of poor silver coins and, if I handed them over to the Exchequer, what recompense would I have got? Royal officials questioning me, hinting I may have stolen it, using every legal nicety to keep the treasure to themselves. How much of this, Sir Hugh, would have found its way into the royal treasury? Kings' clerks are no different from Kings' vintners: everyone has sticky fingers.'

'You could have petitioned the king yourself,' Corbett retorted.

'I thought of that,' Seagrave replied, 'the day you came here. I nearly broke down and confessed but . . .' He shrugged. 'I was committed. I'd waited until the king arrived in York. The great lords, the royal household, clerks, liveried retainers, so many strangers in the city, an opportune time to spend that gold. Royal purveyors were out buying the goods, the markets were doing a roaring trade.' Seagrave's face crumpled, tears rolling down his ashen cheeks. 'Now I have lost everything,' he muttered.

Suddenly the door to the counting-house was flung open and Seagrave's wife entered, two small children clinging to her skirts.

'What will happen?' Her pretty face was now drawn, her eyes dark pools of fear.

'Wait outside, Mistress Seagrave,' Corbett replied. 'The king wants his treasure, not a man's life. What your husband has done is understandable.'

Corbett waited until the door closed. Seagrave had now dried his eyes and was looking expectantly at him.

'What you must do, Master Seagrave,' Corbett declared gently, 'is seek an audience with the king. Take the treasure with you. Do not mention me or my visit here . . .' Corbett paused. 'No, tell him I supped here and that you asked would it be possible to see His Grace.'

'And then what?' Seagrave asked anxiously.

'Throw yourself on the royal mercy,' Corbett continued. 'And then open the sacks. Believe me, Master Seagrave, the king will kiss you as a brother, provided you hand over everything!'

'You mean . . .' Seagrave gabbled.

'Oh, for heaven's sake, man!' Corbett exclaimed. 'You found some gold and spent some of it: that will be taken from your share.'

'Then there will be no fine, no imprisonment?' Seagrave exclaimed.

Corbett got to his feet. 'Master Seagrave,' he replied drily, 'if you play your part well, you'll probably be knighted.'

The tavern master tried to make him stay, saying he would like to reward his generosity. Corbett did remain for a while, finishing his wine and reassuring the flustered Seagrave that his family should fear nothing from him.

'Is this right?' Claverley muttered, seizing a moment when they were alone in the room together.

'What else is there, Roger?' Corbett laughed sharply. 'Seagrave only became greedy. If we punished everyone for that, we wouldn't find enough gibbets in the country.' Corbett held his hand up. 'You are to keep your mouth shut.'

'Sir Hugh, you have my word.'

Once they had finished, Seagrave led them out to the stables where they'd left their horses. The merchant plucked anxiously at Corbett's sleeve.

'Sir Hugh, I have one final confession to make.'

'There's more treasure!' Corbett exclaimed.

'No, it was the day you came here. I thought you were following someone.'

'What do you mean?' Corbett asked.

'Well, the day the king entered York, this tavern, like every other in the city, was very busy. Two Templars came here. One was a senior commander. I knew that by the way he talked. He was balding, grizzle-faced, a short, stocky man.'

'Baddlesmere!' Corbett exclaimed.

'Yes, well, he was accompanied by a young serjeant. A youngish, blond-haired man with a foreign accent. I thought they'd come about the adjoining piece of land so I entertained them and talked about my plans.' Seagrave coughed to clear his throat. 'Now, to put it bluntly, they humoured me. They asked for a chamber, claiming they had matters to discuss, well away from the eyes and ears of the curious. So I obliged: that was early in the morning. About noon the old one left, followed by the younger one, shortly before you arrived . . .' Seagrave's voice trailed off. 'I thought I should tell you.'

Corbett thanked and reassured him. Once they were out of the stableyard he dismounted, leading his horse by the reins. Claverley, staring curiously at him and Ranulf, wondering what was the matter, followed Corbett through the busy, narrow alleyways and streets, then into the silent graveyard of a small church. Corbett sat down on a weather-beaten tombstone, watching his horse lazily munch the long, fresh grass.

'If I was half as clever as I thought I was,' he began, 'then I'd be the most subtle of royal clerks.' He sighed. 'The truth is I blunder about like the hooded man in Blind Man's Buff. If I strike something then it's more chance than skill.'

'You still found the counterfeiter,' Ranulf offered hopefully.

'Mere chance. I thought the wax proved Seagrave was a counterfeiter: it didn't.'

'Why didn't you arrest him?' Claverley asked.

'I've told you,' Corbett replied. 'He was greedy but, still, he's a father, a husband, I don't want his blood on my hands. And now we have Baddlesmere and Scoudas,' Corbett continued. 'They visited the Greenmantle tavern for a love tryst, using Seagrave's desire to purchase some land as a possible pretext. Baddlesmere, to avoid any scandal or rumour, left to join the grand master. More importantly, Scoudas couldn't have attacked me, he was in the tavern. So,' Corbett let his horse nuzzle his neck, 'Baddlesmere and Scoudas were no more interested in attacking the king and myself than the queen of the fairies. They came into York to be together. Baddlesmere and Scoudas were in that tavern all the time.'

'But the warning?' Ranulf asked. 'The map found in Scoudas's possessions: they all bore Baddlesmere's hand.'

Corbett got to his feet. 'I wonder,' he replied. 'Did Baddlesmere have his own suspicions? Did he draw that map in order to help his own inquiries?' He gathered the reins in his hands and remounted.

'Sir Hugh?'

Corbett broke from his reverie and stared down at the undersheriff.

'If you want,' Claverley offered, 'I can ride back with you to Framlingham or accompany you to the Lazar hospital.'

'No,' Corbett smiled. 'As the gospels say: "Sufficient unto the day is the evil thereof".' He extended his hand and grasped Claverley's. 'You did good work, Roger. I shall make sure the king knows of it: I thank you for your courtesy and help.'

'They said you were a hard man,' Claverley told him. He jerked his head back in the direction of the tavern. 'But Seagrave will always remember your compassion.'

Corbett shrugged. 'I have seen more blood and death in the last year, Master Claverley . . .' His voice trailed off. 'Keep well.'

And, urging his horse forward, Corbett left the graveyard. Ranulf stayed to make his own farewells.

'He's homesick,' the manservant whispered, leaning down from his horse. 'Old "Master Long Face" is pining for his wife.'

'And you, Ranulf?' Claverley grinned.

Ranulf pulled his most sanctimonious face. 'Virtue is its own reward, Master Under-sheriff,' he intoned solemnly.

And, with Claverley's laughter ringing in his ears, Ranulf spurred his horse on before 'Old Master Long Face' really did fall into one of his melancholic fits.

Corbett dismounted in the courtyard of the Lazar hospital. A lay brother came out, Corbett whispered to him, and the little man nodded. 'Yes, yes,' he murmured, 'we have been expecting you. Stay here!'

He hurried into the hospital and came back a little later, accompanied by a friar. 'This is Father Anselm, our infirmarian.'

The Franciscan grasped Corbett's hand. 'You'd best come,' he urged, but turned as Ranulf made to join them. 'No,' he apologised. 'I am afraid the knight only asked for Sir Hugh.'

Mystified, Corbett looked at Ranulf, then shrugged and followed the friar in through the door and up the stairs. They went along through the long infirmary where the sick lay on beds on either side. Each bed was cordoned off by dark-blue sheets which hung from steel rods bolted to the wall. The room was clean and fragrant, the sheets and bolsters of each bed a snowy white.

'We do our best,' Brother Anselm muttered. 'Many of these had no dignity in living, at least they'll have some in dying.'

At the end of the room he ushered Corbett into a small chamber, stark and austere. The white washed walls and gaunt crucifix above the bed reminded Corbett of his cell at Framlingham: the 'Unknown' lay propped against the bolsters; his yellow hair, soaked with sweat, fanned out across the pillow. Corbett fought to hide his disgust at the terrible sores and ulcers eating into the man's face. The Unknown opened his eyes and tried to smile.

'Don't worry,' he whispered, the spittle bubbling on his cracked lips. 'I am no beauty, Sir Hugh. Brother, a stool for our visitor.'

Friar Anselm brought one across and, when Corbett sat down, whispered in his ear: 'He has not got much time. I doubt if he'll see the night through.'

Then he left, closing the door quietly behind him.

The Unknown turned his face, closed his eyes, drawing deep breaths, summoning up his last resources of strength.

'You are Sir Hugh Corbett, Keeper of the King's Secret Seal?'

'I am.'

'They say you are a man of integrity.'

'People say a lot of things.'

'A good answer. My strength is ebbing, Sir Hugh, so I'll be brief. Death will be here soon. Who I am, or where I came from does not concern you. I was a Templar. I fought at Acre and, when that city fell, I was taken prisoner and handed over to the Assassins who kept me imprisoned for years in their fortress of the Eagle's Nest.'

The Unknown stirred, moving his limbs to find relief. 'The Old Man of the Mountain,' he whispered, 'released me to cause chaos in my Order, to lay allegations of cowardice.'

'Why?' Corbett asked. 'What allegations?'

'I know a great secret,' the Unknown gasped. 'Those commanders at Framlingham, they were all at Acre. When the city fell . . .' The Unknown stopped, fighting for breath. '. . . Some Templars died. I and others were wounded and taken prisoner, many retreated. But,' his fingers scrabbled at the blankets, 'according to the Old Man of the Mountain, one English Templar was an arrant coward. He deserted his post and, because of that, the Mamelukes took a wall, cutting me and my companions off. On the day I was captured they told me about a Templar knight running away, dropping his sword and shield whilst others died.'

'Which one?' Corbett asked.

'I don't know,' the Unknown retorted. 'But, for years, hidden in that dungeon, I dreamed of returning, of asking the survivors where they were and so account for their actions. When I was released, all the Old Man told me was that the Templar concerned was now a senior officer in the English province.' The Unknown paused again. 'I asked him how he knew the Templar's nationality but not his name.'

'And?'

'He replied that at Acre there were only six English Templars: myself, Odo Tharlestone, Legrave, Branquier, Baddlesmere and Symmes. The coward screamed in English, so it must have been one of them. Now each is a lord! Oh, how they have all advanced themselves while I rotted.' The Unknown smiled weakly. 'I went out into the woods near Framlingham and saw them sweep by in their power.'

'Why would the Old Man release you and send you back?' Corbett asked.

'I've thought of that,' the Unknown replied haltingly. 'The divisions in the Order are well known: further scandal would weaken it even more in the eyes of the Western princes.'

'But now you are dying,' Corbett exclaimed. 'When you were in the woods near Framlingham, why didn't you seek an audience with de Molay?'

'Because . . .' The Unknown closed his eyes. 'Because, Sir Hugh, I want to die clean before God. No, no.' He shook his head. 'That's not the full truth. As I journeyed through Europe I heard the stories about my Order: why should I drag it down further?'

'So why me?'

'My desire for vengeance has gone, Sir Hugh, but justice must be done. You will inform de Molay of what I know. Tell him to ask each of his commanders where they were in Acre.'

'Nothing else?' Corbett asked. 'No details about which wall or which part of the city?'

'The Templars will know,' the Unknown replied. 'They will ask questions. They will interrogate.' He grasped Corbett's hands. 'Swear, Sir Hugh, that you will!'

Corbett stared down at the Unknown's face, so cruelly ravaged by disease.

'You are not frightened by a leper's touch?' the dying man teased.

'I have learnt it takes more than a touch for the contagion to spread,' Corbett replied. 'But yes, sir, whoever you may be: at my time and my choosing, I will tell de Molay.' He placed the Unknown's hand back on the blanket. 'Is there anything else?'

The Unknown shook his head. 'No, my mind's at peace. Now go!'

Corbett rose and walked to the door.

'Sir Hugh!'

Corbett turned.

'I have heard the stories, the terrible fires: whoever it is, he's the coward, I know it.'

Outside in the passageway, Corbett sat for a while on a bench. What the Unknown had confessed was significant, but how and why? Corbett sighed: he'd not tell de Molay – not anyone, he decided, not even Ranulf – until the other pieces of the puzzle were in place.

Corbett and Ranulf reached Framlingham just before dusk. Their ride was quiet, Corbett refusing to answer Ranulf's questions. They found Maltote lying on Corbett's bed, his arms clasping two heavy calf-skin tomes. He woke up with a start, still holding on to the books as he blinked, owl-eyed, up at them.

'Master, I am sorry,' he apologised, 'but I had to wait a while.' He put the books down on the bed beside him.

'His Grace the king?' Corbett asked.

'Well, he's in a fair old rage; closeted in his chamber with de Warenne and the rest. He has ordered the sheriffs to seal all ports. The Templars are definitely out of favour.'

'We know all that,' Ranulf retorted. 'Did he send any messages?'

'We are to return soon. He will take matters into his own hands.'

'And have you discovered anything about the phrases I wrote down for you?' Corbett asked. He sat down beside Maltote and picked up one of the books and opened it. 'For God's sake, Maltote!' he exclaimed. 'What have you brought? "Jerome's Commentary on St Matthew"?'

'It's a bit further on,' Maltote gabbled. 'I showed those

words to the archivist at the minster, and he sent me back with these books.'

Corbett leafed through the pages and a title caught his eye. '"*Liber Ignium*", "The Book of Fires",' Corbett whispered. 'Yes, the same phrase I found in Odo's manuscripts.'

He picked up the second volume, a collection of philosophical writings. Again Corbett leafed through, stopped and smiled. He'd found what he was looking for: '*Epistola de Secretis Operibus Artis et Naturae.*'

'The writings of Friar Roger Bacon,' Corbett explained, 'concerning the secrets of nature. Bacon was a Franciscan, he studied at Oxford. An eccentric recluse, he built an observatory on Folly Bridge and spent most of his time studying the stars.'

'Did you know him?' Ranulf asked.

'Vaguely,' Corbett replied. 'He sometimes lectured in the Schools, a short, stocky man with a sunburnt face and a beard shaped like a spade. Poor eyesight but he had a voice like a bell. Some people considered him witless, others a deep thinker.'

'And how can these books help us?' Ranulf asked.

'I don't know. Perhaps they can't.'

'You have to take great care of them,' Maltote interrupted. 'That archivist made me take an oath and sign an indenture. They are to be returned immediately to the minster library.'

'Does anyone here know you have them?'

'No,' Maltote replied. 'The Templars paid little attention to me. One of the soldiers told me what had happened: the mysterious fire, the deaths of Lord Baddlesmere and the other one. They're whispering that they were lovers.' He paused as a bell began to toll. 'They are having the Requiem now. Only a few know I am here.'

Corbett got up and walked to the window. The sun was still shining but the clouds were beginning to mass, dark and sullen overhead.

'We'll have a storm later,' he remarked. 'Be careful,' he

warned over his shoulder. 'Don't wander round the manor by yourselves.'

'Master.' Ranulf came up beside him. 'I have been thinking. Do you remember the joust? De Molay remarked how Legrave held his lance in his left hand.'

'Yes, yes, I do.'

'And Branquier, he writes with his left hand.'

'What has that got to do with it?'

'Well, the assassin in the library. You described him as helmeted and cloaked . . .'

Corbett turned and clapped Ranulf on the shoulder.

'Well done, oh sharpest of clerks!' he cried. 'Maltote, bring those books. Ranulf, you have an arbalest. Come on, let's go back to the library.'

Corbett hurried out of the chamber. Ranulf hung back to inform Maltote in hushed tones what had happened since he had left. He told him about Seagrave and the visit to the Lazar hospital, swearing the young messenger to secrecy.

'Or,' Ranulf muttered darkly, 'Corbett will see you reduced to the lowest scullion in the royal kitchens.' He stopped speaking abruptly as Corbett came back into the room.

'I've been waiting!' he snapped. 'Maltote, bring those books! Ranulf, your crossbow!'

Outside the day was dying. The sky was purple-black and, in the distance, came the first faint rumble of thunder and the faint flash of lightning above the forests to the north of the manor. They made their way past the church where the Templars were still gathered, the faint strains of the Requiem Mass echoing eerily through the stained-glass windows. The library was unlocked but dark. Corbett lit a few candles, making sure their capped hoods were secured, then walked down to where he had been sitting when the assassin struck. He told Maltote and Ranulf to stay by the door, then instructed his manservant to pretend he was attacking him.

'I am right-handed, Master,' Ranulf called. 'As most men

are: I hold the arbalest steady with my right and pull back the winch with my left.'

Corbett studied him.

'If I was left-handed.' Ranulf continued, 'then it would be the other way round, like this.' He moved the arbalest to the other hand, holding it more clumsily as he winched back the lever.

Corbett closed his eyes, trying to recall that fateful afternoon. He shook his head and opened his eyes.

'Do it again, Ranulf. Walk forward slowly.'

Ranulf obeyed. Maltote, still holding the books, stood by the door.

'Well, Master?' Ranulf asked, now only a yard away from him. 'Can you remember?'

'He held it in his right hand,' Corbett declared. 'Yes, definitely his right.'

'So, the assassin could have been Symmes or de Molay? Legrave and Branquier are left-handed. Baddlesmere's a blackened corpse, and the same goes for Scoudas. Moreover, we now know, or think we do,' Ranulf continued, 'that neither Baddlesmere nor Scoudas had a hand in this business.'

Corbett just shook his head and extinguished the candles. They walked out of the library, back across the square. The Templars were now leaving the chapel; de Molay, surrounded by his commanders, beckoned Corbett over.

'Sir Hugh.' The grand master forced a smile. 'We wondered where you were. We even thought you might have forgotten us.'

'King's business in York,' Corbett replied. He glanced quickly over his shoulder and thanked God Maltote had had the sense to hide the books under his cloak.

'We buried our dead,' de Molay continued flatly, staring up at the darkening sky. 'And it seems their passing will not go unnoticed by the weather. Sir Hugh, we have certain decisions to make. You will be our guest at dinner tonight?'

'No funeral obsequies?' Corbett asked.

'Not for Baddlesmere!' Branquier snapped, stepping forward. 'Sir Hugh, this business is finished.'

'And Baddlesmere is the guilty party?' Corbett retorted.

'The evidence points that way,' de Molay replied. 'His lustful relationship with Scoudas; his resentments; the map of York showing where the king was stopping; the Assassins' warning. What further proof do we need? Royal writ or no, we have been prisoners here far too long. In three days' time I intend to go into York to seek audience with the king. My companions here also have business. We cannot wait. These matters are resolved: Baddlesmere was the guilty party.'

'I don't think so,' Corbett replied.

The Templar commanders, openly hostile, now took up a more threatening stance. They moved round him, throwing back the white ceremonial robes of their Order, hands touching the swords and daggers in their belts. Corbett stood his ground.

'Don't threaten me, Grand Master.'

'I am not threatening,' de Molay retorted. 'I am sick and tired of the intrigue and the mystery, the fires and the murder of old companions. Those things are a tragedy, but I am a French subject, Grand Master of the Order of Templars. I object to being a prisoner in one of my own manors.'

'Then go if you wish, Grand Master. But I tell you this, everyone of you will be arrested as a traitor. And don't quote Baddlesmere's name to me. He may have been a sodomite, a man who grumbled, but he was totally innocent of any crime. The day the king was attacked in York he was closeted with his lover in a chamber at the Greenmantle tavern. He'd left before I was warned. Nor could Scoudas have had that warning pushed into my hand, or tried to kill me as I went through York.'

De Molay's gaze faltered. 'But the map?' he questioned. 'The warning? The receipt of monies?'

'Aye, I've reflected on that,' Corbett replied. He glanced sideways at Symmes, his dagger half-drawn from his belt.

'Keep your hand away from your dagger,' he warned. 'And look after your pet weasel.'

Symmes's good eye glared at de Molay, who nodded imperceptibly.

'You were telling us about Baddlesmere,' the grand master said.

'Baddlesmere believed that the assassin was a member of his Order,' Corbett continued. 'He was making his own inquiries. He drew that map for some purpose which, at this moment in time, I don't understand. He also transcribed that warning so as to study it more closely. To put it bluntly, Grand Master, the man I am hunting still lives and breathes. Poor Baddlesmere died as a pretext, nothing more.'

They all turned as a serjeant ran up and, pushing his way through, whispered into de Molay's ear.

'What's the matter?' Corbett asked.

'Something or nothing,' the grand master replied. 'But one of our squires, Joscelyn, is missing, probably deserted.' De Molay looked over Corbett's shoulder at Ranulf. 'Tell your manservant to lower that arbalest.' De Molay raised his hands, snapping his fingers. 'The rest of you follow me. Sir Hugh,' he smiled apologetically, 'you are still our guest. Do join us for supper tonight.'

Corbett stood his ground as the Templars swept away in a flurry of cloaks, their boots crunching on the pebbles. Maltote gave a groan and crouched down.

'Master, these books weigh like a sack of stones.'

Ranulf tucked the crossbow bolt back into his pouch. Corbett turned clumsily. His legs felt heavy as lead. He moved his neck to ease the cramp.

Ranulf asked, 'Do you think Baddlesmere was killed because he knew too much?'

'Possibly,' Corbett replied. 'But I still don't see any pattern to these killings. The grand master is correct: we cannot detain him here for much longer.'

'And would the king arrest them?'

'I doubt it. De Molay is a lord in his own right, as well as a subject of Philip of France. The king could huff and puff, detain him at some port and threaten to confiscate Templar goods. But de Molay would eventually leave and appeal to the Pope.'

'And so the killer will walk free?'

'On this occasion, Ranulf, he might well do that. But let's not disappoint our hosts. We have to wash and change.'

They returned to the guesthouse. For a while Corbett sat studying the books Maltote had brought. He read the first chapters of Bacon's work, though he could find little there of interest. He cradled the book in his hands and remembered the Unknown's dying gasps in the Lazar hospital. What, he thought, was the significance of his confession: allegations about cowardice amongst the Templars at Acre so many years ago? Was the coward here at Framlingham? Outside the storm broke: the rain splattered against the window, the thunder crashed over the manor house, whilst the lightning illuminated the trees and grounds in great bursts of white light.

'Is there anything interesting in the books?' Ranulf asked, coming up beside him.

Corbett scratched his head. 'Nothing.' He got to his feet. 'It will wait.' He took off his jerkin. 'I wonder what will happen now?'

Ranulf just stared at him.

'I wonder if the true assassin thought I'd be happy with naming Baddlesmere as the assassin?'

'So, we are still in danger?' Ranulf asked.

'Possibly. But come . . .' He paused at the tolling of the bell, almost hidden under the rumble of thunder. 'Our hosts await us.'

They finished their preparations, putting their cloaks on, and ran through the rain and into the main door of the manor. De Molay and his commanders were waiting in the hall. Corbett had to hide a shiver at the scene. Outside the windows, thunder crashed and lightning flared. In the hall itself, all the torches had been lit, and a row of candles along the table threw long shadows which danced and moved against the wall. Corbett and his companions received a frosty welcome. De Molay indicated with his hand where they should sit: Corbett on his left, Ranulf and Maltote further down the table. The grand master said grace, then servants brought out the dishes from the kitchen. Corbett found it difficult to eat, scrupulously studying his goblet, only sipping from it after the others drank wine poured from the same jug.

'You don't trust us, Sir Hugh,' de Molay murmured, popping a piece of bread into his mouth.

'I have enjoyed more festive banquets,' Corbett replied.

The meal continued. Legrave attempted a conversation, but de Molay was lost in his own thoughts, whilst Symmes and Branquier gazed stonily down at the table, determined to ignore Corbett and his companions. The meal was drawing to an end when there was a loud knocking on the door. Corbett turned in his chair as a serjeant ran in.

'Grand Master!' he gasped. 'Grand Master, there are royal soldiers here!'

De Molay half rose from his chair, his surprise cut short as the door crashed open and a rain-sodden captain of the royal guard strode into the hall. Behind him, two of his men pushed a chained, manacled figure, the prisoner's cloak dripping with water.

'Grand Master,' the captain declared, 'I apologise for the inconvenience caused by our abrupt arrival. We believe this is one of your men.'

Grabbing the prisoner, he thrust him forward, pulling back the cowl. Corbett stared in utter disbelief at the unshaven, rain-soaked face of Sir Bartholomew Baddlesmere.

Chapter 12

Immediate consternation broke out: the commanders leaping up, daggers drawn, chairs falling back. More soldiers rushed into the hall, swords out, arbalests loaded. The captain of the royal guard rapped out orders, his men gathered in a small circle facing outwards round their prisoners, weapons ready. Corbett recovered from his surprise and shouted for silence. Whilst he did so, he gazed quickly at the Templar commanders; all of them, de Molay included, looked as if they had seen a ghost.

'There will be silence!' Corbett roared. He drew from his pouch the Secret Seal he always carried. 'Every man here will put away his weapons. I am the king's commissioner.' He continued at the top of his voice. 'I carry the Royal Writ. It is treason to oppose me.'

His threats eased the tension: swords were sheathed, de Molay rapped out orders. The Templar serjeants withdrew, the royal guard also relaxed. Corbett approached their captain, who now took off his heavy conical helmet. He cradled it in his arms, wiping the sweat and water from his face. His prisoner stood swaying, oblivious to what was going on around him.

'Sir Hugh.' The captain stretched forth his hand. 'Ebulo Montibus, Knight Banneret. I bring greetings from the king.'

Corbett clasped his hand.

'I never thought,' the captain continued, 'that I would receive such a welcome. After all, the man has done no wrong.'

'It's a long story, Captain.'

Symmes came forward: he caught Baddlesmere just before he fell and helped him to a chair.

'If he's done no wrong, why is he chained?' Branquier snapped. He filled a goblet of wine and passed it down to the prisoner.

'It's quite simple,' Montibus snorted. 'The king's proclamation was very clear: no Templar was to leave Framlingham Manor.'

'And where did you find him?' Corbett asked.

'Trying to smuggle his way through Micklegate Bar. He wore no Templar livery but the saddlebags he carried contained enough evidence about who he was. The city bailiffs arrested him. He was detained in the castle and the king ordered him to be brought back here.' The captain smacked his lips and looked at the table. 'It's a witch's night,' he continued. 'My men are cold, hungry.'

'Then be our guest.' De Molay intervened smoothly. 'Legrave, take our guests into the kitchen. The chains can be removed, can't they?'

Montibus agreed. Baddlesmere's leg irons and wrist gyves were unlocked, falling to a heap on the floor. Baddlesmere, however, sat like a man poleaxed. Now and again he would blink or drink greedily from the goblet. His escort disappeared into the kitchen; only Montibus stayed. Corbett took his seat. Maltote stood staring, open-mouthed, like a cow over a hedge.

Ranulf, delighted by the surprising diversion, grinned from ear to ear. He came down and whispered an Corbett's ear, 'Nothing is what it appears to be, eh, Master?'

'Did he commit a crime?' de Molay asked.

'Not that we know of,' Montibus replied. 'Except that he broke the royal prohibition.'

'It's the first time ever,' Ranulf remarked with a laugh, retaking his seat, 'that I have sat at table with a man who is supposed to be dead, buried and his Requiem sung.'

'Shut up!' Branquier snarled, his face white with fury.

Ranulf just smiled back. Baddlesmere slammed the goblet down on the table. He gave a deep sigh then slouched forward, shoulders hunched, the tears rolling down his cheeks. Montibus was ignoring all this, piling the trancher in front of him with scraps of chicken and pork. He began to eat hungrily then, struck at last by Ranulf's words, and by the tense silence, looked up. 'What is this?' His face grew serious as he stared round at the company. 'What did you mean, a man who's supposed to be dead and buried?'

'Captain,' Corbett intervened. 'Eat your food and drink your wine. You and your men can stay the night. I am sure the grand master's hospitality will extend to that. Sir Bartholomew, there are questions I must ask, though this is not the place.'

'No, it is not,' de Molay remarked, rising to his feet. 'Branquier, Sir Hugh, bring Baddlesmere to my chamber.'

Corbett whispered to Ranulf to look after the royal guard, then followed a shuffling Baddlesmere, held by Branquier, out of the hall and along the corridors into the grand master's chamber. For a while Baddlesmere just sat muttering to himself, rubbing his mouth and staring vacuously around.

'He's lost his wits,' Branquier commented.

'Sir Bartholomew,' de Molay thundered. 'You must tell us what happened! Your chamber was burnt. The corpses of two men were found on the bed, blackened and burnt beyond recognition. We thought one of them was you.'

Baddlesmere lifted his head. 'I am a worm and no man,' he intoned. 'My sins, my sins are always before me!'

'What sins?' Corbett asked quietly, moving the stool so he sat directly opposite the Templar. 'What sins, Bartholomew?'

Baddlesmere lifted his head. 'The sin of sodomy,' he rasped. 'Which cries out to God for vengeance.'

'And yet,' Corbett replied, quoting from the Bible, '"though your sins be as scarlet, they shall be as white as snow." You loved Scoudas, didn't you?'

Baddlesmere plucked at a loose thread in his rain-sodden hose.

'I became a Templar,' he began slowly, 'as a young man. I wanted to be a knight in shining armour, dying for the Cross. No, even before that, as a child: I used to sleep in my mother's room. She would bring men home. I'd hear her groaning and scrabbling in the bed. I was only a stripling. By the time I was fourteen, I knew I could never take a woman. I wanted to be pure, cold as ice and white as snow: clean and God-fearing before the Lord.' Baddlesmere pulled a face. 'And so I was. I became a Templar, a warrior, a monk, a priest. I had temptations of the flesh but I could control them, until I met Scoudas. At first I loved him like the son I never had but always wanted. His skin was smooth, white as satin . . .'

'And on the morning you went to York,' Corbett interrupted, 'you saw Murston being gibbeted and then went to the tavern, the Greenmantle?'

Baddlesmere nodded.

'And Scoudas went with you?'

'Yes, we shared the same chamber. However, Scoudas had changed. He began to threaten me, insinuate that he would complain.' Baddlesmere paused. 'He shouldn't have done that: he mocked me as an old man, telling me that he had met someone else, Joscelyn, a member of Branquier's retinue. I left in a temper, rejoined de Molay and journeyed back to Framlingham.'

'And the night of the fire?' Corbett asked.

'Scoudas came to my chamber. I thought he'd come to make his peace. Joscelyn was with him. They sat and baited me, threatening to disgrace me. I couldn't bear their taunts any longer. I walked out of the room, slamming the door behind me, their laughter ringing in my ears. The manor was quiet. I'd left my wine in my chamber so I took a jug from the buttery and went into the grounds. I deliberately hid myself because I didn't want to meet or talk to anyone. I went around the maze and across into the trees. The night was warm. I fell asleep. I was tired and exhausted. I'd drunk a little too much. When I woke, it was dark, though I could see the sun was about to rise. I got up stiff and sore. I was about to go back to the manor when I heard the cries and saw the flames. Even from where I stood, the smoke hung heavy in the air.' He paused and scratched his chin.

'And you fled?' Branquier asked.

Baddlesmere paused as the door opened and Symmes and Legrave slipped in.

'The royal guards are feeding their faces,' Symmes barked. 'And, when they've finished at the trough, I will show them their sties.'

Corbett ignored the insult. 'Why did you flee?' he asked.

'I suppose I panicked,' Baddlesmere replied. 'It was obvious someone had died in the room. I would be blamed. Whatever I did, I'd be damned. My secret sin would be revealed. Worse, I might be accused of starting the fire and held responsible for the other deaths. It was quite easy: I had my saddlebag with me so I simply climbed the wall. For a while I stayed in the open countryside around York, but I needed a horse and a change of clothing.' He flailed his hands. 'The rest you know.'

'You guessed someone was in your chamber?'

'I went as close as I could to the manor house, I could tell from the shouts and cries. I started to think: was the assassin after my life? Even if I could prove my innocence, they'd still say I killed Scoudas.' He put his face in his hands and sobbed quietly.

'Joscelyn died too,' Corbett remarked.

'But why?' Baddlesmere asked. 'Both men were young and vigorous. They could have escaped.'

'You left a jug of wine?' Corbett insisted.

Baddlesmere blinked slowly.

'The wine?' Corbett repeated. 'How much did you leave?'

'A jug, five or six cups.' Baddlesmere's jaw sagged. 'You

are saying it was tainted? They were poisoned or drugged?'

'That is the only explanation.'

'But I wouldn't hurt him!' Baddlesmere wailed. 'I would never hurt Scoudas!'

'When did you put the wine in your room?'

'Early in the afternoon: the best Rhenish. I placed it in a bowl of cold water to chill.'

'And did you drink it?'

'Yes, yes, I did, half a cup: then Scoudas and Joscelyn arrived. I became so angry at their taunting, I threw the cup on the floor and left.'

'Sir Bartholomew,' Corbett continued, 'all your possessions were destroyed in the fire but, amongst Scoudas's, we found a map of York and the assassins' warning, both in your hand, as well as a receipt signed by Murston for monies received.'

Baddlesmere's eyes took on a secretive, cunning look: the change of mood was so quick that Corbett wondered whether the man was fully in his wits, or even if he might truly be the assassin, Sagittarius.

'The papers,' Corbett insisted, 'please. Why should Scoudas be holding these papers?'

Baddlesmere coughed and licked his lips. 'I'd like some wine, Sir Hugh.'

Branquier filled a cup from the side-table and thrust it in his hands.

'Answer my question,' Corbett insisted.

'You have no authority here,' Branquier broke in.

'Yes he has,' de Molay snapped. 'Sir Bartholomew, answer the question!'

'Yes, I'll answer your question.' Baddlesmere sat up. 'Though I don't like snooping clerks. Whatever my sins, I'm still a Templar. I resent you, Corbett. I resent you being here. The Order has its own rituals and rule.'

'The papers?' Corbett demanded harshly.

'I was making my own inquiries,' Baddlesmere snapped

back. 'I drew that map and the warning to help myself. I gave a copy to Scoudas and asked him to keep his eyes and ears open. If my chamber hadn't burst into flames, you'd have found other copies there as well.' He shrugged. 'I know nothing about a receipt for Murston.'

'Why did your room burn?' Corbett asked.

'I don't know.'

'There was nothing in it which could start such an inferno?'

'Nothing. Clothing, parchment, some books but nothing else!'

'An oil-lamp?' Corbett asked.

'I said nothing.' Baddlesmere's eyes slid away. Corbett knew this disgraced Templar had his own suspicions.

'What will happen to me?' Baddlesmere whispered. His eyes pleaded with de Molay.

'You will be confined to a chamber on bread and water,' the grand master replied. 'And, when these matters are finished and the king's clerk has left us alone, you will stand trial before your peers. The Crown, if it so wishes, may also punish you for defiance of its writ.'

Baddlesmere nodded. 'I'll be broken, won't I?' he murmured as if to himself. 'I'll have my spurs hacked off, my knighthood removed. Sir Bartholomew Baddlesmere, Commander of the Order of the Temple, reduced to a kitchen scullion in some lonely castle.' He clenched a hand, glaring at Corbett so furiously that the clerk's hand dropped to the hilt of his dagger. Behind him he could feel the hate of Sir Bartholomew's companions: disgraced though Baddlesmere was, like any enclosed community, the Templars deeply resented the intrusion of outsiders. Corbett got to his feet.

'Grand Master, I am finished. I must insist that Sir Bartholomew is kept secure.' He walked to the door.

'Corbett!' Baddlesmere was staring oddly at him. 'Truth stands on the bank.'

'What do you mean?'

Baddlesmere began to laugh, shaking his head, gesturing at him to go. Corbett bowed at de Molay and left for his own chamber. Ranulf and Maltote immediately began to question him.

'I don't know,' Corbett replied. 'I don't know if Baddlesmere is telling the truth, has lost his wits, or whether he is actually the assassin. Maltote, where are those books?'

The messenger pulled them out from beneath the bed.

'We'll all sleep in this chamber,' Corbett declared. 'But for tonight – ' he eased himself on the bed and opened one of the books – 'I'll see what secrets these hold.'

Corbett spent the night reading and rereading different pages whilst his companions snored, sleeping as peacefully as babes. Sometimes Corbett's eyes would grow heavy. He dozed for a while and then shook himself awake, going across to splash water on his face or replenish the candles when they burnt too low. At last he could do no more. The last chapters of Bacon's work were a mystery but Corbett felt elated. He knew the source of that mysterious fire and, just before dawn, drifted into nightmares lit by the roaring flames of the Devil's fire.

Ranulf shook him awake. 'Master, it's ten o'clock.'

Corbett rose and groaned, shielding his eyes against the sunlight pouring in through the open shutters.

'Maltote and I have been up hours. We broke our fast in the refectory, gobbling away whilst the community just glared at us. Montibus has gone.'

Corbett groaned. 'Oh, no!' He swung his legs off the bed and rubbed his face, pushing the books away. 'I wanted him to stay. He might have afforded us some protection.'

Ranulf's face became serious. 'The Templars wouldn't attack us surely, not royal envoys?'

'Oh, not attack, but you or I, my dear Ranulf, could suffer some dreadful accident.'

'Tell him what we found,' Maltote urged from where he sat perched on a stool busily sewing a stirrup leather.

'Oh yes.' Ranulf handed Corbett a rag tied in a knot at the neck.

'Undo it carefully, Master.'

Corbett did so and stared at the burnt leather fragments.

'What's this?' He touched one piece and it crumbled into flakes. One small part, however, still remained firm and smooth.

'It's leather,' Ranulf explained. 'Scraps of leather. We found them in the woods where those scorch-marks were: little pieces blown about by the breeze.'

Corbett placed the rag carefully on the bed. He took each scrap, scrutinising it closely before putting it back. He then got to his feet, stretched, and took off his jerkin and shirt. He went across to wash his face and hands, telling Maltote to get some hot water from the scullery as he also wished to shave.

'Well?' Ranulf asked anxiously. 'What do you think?'

'They are burnt scraps of leather,' Corbett replied, rubbing his hands with the small bar of soap he'd bought from a merchant in Beverley. 'They may be fragments of a sack used to carry what the Ancients called "Devil's fire".'

Ranulf immediately began to question him, but Corbett just shook his head and, when Maltote returned, concentrated on his shaving, asking Ranulf to hold the mirror steady in his hands.

'Once I am finished,' Corbett smiled at Ranulf, 'get me some food from the kitchen – but make sure you see who handles it. Whilst I eat, I'll tell you a story.'

As Corbett dried himself off, Ranulf hurried out and returned with a linen cloth bearing loaves and a stoup of ale.

'So,' Corbett rubbed his chin and sat down at the table. 'Now I have finished my ablutions, let me tell you what those books contained. First, the fire is not from hell, it's man-made.'

Corbett bit into one of the loaves, Ranulf shuffled his feet impatiently.

'At first,' Corbett continued, 'I thought the fire could have been started by some form of oil but that's not safe. Sometimes oil is difficult to burn, especially when it congeals. Now Brother Odo, God rest his soul, also realised this. He must have examined his chronicle and recalled the fire missiles the Turks threw into Acre. Now these were nothing extraordinary: a mixture of tar and pitch, poured over some rags, torched as they lay in a catapult, then cast in amongst the defenders. I've seen the same happen at sieges: straw or rags coated with sulphur and then lit.

'But this fire is different. Odo realised that. A student of warfare, he recalled two books. The first is an ancient tract called the "*Liber Ignium*" or "Book of Fires". The second is much more interesting: Friar Bacon's letter, "De Secretis Operibus Artis et Naturae". Now both these works describe a very dangerous substance, a mixture of elements which, if exposed to the naked flame, creates fire difficult to put out even with water.'

'And you think this caused these murders?' Ranulf asked.

'Perhaps. The "*Liber*" describes the mixture as sulphur, tartar and a substance called "*Sal Coctum*" or cooked salt. Bacon is more specific: he mentions a substance called saltpetre. Now Friar Bacon conceals his discovery behind riddles and anagrams but, if he is to be believed, this saltpetre mixed with sulphur and tartar will ignite immediately.'

'But you said,' Ranulf declared, 'that Bacon was regarded by many as witless.'

'I doubt it,' Corbett replied. 'Friar Bacon acquired his learning from the Arabs. According to them, this substance was known to the ancient Greeks as well as the armies of Byzantium which used it to destroy a Muslim fleet; hence its name: "Greek" or Sea fire".'

'And, of course,' Ranulf added, 'all the Templar commanders have served in Outremer. They might know of this secret.'

Corbett popped a piece of bread into his mouth. 'More importantly, the Templars have some of the finest libraries in the world, especially in London and in Paris,' he said. 'However, though de Molay and his companions might know the secret, they are too engrossed in what is happening to their Order: all they can see are these dreadful deaths and the consequent scandals.' Corbett sipped at the ale. 'Brother Odo was different: more detached, more serene, he was a born scholar. The assassination of Reverchien must have stirred memories. He was searching for what I've found.'

'But can you prove all this?' Ranulf asked.

'If necessary but—'

The door was abruptly thrown open and de Molay burst into the room. 'Sir Hugh, you must come immediately! It's Baddlesmere . . .'

The grand master strode out, leaving Corbett no choice but to follow, Ranulf and Maltote hurrying behind. De Molay strode ahead, not even bothering to look back. He went round the back of the manor into the servants' quarters, up a flight of stairs and along a narrow passageway. The guards outside the chamber opened the door, de Molay went in and Corbett followed.

'Oh, my God!'

The clerk immediately turned away. Baddlesmere, dressed in shirt and hose, swung from the end of a sheet which had been tied round one of the rafters. He looked grisly yet pathetic: his face had turned a dark purple, eyes popping, tongue clenched between half-opened lips. His corpse twirled like some grotesque doll in the breeze coming through the arrow-slit window. Corbett drew his dagger and, helped by Ranulf, got the corpse down and laid him on the trestle bed. De Molay stood just inside the door, his face marble-white, dark circles round his eyes. He opened his mouth to speak but instead just shook his head.

'Grand Master, what did you say?'

De Molay's lips moved but no sound came out. Instead he clutched his stomach, pushed Corbett aside and rushed out towards one of the latrines built into an alcove in the corridor.

They heard him being violently sick.

'Is it suicide?' Ranulf whispered.

Corbett studied the corpse, examining the nails carefully, the position of the knot behind the left ear. He lifted the shirt, examined the man's torso, then sawed through the knot with his dagger. He tried to arrange the corpse in as dignified a pose as possible and covered it with Baddlesmere's cloak.

'He committed suicide,' Corbett muttered. He pointed up at the rafters then at the bed. 'So simple, to walk from life into death. Baddlesmere stood on the bed, fashioned that noose, put it round his neck and kicked the bed away.'

'What's this?' Ranulf leaned across the bed and pointed to a carved scrawl on the wall.

Corbett studied this carefully and, looking amongst Baddlesmere's possessions, realised the dead man had carved this, using the buckle of his belt, now worn down on one corner.

'What does it say?' Ranulf asked.

Corbett studied the words. '"*Veritas*," he read, '"*Stat in ripa*."' 'Truth stands on the bank,' he muttered. 'What on earth did Baddlesmere mean by that? The tag usually reads, "Veritas stat in media via"; "Truth stands in the Middle way".'

'I found him hanging!'

Corbett whirled round: de Molay stood in the doorway.

'He was here last night, with a jug of water and bread. Two guards stood outside.'

'And they heard nothing?'

De Molay shook his head. 'They heard him moving around early in the morning: he was singing the "*Dies Irae*". You know the sequence from the Mass of the Dead. How does it go, Corbett? "O Day of Wrath! O Day of Mourning! Heaven and Earth in Ashes Burning".'

'"See What Fear Man's Bosom Renders,"' Corbett continued, '"When from Heaven the Judge Descendeth on Whose Sentence All Dependeth!"'

De Molay knelt by the bed, crossing himself. When the others came, Branquier, Legrave and Symmes, Corbett walked back down the stairs and out into the fresh air. De Molay joined him there, Legrave beside him.

'Before you ask, Grand Master, Sir Bartholomew committed suicide.' Corbett shrugged. 'Overcome by remorse, fearful of what he had been implicated in, unable to accept the disgrace.'

'I came up,' de Molay remarked, 'just to greet him as a brother.' He glanced at Legrave. 'He can't be buried in hallowed ground.'

'But, Grand Master,' Legrave exclaimed, 'he was my brother as well! I knew Sir Bartholomew. We fought at Acre together.'

De Molay glanced expectantly at Corbett.

'Charity lies at the root of all laws,' Corbett declared. 'I do not think Christ will judge him as harshly as you do.'

'Strange,' de Molay murmured. 'All these deaths by fire. When I was a child, Corbett, playing in the fields outside Carcassone, I taunted a witch, an old woman, who lived in a shabby hut built against the wall overlooking the ditch. With all the foolishness and ignorance of youth, I shouted that she should burn. She approached me, eyes gleaming. "*No, de Molay*," she screeched back. "*You will die in fire and smoke!*"' De Molay rubbed his eyes. 'I always wondered what she meant. Now I know: there are different forms of fire and there are different kinds of death.'

And, not waiting for an answer, the grand master spun on his heel and walked away. Legrave followed him. Corbett watched them go then beckoned Ranulf and Maltote over.

'Get your horses ready,' he ordered. 'I want you to go to York. Seek out Claverley.' He dug into his pouch and handed them a small scrap of parchment. 'Scour the city, buy these mixtures, but keep each separate. Claverley will assist you.'

'Where shall we look?'

'Among the charcoal-burners of the city. It may take some time, but remember what I said: keep each substance separate

211

and bring them back as soon as you can.'

Within the hour, Ranulf and Maltote had left the manor. Corbett decided to stay in his own chamber. He examined this carefully, locking the shutters on the window before going out to find a long ash pole to lie across the bottom of the door. As he did this, Corbett noticed the gap between the door and floor. For a while, he stood and stared at the long piece of leather hung on the back of the door to exclude draughts. Corbett smiled. 'I wonder,' he murmured.

He had a vague idea how each of the victims had died, but not of the motive or the identity of the assassin. He laid out his writing implements on the table and, for a while, studied what he had written, trying to recall conversations, incidents, gestures and expressions. His mind kept going back to Baddlesmere's death scene: the corpse swaying slightly and that enigmatic inscription carved on the wall.

'Truth doesn't stand on the bank,' Corbett murmured. 'It stands in the middle way. What did Baddlesmere mean by that nonsense?'

He slept for a while, then got up and went down to the kitchen to beg for some food; a surly, hard-eyed retainer almost flung it at him. Later in the afternoon there was a knock on the door, de Molay asking if all was well? Corbett shouted that it was and returned to his studies. He decided to concentrate on the first item of evidence: the assassins' warning. Once again Corbett noticed how there were two versions.

'Why, why, why?' Corbett muttered to himself. 'Why are they different?'

There was the message left in St Paul's with which the Baddlesmere version agreed, as did the words spoken in the library: these three differed slightly from Claverley's and the one pushed into his hand on Ouse bridge. Every story, Corbett thought, has a common source, be it a love poem or some message. It only changes when it's passed on. Baddlesmere learnt about the warning when the king met de Molay and the other Templar commanders at the Priory. But why was the warning delivered to him on Ouse bridge the same as that given by Claverley? Corbett's hand went to his face.

'Oh, sweet God!' he murmured. 'So much for your fine logic, Corbett!'

He returned to his scribblings, following a new direction, concentrating on when the warnings were given as well as the recent attack on him in York.

Corbett looked up. 'The Templars may have been in York when the warning was passed,' he whispered, 'but they were definitely gone when I was attacked.'

He snatched his pen up. Ergo, he wrote, the attack was planned by someone else. Corbett nibbled the tip of the quill. Once he had suspected Baddlesmere and Scoudas; in reality both men were innocent, more absorbed in their own sin than anything else. Corbett drew two circles on the parchment, then drew a line joining them. He got up, opened the shutter and stared out at the dusk. Some of the riddle was resolved, the how and the why, but who? Whom did Baddlesmere suspect? And what did that inscription mean? Was it a pointer to the truth? A warning to the assassin, or both? '*Veritas stat*' Corbett translated as 'Truth stands', but '*in ripa*'? He went back and began to play with the words, changing them round, but this proved nothing. He picked up the warning the little boy had given him on Ouse Bridge, then he looked down at his jottings: did I, Corbett wondered, tell anyone about that? And, if not, who amongst the Templars mentioned it? He racked his brains but his eyes were growing heavy. He made sure the door was secure, wrapped his cloak around him and lay down on the bed.

Chapter 13

Ranulf and Maltote returned later the next morning. Both were unshaven, rather bleary-eyed, but loudly protesting how they'd only found what Corbett had ordered after a thorough search. Night had fallen, the curfew had been proclaimed, the city gates shut, so they'd hired a room in a tavern just near Botham Bar Gate.

'Aye, and you tasted the local ale?' Corbett observed crossly.

Ranulf held his hands up, his eyes round with innocence.

'Master, a mere drop, a mere drop.'

'Let us see what you have brought,' Corbett snapped.

Ranulf undid the saddlebag and brought out three large pouches, each containing a powder. Corbett opened, sniffed and felt each of them carefully. The smell was acrid but not pungent.

'In the open air,' he observed, 'it would raise no alarm or suspicion.'

They slipped out of the guesthouse, around the manor and into the maze. Corbett took his hornspoon out of his pouch and, following Bacon's instructions, carefully mixed the powders together. He stirred them with his fingers until all three substances were mingled. He then piled it in a heap, took a lighted candle out of Ranulf's hand and placed it near the fire, urging Ranulf and Maltote to stand back. The candle flame gutted and went out. With some difficulty Corbett relit it. This time the flame was stronger, the candle melted, the flame moving back to where the dark powder lay in a small heap.

Corbett's heart sank in despair but then the flame caught the powder, there was a crackle and the flames leapt greedily into the air, scorching the earth beneath. Corbett studied the flames' blueish tint whilst Ranulf and Maltote stared in amazement.

'I've never seen oil burn so quickly or so fiercely,' Ranulf muttered.

'I've seen something like it,' Corbett declared. 'When farmers burn the dry stubble in autumn: sometimes the fire runs faster than a man.' He stamped on the flame, wary lest it raise the alarm.

They left the maze and walked into the ring of trees where Corbett picked up a dry stick. Once again he mixed the substance: he smeared the wood, leaving one end free which he lit with Ranulf's tinder. This time the effect was even greater. The flame, as soon as it reached the substance, burnt so fast and greedily that Corbett had to stamp it out with his boot.

'You should have used gloves,' Ranulf remarked, watching his master clean his hands on his jerkin. 'A thick, leather pair of gauntlets.'

Corbett looked down at his hands then back up at Ranulf.

'Gloves?' he whispered. 'Do you remember the leather fragments you found? Gauntlets!' he exclaimed. 'That's the only trace the assassin left.'

'What do you mean?' Ranulf asked.

'The fragments of leather,' Maltote volunteered, 'that we found near the scorch-marks: the assassin must have burnt the gauntlets he used.'

Corbett walked deeper into the trees. He now knew who the assassin was, but how could he prove it? What evidence could he offer? He told Ranulf to conceal the bags of powder and they returned to the guesthouse. Corbett asked his companions to find something to eat whilst he returned to studying Baddlesmere's map.

'It's not of the entire city,' Corbett murmured, 'but only the area around Trinity.'

He then studied the inscription Baddlesmere had written on the wall. Last night Corbett had thought the words formed an anagram, a complicated puzzle or riddle. He translated them back into English, rearranging the letters, but all his conclusions were nonsense. Finally he translated them into French and clapped his hands in surprise: Baddlesmere, too, knew the identity of the assassin. However, in those last moments before death, he could not bring himself to name his brother Templar, so he had purged his conscience by leaving this mysterious phrase.

Ranulf and Maltote returned, bringing food from the kitchen. By Corbett's face, Ranulf realised that 'Old Master Long Face' was closing his trap. 'Drawing up a bill of indictment,' he whispered to Maltote. 'Like any hanging judge.'

'You do know, don't you?' he called out.

Corbett put his pen down and turned. 'Yes, I know the assassin and I think I can prove it.'

'Logic,' Ranulf exclaimed, 'as always.'

Corbett shook his head. 'No, Ranulf, not logic. I applied that and made a dreadful mistake. You work on a premise and then believe that everything will fit into place.' He rose and stretched. 'Because of my arrogance and because of my logic, I made a terrible error. Poor Baddlesmere was closer to the truth than I.'

'What's a premise?' Maltote asked, his mouth full of bread and cheese.

'You start with a statement,' Corbett replied. 'Such as "All Men drink ale; Maltote is a man; therefore he drinks ale." But the premise is wrong. All men don't drink ale: it's not an undisputed fact. Therefore, every statement you make based on that must be wrong.' Corbett pulled his stool over to where his companions sat with their backs to the wall, sharing the bread and cheese piled on a pewter plate. 'I believed there was a coven in the Templar Order intent on wreaking vengeance against the Crown both here and in France. I therefore concluded that the murders here at Framlingham and elsewhere were

217

merely the work of that coven. I was wrong.'

'So, what is the truth?' Ranulf asked.

Corbett shook his head. 'Eat your bread and cheese.' He paused as he heard a sound in the gallery outside. 'We have to leave here as quickly as possible,' he urged. 'Ranulf, pack our bags; Maltote, go down to the stables, saddle the horses. I want to be gone within the hour.'

Maltote grabbed a chunk of cheese and hurried out. Ranulf took one look at Corbett's drawn face and hurriedly packed their belongings. Corbett carefully put away his writing implements, checking the chamber, ensuring they had left nothing behind.

'Hide the books Maltote brought,' he hissed. 'And the three bags of powder?'

'They are kept separate,' Ranulf assured him.

They left the guesthouse and went down to the stableyard. Maltote had already led their horses out: he was busily trying to harness the small but evil-tempered sumpter pony. Corbett helped, checking harness and saddle girths. He was surprised at the silence of the manor, then he heard the clink of metal behind him and Ranulf's muttered curse. He swung round: the mouth of the stableyard was now cordoned off by Templar soldiers, helmeted and armed, each carrying an arbalest. On either flank stood their serjeants and officers.

'Mount,' Corbett ordered. 'If necessary, ride through them!'

Corbett edged his own horse forward. An order rang out: one of the crossbowmen raised his crossbow and a bolt whirred through the air over Corbett's head. Fighting to control his panic as well as his restless horse, Corbett rode on. Again the order was issued. This time the crossbow bolt whirred past his face; another smacked the cobbles in front of his horse, making it whinny and shy.

'That's as far as I'm going,' Maltote muttered.

Corbett reined in his horse: de Molay came out of the buildings and walked through the line of men. The grand master was dressed in half-armour, as were the other commanders, his hands resting on the pommel of his sword. He came up and grasped the bridle of Corbett's horse.

'You are not leaving us, Sir Hugh, without so much as a fond farewell?'

'You have no authority,' Corbett retorted. 'I intend to ride through and you must take the consequences!'

'Please.' De Molay's red-rimmed eyes had a pleading look. 'Corbett,' he whispered. 'You know the assassin, don't you? Your face betrays you.'

'These matters are for the king to decide upon,' Corbett replied.

'No, Sir Hugh, this is Templar land. I am the grand master. I must have some control, some say in what happens here. Templar justice is just as thorough and exacting as any king's.'

Corbett relaxed in the saddle. 'You know the murderer, don't you, Grand Master?'

'Yes, yes, I think I do: proving it is another matter.'

'And if I stay,' Corbett volunteered, 'I have your word that justice will be done and I will be allowed to go on my way?'

De Molay raised his hand. 'My oath on the Cross.'

Corbett dismounted. 'Then send four of your men to York. Don't worry, I will give them warrants and passes. They are to go to Monsieur Amaury de Craon, Philip IV's envoy at the archbishop's palace.' Corbett made sure he kept his voice low. 'Tell him what you like but invite him to come here as your guest. Say you wish to reveal secret matters affecting the Crown of France. Couch your letters in the friendliest terms.' Corbett glanced up at the pale-blue sky. 'It's about noon now. He's to be here by dusk.'

'I, too, studied Bartholomew's message scrawled on the wall,' de Molay retorted. 'It fits other pieces, fragments, mere morsels.'

'You should have told me,' Corbett replied.

'By nightfall we will all know,' de Molay whispered.

Corbett turned, telling Ranulf and Maltote to dismount: their horses were to go back to the stables, their baggage to the guesthouse. The Templars stood aside and Corbett returned to his own chamber. Guards soon followed, taking up position in the gallery.

'We should have rode on,' Ranulf declared, throwing the baggage to the floor, his face red with anger. 'They wouldn't have dared!'

'There was only one way of knowing that,' Corbett retorted. 'And I wasn't prepared to find out.'

He sat at the table and began to write out a short letter to the king as well as letters of permission allowing the Templar messengers into York. He sealed these hurriedly and Ranulf gave them to one of the guards outside. Corbett was then forced to kick his heels and wait, ignoring Ranulf's constant questioning, or Maltote's hushed observations about how many Templars were on guard.

In the afternoon they went for a walk and the guards followed. Ranulf counted at least a dozen. Corbett was tempted to seek an audience with de Molay but decided not to. He was still not fully sure, and concluded it was best that he wait until de Craon's arrival. He told Ranulf and Maltote to go back to their chamber and went into the Templar church. For a while he sat in the Lady Chapel, staring up at the dark mahogany, beautifully carved statue of the Virgin and Child. Above this was a small rose window with painted scenes from the life of Christ. For a while Corbett prayed: the statue and paintings reminded him of the small parish church near his father's farm.

I should go back there, Corbett thought: make sure my parents' tomb is well kept. He stared up at the window. Perhaps he could buy painted glass to light the dark transept where, under cold, dank slabs, his parents lay buried. He smiled; his mother would have liked that. She used to take him to church on afternoons like this, when his father and elder brothers were busy working on the land. She would describe the painted scenes on the walls or rood-screen: that's how Father Adelbert had come to know him and later agreed to school him.

'You are to work hard, Hugh,' his mother would say. 'Remember, great oak trees always start as little acorns.'

'I wish you were here!' Corbett whispered.

What would she have thought of him now, away from his second wife and child, preparing to confront a murderer and see justice done? That was his father's legacy: a former soldier who had fought in the civil war, his father had constantly preached about the need for a strong prince, good judges and sound laws. Corbett sighed. He got up from the small prie-dieu and walked back to the door of the church where his guards were waiting. He still wasn't sure what he would do: how he could trap the murderer? Evidence was one thing, proof was another. He turned and looked back at the rose window and the stories painted there: a vague idea formed in his mind.

'I want to see de Molay,' he told the guard. 'Now.'

The serjeant in charge shrugged his agreement and took Corbett around the manor house to the grand master's cell. De Molay had been busy: servants were packing chests and coffers, the bed was stripped, the desk had been cleared of all parchments and inkhorns.

'You are leaving, Grand Master?'

De Molay gestured at the retainers to go.

'You are my prisoner, Hugh,' he remarked drily. 'Whatever happens tonight, I will go back with you into York as your prisoner to meet the king.' He cocked his head to one side. 'You have not come about that, have you?'

'No,' Corbett replied. 'I have come to ask a favour. I wish you, Branquier, Symmes and Legrave to write out an account of all that has happened since your arrival in England.'

'Why?'

'Because I want it.'

'What will it prove?'

'Nothing – well, not really,' Corbett lied. 'But tell your commanders that, after my meeting with Monsieur de Craon, they may well wish to lodge their own complaint against me. Such an account might be useful.' Corbett went back towards the door. 'There are still a few hours left,' he called out. 'Plenty of time before dusk.'

Corbett returned to the guesthouse and dozed for a while. Food was brought in from the kitchen and, late in the afternoon, one of de Molay's retainers came to tell him that Monsieur de Craon had arrived and would Sir Hugh prepare himself? About an hour later Corbett, Ranulf and Maltote went into the refectory. The Templars were already assembled around the great table. De Craon rose as Corbett entered, his craggy face wreathed in smiles.

'Sir Hugh, the grand master says you are leaving, though there are matters we should discuss.'

Corbett limply shook de Craon's extended hand, fighting back the urge to smack that sharp, wily face. 'He's two people,' Corbett had once told Maeve. 'There's de Craon the envoy, but in his eyes you can see something else, dark and malevolent.'

Branquier, Symmes and Legrave were also there, as well as one of de Craon's black-garbed clerks: a young man, pale-faced with watchful eyes, his mousy hair cropped close to his head. He was there as de Craon's witness.

As soon as they took their seats, de Craon rose.

'Grand Master, I welcome Sir Hugh Corbett, but I was given to believe that you wished to consult me. Why is he present?'

De Craon's lawyer was already writing, busily recording his master's protests. De Molay smiled. His face became youthful, as if he thoroughly enjoyed baiting Philip's envoy. Corbett wondered what the real relationship between the grand master and the king of France was. De Craon, confused by de Molay's smiling silence, sat down.

'Sir Hugh is here,' de Molay rubbed his hands slowly together, 'because he is a hunter of souls and the searcher out of secrets.' He glanced down the table at Corbett. 'Time is passing,' he murmured. 'Darkness is drawing in.'

Corbett rose and walked to the end of the table so they could all see him and he watch them. Ranulf, as instructed, stood near the door, Maltote beside him; both had rested their loaded arbalests against the wall.

'Once,' Corbett began, 'there was a king of France, saintly but warlike; the holy Louis who wanted to plant the standard of the Cross on the towers of Jerusalem. He failed, died, and a martyr's crown was his reward.'

De Craon, his anger forgotten, was now looking curiously at him.

'At that time,' Corbett continued, 'this saintly king was helped by the Templars, a great fighting order of monks, founded on a rule drawn up by St Bernard himself. They were imbued with a vision, the capture and defence of the Holy Places in Outremer. The years passed, fortunes changed, and we now have a king of France, St Louis's descendant, Philip Le Bel, who would prefer to see his standards flying over the towers of London and Antwerp.'

'This is impossible!' De Craon sprang to his feet.

'Sit down!' de Molay snapped. 'And that's the last time you interrupt, sir!'

'But Philip's dreams crumbled,' Corbett continued, matter of factly. 'So he spun another dream. What he can't get by force, he'll acquire by stealth. His daughter is to marry our king's only son, so Philip knows that one day his grandson will sit on the English throne. Philip has to pay for this. He must collect a huge dowry, but his coffers, like those of Edward of England, are empty, so he looks around and sees the great Templar Order with its manors, farms, cattle and treasure. He watches closely because the Order has lost a great deal of its idealism. There are whispers of scandals; sodomy, drunkenness.'

Corbett glanced down the table and noticed Symmes's scarred face blush slightly. 'There are several rituals,' Corbett continued, 'gossip about covens and cabals; and a subtle plan forms in Philip's devious soul . . .'

De Craon made to rise but de Molay's hand went out and pressed him firmly down in his chair.

'The Templar Order itself,' Corbett continued, 'does leave a lot to be desired. There is a rottenness in it, but the Order is protected by the Holy Father in Avignon. Anyone who moves against the Templars moves against the Papacy, and Philip can't do that. He bides his time and selects his man: a Templar who will do for his Order what Judas did for Christ: betrayal with a kiss.'

The Templars stirred. Corbett fleetingly wondered how many of them had at least considered the path which the assassin had trod. Only de Molay remained impassive, hands before his mouth. He watched Corbett with the look of a hunting cat.

'A new grand master to the Order is elected.' Corbett leaned on the table. 'He holds a Grand Chapter in Paris. He wishes the Order to be revitalised and loudly proclaims his intention to make a progress through all its provinces. England will be first. He leaves Paris, lands in Dover and travels to London but, before he leaves France, the scandal breaks. A Templar serjeant, stupid and witless, is captured on suspicion of trying to kill Philip of France. A degenerate, probably dabbling in the occult, this Templar is handed over to the Inquisition. I suppose,' Corbett smiled thinly, 'if I was hung in the dungeons of the Louvre and left to the subtle cruelty of the Inquisition, I would swear black was white and white was black. God forgive me, I might even deny my faith, my family, even as I cursed myself as a coward. For that serjeant it was easier: bitter and resentful, he readily answered the Inquisitor, damning himself and the Order he once served.'

Branquier pushed himself forward. 'Are you saying that the serjeant was no assassin?'

'He was no assassin,' Corbett replied. 'A mere dupe. Philip was not attacked in the Bois de Boulogne or crossing the Grand Ponte: that was only to make us believe a sinister plot existed. There is no "Sagittarius",' Corbett continued. 'Or secret covens or cabals amongst the Templars: just a great deal of grumbling which a sinister Judas was willing to exploit.' He glanced at de Craon, who snatched the quill from his scribe's fingers.

'In England,' Corbett continued, 'the real plot began. King Edward had once fought in Outremer. The Assassins had tried to kill him. Such memories die hard and, naturally, when the Assassins' warning was pinned on the door of St Paul's, Edward paid heed. Such news chilled his blood. He came to York to hold a great council. He met our noble envoy de Craon to discuss the marriage terms. Our king, too, is bankrupt, so he also sought a loan from the Templar Order.'

'But the warning in London?' Branquier shouted.

'Oh, that was pinned to the door by one of you. A Judas who had become Philip of France's secret agent.'

'This is nonsense!' De Craon snapped. 'Stupid speculation . . .'

'Wait awhile,' Corbett replied. 'Now, when the traitor was in London, he not only nailed that message to the door of St Paul's, he also visited certain London merchants to purchase quantities of saltpetre, sulphur and other substances. This Templar had once served in Outremer where he had learnt of a mysterious fire which burns so fiercely that not even water can quench it: mingled with other substances and exposed to a naked flame, it seems the fires of Hell have erupted.'

'I have heard of that.' Symmes now put his pet weasel on the table: he stroked its ears and offered it a tidbit of dried meat. The Templar's good eye gleamed. 'We have all heard of it!' he exclaimed. 'The Byzantines used it to burn a great Muslim fleet.'

'No secret really,' de Molay interrupted. 'Certain books

225

discuss such a fire, and did not your Franciscan scholar, Bacon, analyse such mysteries?'

'The assassin certainly did,' Corbett answered. 'And it would not be difficult. Both the libraries in Paris and London are visited by scholars from all corners of God's earth. The fire itself is easy to make, once you know what to buy and how to use it.' Corbett now kept his eyes firmly on de Molay. 'Now this assassin,' Corbett continued, 'arrived in York. He mingles the substances and experiments with it here at Framlingham, in the woods, away from the inquisitive. Even so, the gossip begins. How the Devil's fire is seen. So, one night, he leaves the manor and goes along the lonely road towards Botham Bar. He hobbles his horse and, once again, experiments with the strange fire, perfecting its use. At the same time, being a consummate archer, he practises with an arbalest, loosing fire arrows into a tree: even in the dark his aim is true.

Now, all should have been well. However, on that night, a relic-seller, Wulfstan of Beverley, probably half-drunk, had left York to sell his tawdry goods in the villages beyond. Wulfstan, curious, ever eager for new stories, saw the fires, so he pushed his nag off the path and into the trees. The killer cannot allow this. Wulfstan will remember both his face and horse. He draws his great two-handed sword and strikes with such a great and powerful blow that he severs poor Wulfstan in two.'

'That death?' Branquier barked.

'Yes, that death,' Corbett echoed. 'As Wulfstan's horse bolts into the darkness, the assassin realises he has human flesh to play with. The fire will also destroy the identity of the victim. The remains are set alight but the assassin hears the cries of two good sisters and their guide, so he goes deeper into the trees and waits until they pass. He then leaves, removes the arrows from the trees: the burnt patches, the scratches on the bark and Wulfstan's mangled, burning remains are the only traces left.'

'Who?' de Craon shouted. 'Who is this assassin?'

226

'In a while,' Corbett taunted back. 'This assassin, Monsieur de Craon, is now ready to spread his web. Murston was a Templar serjeant, someone very much like the one who is lured into Paris. On the night before Edward of England enters York, Murston is told to go to a tavern near Trinity where the king will pass. He is ordered to hire a chamber and wait there.'

'Murston was a killer,' de Molay interrupted. 'An assassin.'

'He was no assassin,' Corbett replied. 'Just a stupid man, carrying out the orders of a superior officer. He stays the night like a good soldier would: the king enters York and so do you, Grand Master, with your commanders. However, one of them slips back along the streets to the tavern where Murston is waiting. He goes upstairs, slits Murston's throat and takes the crossbow Murston brought into the city. When the king processes up Trinity, the assassin fires two bolts, narrowly missing His Grace.'

Corbett turned and pointed to a chair standing in the corner, gesturing at Maltote to bring it across. Corbett sat down, easing the cramp in the small of his back.

'Murston was dead before those bolts were ever shot,' he continued. 'Greek fire has already been sprinkled over his corpse. Once the second bolt has been loosed, the assassin ignites the powder and flees down the stairs. He protects his face and body in a ragged cloak he'd bought from some beggar. I was the first to reach that garret but the assassin was already gone, leaving me to wonder how a man like Murston could shoot two crossbow bolts and then be half-consumed by those yellow-blue flames.'

'Did the assassin intend to kill the king?' de Molay asked.

'No, that was just the start. What the assassin really wanted – what Philip of France wanted – was to create a great scandal in the Templar Order.'

'Why?' Branquier shouted.

'So that the English crown would launch an attack upon the Order, seizing its properties, filling the exchequer with its treasure. And what Edward started in England, Philip of France would soon finish. And if the Holy Father complained?' Corbett shrugged. 'Philip would simply point to Edward of England, saying he was only imitating what his brother king had already done. Philip would destroy the Order, seize its lands and treasure, fill his own coffers as well as remove a movement which constantly reminded him about how his saintly grandfather had gone on Crusade. However, the Pope would hold Edward as the main culprit. Now the assassin knew that I would be sent to investigate. Hence the warning, followed by the attempt to kill me near the Shambles.'

'But we were all gone from York by then,' de Molay intervened. 'No Templar was in York when you were attacked.' The grand master spread his hands. 'True, one of us could have sent that warning to you but . . .'

'You never sent the warning,' Corbett declared. 'Nor was the mysterious archer a Templar. Was he, Monsieur de Craon?'

The Frenchman's eyes never flickered.

'Only you,' Corbett continued, jabbing his finger at de Craon, 'knew when I left for the archbishop's palace. You had me followed. You or one of your creatures also arranged that attack and, in doing so, deepened the mystery.'

'And Reverchien?' Legrave said hoarsely, not moving his head. 'None of us was at the manor when Reverchien died.'

'No, no,' Corbett replied softly. 'But you were there the day before he died: that was when the assassin entered the maze, carrying the Greek fire. He went to the centre. On the stone plinth, before the cross, are three candles on their metal stand. The assassin sprinkled the Greek fire over the candles, coating them, the stone plinth and the steps where Reverchien always knelt.'

'Of course,' Branquier breathed. 'And the old Crusader lit those candles, saying his prayers, his mind on God.'

'Yes,' Corbett replied.

He turned and gestured at Ranulf in the corner. The

manservant came over, carrying a small bowl. Corbett placed it on the table. He smiled apologetically at de Molay.

'I borrowed it from the scullery.'

He rose and brought back one of the many candles which burnt in their holders along the windowsill.

'In the bowl,' Corbett explained, 'is a very small portion of the powder which causes Greek fire.' He glanced up as the Templars pushed back their chairs. 'No, there's no danger.' Corbett took a long piece of dried vellum from his pouch, placed it in the bowl and lit one end. The flame licked it greedily, running down into the bowl. Even Ranulf jumped in alarm at the small, angry flame which shot up into the air. 'Reverchien did that,' Corbett said, pulling the bowl towards him and peering warily at the black scorch-mark inside.

'Reverchien lit those three candles, saying his prayers, unaware in the poor light before dawn of the death-bearing powder around him. The candles are lit. The substance is caught. The flames run down the candle stem, catching the powder on the step. It turned Reverchien into a living blaze. How subtle a way to kill your victim when you are far from the place of his death. And the flame burns fiercely,' Corbett explained, pushing the metal bowl along the table. 'Not only is it difficult to douse with water but the fire roars, leaving no trace of what caused it or how it began.'

Corbett retook his seat. 'The other deaths were similar. Peterkin the kitchen boy puts on an apron and oven cloths, not knowing they have been coated with that same powder. As he rakes the burning ash, Peterkin has a faint suspicion of what was happening before he died. Remember, his companions in the kitchen were discussing Reverchien's death and the other strange happenings. Peterkin made a joke about the air being tinged with sulphur. It was, on the very cloths he was wearing. The rest you know,' Corbett continued, staring at the murderer. 'A piece of hot ash or burning charcoal caught the cloths around his hand. The man tried to beat them out against his apron. Of course, the fire spread and Peterkin dies.'

'But why?' Symmes asked. 'Why a poor cook?'

'Because the assassin wanted to create terror. Spread the rumour, deepen the darkness, how the Templars were cursed, not only harbouring a possible regicide and killing each other, but allowing the flames of hell to burn freely and fiercely even amongst the innocents in their midst.' Corbett played with the Chancery ring on his finger. 'On a more practical level, Peterkin's death led to the flight of all the servants from Framlingham. Servants are curious, they look for the unexpected. Peterkin's death ended that and so protected the assassin.'

'And who, sir, is that?' Legrave snarled.

'Why sir, you sir,' Corbett remarked quietly.

Chapter 14

De Molay took some time to calm the subsequent uproar. Legrave rose and lunged at Corbett but Symmes, sitting between them, pushed back his chair. De Craon sprang to his feet, snapping his fingers at his black-garbed clerk as if they were on the point of departure. Corbett knew his old enemy and recognised the mummery for what it was: de Craon would only leave when it was to his advantage. Corbett was pleased the other Templars did not spring to Legrave's defence. There were shouts of disapproval, looks of concern, but the grand master's stern face and Branquier's troubled gaze reassured Corbett.

They know something, he thought; what I have said has touched secrets they harbour.

At last Legrave, red with fury, was forced back in his chair.

'You have no proof!' he spluttered.

'I will come to that in due course,' Corbett replied, 'when I have described the other deaths. Poor Brother Odo. You caught him as he went out to fish, didn't you? Waiting for him amongst the trees near the entrance to the jetty. I saw no blood there so you must have struck him a blow on the head, probably cracking his skull. Then you lowered him into the boat, fastening him upright in the seat, whilst in the stern and prow you sprinkled the Greek fire. The oars were tied to the old man's hands and fastened to their ratchet rings; the fishing line was slipped between the dead man's fingers and *The Ghost of the Tower* pushed out into the centre of the lake. A common sight here at Framlingham: old Odo dressed in his usual cloak and cowl, bending over a fishing rod, his boat bobbing on the lake. You hid amongst the trees, shot a fire arrow into the boat, and so the terror spreads. If a man like Odo, a hero of his Order, is devoured by the flames of hell, who can be safe? What is wrong at Framlingham? What is wrong with the Templars? And so the pool of poison spreads.'

'Why Odo?' de Molay asked. 'Why a gentle old man?'

'Because he was a scholar,' Corbett replied.

'And Baddlesmere?'

'Because he was a source of scandal,' Corbett continued. 'Legrave knew about Baddlesmere's little secrets, his passion for young men and the chilled white wine standing in his chamber. A sleeping potion was sprinkled into the jug; the fire powder spread on the floor beneath the rushes as well as along the leather sheet which hung against the door to keep out the draughts. Only Baddlesmere is not present: there's been a lovers' quarrel. Scoudas and Joscelyn drink the wine. Night falls whilst Baddlesmere sulks amongst the trees.' Corbett looked at Legrave's ashen face. 'And back you go, possibly carrying a small bowl containing a piece of burning charcoal. You slip that under the door. The rushes are dry, the powder is caught, the fire rages whilst those two drugged young men slip into death.'

'Grand Master.' Legrave pushed himself away from the table but, as he did so, Symmes placed his pet weasel on the floor; the creature scampered off into the darkness as its master caught Legrave's arm.

'I think you'd best stay, Brother,' Symmes remarked quietly. 'What Corbett says makes sense.'

'Of course,' Corbett continued. 'There was a connection between Baddlesmere and Brother Odo's death. The librarian was becoming curious. He was beginning to remember stories about the mysterious fire from the east. Legrave, however, was watching him. Perhaps Odo talked to him, told him what he was doing: that's why you came back into the library when I was there. If that door had not opened,' Corbett snapped, 'you'd have killed me as well!'

Legrave stared back, glassy-eyed, jaw tense. He kept gulping and glanced quickly at de Craon who refused to meet his gaze.

Corbett sighed: that glance alone confirmed his suspicions.

'For all his faults,' he continued, 'Baddlesmere was also edging towards the truth: he wondered who could have been behind Murston's death. On the morning the king was attacked, Baddlesmere knew where he was and where the grand master had gone. He also reached the conclusion, as I did, that two of his companions, Symmes and Branquier, had been at the other end of York near Botham Bar well away from Trinity when the attack was carried out.'

'That's true,' Branquier interrupted. 'Baddlesmere kept questioning all of us: where we had gone, which streets we'd walked down.'

'Even which taverns we'd drunk in,' Symmes added drily.

'But I was with the grand master,' Legrave shouted. He glanced down the table but de Molay just stared at him.

'The grand master was with the goldsmiths for at least two hours,' Corbett replied. 'You were supposed to stay outside.'

'And I did.'

'But if you look at Baddlesmere's map of York, you can travel from Stonegate to the tavern in Trinity where Murston was in a matter of minutes.'

De Molay took his hands away from his mouth. 'Sir Hugh speaks the truth,' he declared. 'We visited two goldsmiths on that street. On one occasion I came out and did not find you there.'

'I was amongst the stalls,' Legrave cried.

'Oh, yes, so you were,' Corbett declared. 'Buying what?'

Legrave licked his lips.

'Gloves,' Branquier replied, 'or gauntlets: that's what you told us.'

'Where are these?' Corbett asked. 'You bought more than one pair. Different stall-owners will attest to that. Why should any man want more than one or two pairs of gauntlets? You are a soldier-monk, Legrave, not some foppish courtier.'

'Where are the gauntlets?' de Molay demanded.

'Oh, you'll find them gone,' Corbett interjected. 'You see the powder Legrave used can be very dangerous. It leaves a stain: the grains become embedded in the cloth. Once used, they must be destroyed. Legrave did this. He burnt them in isolated spots in the manor. My companions found the remains.'

'You are lying! You are lying!' Legrave beat the table with his fists.

'We can search your chamber,' Corbett offered. 'We could ask you to produce these gauntlets. Who knows what we might find there. Some traces of the substances you used? It would leave its mark on boots and clothes. Perhaps traces of blood on a knife or sword?'

'Ralph.' Branquier leaned forward, looking down the table. 'You have the opportunity to answer these charges.'

Legrave refused to look up.

'Baddlesmere, too, studied the Assassins' warning,' Corbett continued. 'You see, the warning nailed to the doors of St Paul's Cathedral read as follows:

KNOWEST THOU, THAT WE GO FORTH AND RETURN AS BEFORE AND BY NO MEANS CAN YOU HINDER US.

Corbett closed his eyes.

'KNOWEST THOU, THAT WHAT THOU POSSESSES SHALL ESCAPE THEE IN THE END AND RETURN TO US.
KNOWEST THOU, THAT WE HOLD YOU AND WILL KEEP THEE UNTIL THE ACCOUNT BE CLOSED.

'That is the warning I read out at the priory when I was present with the king. However, the warning given to me on Ouse Bridge read a little differently:

KNOWEST THOU, THAT WHAT THOU POSSESSES
SHALL ESCAPE THEE IN THE END AND RETURN
TO US.
KNOWEST THOU, THAT WE GO FORTH AND
RETURN AS BEFORE AND BY NO MEANS CAN
YOU HINDER US.
KNOWEST THOU, THAT WE HOLD YOU AND WILL
KEEP THEE UNTIL THE ACCOUNT BE CLOSED.

'And the same is true of the warning which Master Claverley took from Murston's gibbet.' Corbett shrugged. 'It was that which made me wonder. Were there two parties to this macabre game? Legrave in England and de Craon in France? Legrave posted the warning at St Paul's when the Templars passed through London. De Craon passed me the second rendering of the message as I travelled through York. He also had one of his clerks display one on Murston's gibbet just to deepen the mystery.' Corbett smiled bleakly at the Frenchman. 'You'll have to tell your master in France that you made a terrible mistake: you copied out a message wrongly.'

The French envoy did not stir but sat, head back, staring up at the ceiling, running his hands through his sparse red beard.

'But what's this connection?' Symmes asked. 'How did you know Legrave and de Craon were fellow conspirators?'

Corbett turned to him. 'Because on my arrival here – and you may not recall this – I told you that I had received a similar death threat but I did not tell you where. Later on, in discussion with all of you, Legrave casually remarked on how I was threatened as I crossed Ouse Bridge. How did he know that unless he and de Craon were fellow conspirators?' Corbett pointed to Symmes. 'You have written out your account, as the grand master ordered, of this whole sorry tale?'

The Templar nodded.

'And you, Branquier?'

'Of course.'

'And Legrave?'

'I was too busy,' he retorted.

'Whatever,' Symmes barked. 'I never knew about the warning being given on Ouse bridge.' He pointed at Legrave. 'Yet I do remember you saying it and Branquier kept a record of that meeting.'

'But this manor has been secured,' de Molay explained. 'None of us could enter York, nor has Monsieur de Craon been here.'

Corbett asked. 'If you wanted to correspond with someone just beyond the walls of this manor, would it be difficult? Baddlesmere found it very easy to slip away. I am sure Monsieur de Craon has envoys and clerks to run his errands – and so each kept the other informed about what was happening.' Corbett paused and stared at the window. The storm had passed but the rain was still splattering against the windows. 'In the end,' Corbett murmured, 'I must confess, I made a terrible mistake.' He glanced round the table. 'I thought this Order was rotten but, as in any community, there are bad and there are good. Grand Master, for my suspicions against you and the rest of your brothers, I apologise.' Corbett rubbed his face. 'But I am tired and my heart is elsewhere. "*Veritas in ripa*",' he murmured. 'Truth stands on the bank.' He stared at Legrave. 'That's what Baddlesmere scrawled on the wall of his cell before he hanged himself. He, too, had guessed the identity of the assassin. Perhaps he had seen something. Perhaps he had reflected on how close Legrave had been to Trinity when the king had been attacked. Perhaps he remembered what an excellent archer Legrave had been. A born warrior, he was not left-handed or right-handed but ambidextrous, who could shift a lance so easily from one hand to another. When I recalled the assassin in the library and asked my servant to play the part, I became confused until I remembered how the assassin kept moving the crossbow from hand to hand.' Corbett looked at the grand master. 'You know what the inscription meant?'

'Yes, yes, I do,' de Molay replied. '"*Ripa*" in Latin means bank, but in French bank is "*la grève*".'

Corbett pushed back his chair. 'Baddlesmere knew that,' he said. 'But he could not betray an old friend, a brother of his Order. Moreover, he lacked any evidence so, in leaving that cryptic message, he purged his conscience.' Corbett rose to his feet. 'I have finished, Grand Master,' he declared, 'there is no secret coven or conspiracy amongst the Templars but instead, as I have described, there has been an attempt to bring the Order into discredit, to provoke Edward of England into seizing it and thus pave the way for Philip of France to act. Legrave was their tool but the conspiracy had its roots – ' Corbett glanced at de Craon – 'with those dark souls who advise the French king.'

'I, too, am finished.' De Craon sprang to his feet, his chair crashing back to the floor. 'Grand Master, I refuse to stay here and listen to this nonsense: these insults offered to myself and my master. A formal protest will be lodged both with Edward of England and the Temple in Paris.'

'You can go when you want,' de Molay uttered drily. 'As you say, you are an accredited envoy. I have no power over you.'

De Craon opened his mouth to reply but thought better of it and, with his black-garbed clerk following, strode out of the room. Only when he passed Corbett did his eyes shift; the clerk flinched at the malevolent hatred in the man's eyes. Corbett waited until the door slammed behind him and listened to de Craon's fading shouts for his horses and the rest of his servants to join him.

'He will return to York,' Corbett declared, 'then protest

most effusively to His Grace and, by this time tomorrow, he will be travelling to the nearest port for a ship back to France. Now I, too, must go.'

He glanced at Legrave who sat, hands clasped together, staring into the darkness, his lips moving wordlessly. Corbett still hoped to spare this man the ultimate degradation.

'You cannot go,' de Molay declared.

'But you gave your word.'

'When these matters are finished!' de Molay snapped. 'And they are not finished yet!' He turned. 'Sir Ralph Legrave, Commander of this Order, what answer do you make to these accusations?'

Symmes, sitting next to the accused, grasped him by the arm and shook him. Legrave pulled his arm away as if he could see something in the shadows on the other side of the hall.

'What answer do you make?' de Molay demanded harshly.

'I am a Templar,' Legrave replied.

'You are accused of terrible crimes,' Branquier retorted. 'Your chamber and possessions will be searched!'

Legrave shook himself from his reverie. 'There's no need for that.' He ran a finger round his lips. 'Search my room and you'll find the evidence.' He chewed the corner of his lip and glanced fleetingly at Corbett. 'They might not find it but you will. De Craon warned me about you. I should have killed you immediately. We all deserved to die.' His voice rose. 'We are the Templars, men devoted to war against the Infidel. Now look at us: bankers, merchants, farmers. Men like Brother Odo living on past glories. Reverchien and his stupid pilgrimage every morning; Baddlesmere with his boys; Symmes and his drinking; Branquier and his accounts. What hope is there for any of us? I came into this Order because of a vision just as noble, just as holy as the search for any Grail.' He jabbed a finger towards de Molay. 'Philip of France is right. Our Order is finished. Why should we hug our riches to us? The Order should be dissolved, united with others, given a fresh purpose.'

'And you?' Corbett asked, curious at what Philip had offered this Judas.

'To be a knight banneret at the French court,' Legrave answered. 'Yes, to have manors and estates, a release from my vows. The opportunity to make up the time lost; to marry, to beget an heir. At least there's purpose in that. Sooner or later the storm will come, and the house of the Templars, built upon sand, will shatter and fall; and great will that fall be.'

Corbett went and stood over him. 'You're a liar,' he accused. 'You were a coward: you betrayed your Order years ago at Acre.'

Legrave's head snapped back at the hiss of anger from his companions.

'What, what are you saying?' he stuttered.

'I met a knight, a Templar in the Lazar hospital in York. A man kept prisoner for years by the Assassins: he did not give me his name. He called himself the "Unknown" but he talked of an English Templar who ran from his post in Acre and doomed his companions.'

'I have heard of such rumours,' Branquier interrupted.

'You ran, didn't you?' Corbett asked. 'And the French found out. They not only offered you wealth but threatened to reveal your cowardice.'

Legrave just nodded and, putting his face in his hands, sobbed quietly.

'You admit the charges?' Branquier whispered.

'He must stand trial,' Symmes barked.

'He has stood trial,' de Molay replied, rising to his feet. 'And has been found guilty.'

The grand master drew his great sword from its scabbard hanging on the corner of his chair. He walked down the other side of the table then stopped, glaring down at Legrave. He held the sword up just beneath the hilt like a priest holds a cross.

'I, Jacques de Molay, Grand Master in the Order of the Templars, do find you, Sir Ralph Legrave, knight of that same order, guilty by your hand of the terrible crimes of murder and treason. What have you to say?'

Legrave raised his head.

'Sentence is passed,' de Molay intoned. 'Execution will be carried out at first light tomorrow.'

'You cannot do that!' Corbett exclaimed.

'Go back to your Chancery!' de Molay retorted. 'Look amongst the deeds and muniments, your royal charters and licences. I have the power of the axe, the scaffold and the tumbrel, Brother.' De Molay looked back at Legrave. 'I ask you for the final time: do you have anything to say?'

'Nothing,' Legrave replied. 'Except, Grand Master . . .' He stared round the hall, seeing it for the last time. 'All this will pass,' Legrave whispered, 'for our cause is finished. Our days are numbered. Our house will surely fall.'

De Molay went towards the door and came back, leading a group of serjeants. Symmes pulled Legrave to his feet. De Molay removed Legrave's swordbelt, the sign of a knight.

'Give him a priest,' de Molay rasped. 'Let his sins be shriven.'

The prisoner turned and, without a backward glance, was led out of the hall.

Corbett went towards the grand master, hands extended. 'Sir, I bid you adieu.'

De Molay grasped his wrist; Corbett grew alarmed as the Templar seized it, holding it with all his strength. Ranulf cursed and stepped forward.

'You are our guest,' de Molay declared. 'It is too late for you to return. You are the king's commissioners. You must be his witnesses to our justice.'

Corbett's heart skipped a beat. De Molay was right. Legrave's execution would have to be witnessed. The king would demand that.

'You object?' de Molay asked curiously, still gripping Corbett's hand.

'I do not like to see any man die,' Corbett replied. 'Least of all at the block.'

De Molay released his hand. 'It will be swift,' he murmured. 'So, sir, tell your servant to withdraw. Branquier and I have something to tell you.'

'Master,' Ranulf protested. 'It is not—'

'Sir Hugh is safe,' de Molay reiterated. 'No harm will come to him. You have my oath.'

Corbett nodded; Ranulf and Maltote reluctantly went to the door.

'Wait for him in the guesthouse,' the grand master called out. 'He may be some time. You have nothing to fear.'

Once the door closed behind them, de Molay gestured Corbett to sit, he and Branquier on either side of him.

'You suspected,' Corbett began.

'I understood Baddlesmere's riddle,' de Molay replied. 'Though I could not see how it could be true.'

'And Philip of France's meddling?'

'The thought crossed my mind,' de Molay replied. 'At the Chapter in Paris, Legrave was often missing. I wondered if he was meeting some of Philip's coven. The French king has always found us an irritation. We constantly remind him about how his sainted grandfather went to the aid of the Holy Places in Outremer. But something else; about eighteen months ago Philip, now a widower, actually applied to be admitted into our Order.'

'Why?' Corbett exclaimed.

'For the glory. Perhaps our treasure. Or to learn our Great Mystery.'

'What Great Mystery?' Corbett asked.

De Molay looked across the table at Branquier.

'He deserves to know,' he remarked quietly.

Branquier breathed out noisily.

'I have decided,' de Molay repeated. He loosened the collar of his shirt, took out a gold reliquary, covered at the front by a piece of thick glass, and placed it on the table. He pulled the candle closer.

'What is it?' Corbett asked.

'A piece of the true cross,' de Molay explained. 'Taken before we lost it at the Battle of Hattin. Put your hand over it.'

Corbett obeyed.

'Now swear,' the grand master insisted, 'that what you see tonight, you will not describe, or hint at in any way, to another living soul.'

'I swear!' Corbett replied. He knew the Templars were about to reveal the Great Mystery of their Order: the source of all their secret rituals, hidden chambers, and ceremonies held at the dead of night.

'I swear,' he repeated, 'by the Saviour's Cross!'

De Molay slipped the reliquary back round his neck and, without another word, he and Branquier led Corbett out of the hall. They went up the stairs on to the gallery towards the secret chamber, still closely guarded by a company of soldiers. De Molay unlocked the room but he did not take Corbett aside. Instead, he came out carrying the tapestry Corbett had noticed hanging there on his first visit. The Templar soldiers stood like statues, heads lowered as Corbett was led up another flight of stairs and into a secret chapel. The tapestry was hung on a small hook thrust into the rim of the altar standing on the dais. Sconce torches were lit, as were the candles and the dark chamber flared into light. Three cushions were placed on the floor. Branquier gestured at Corbett to kneel, the Templar beside him. De Molay then played with the wooden rim round the tapestry. He took this and the tapestry away, revealing a pale linen sheet. Corbett could see the cloth was very old, yellowing with age, with a faint outline on it. De Molay then put two candles on either side of the sheet, etching more sharply the image it held. He came and knelt beside Corbett.

'Look, Sir Hugh,' de Molay whispered. 'Look and adore.'

Corbett stared. As he did so, he lost all awareness of his two companions or the chamber. His eyes adjusted to the contrast of light and dark, his heart skipped a beat, and he felt the sweat break out on his body: the image, as if painted in a rusty coloured substance, depicted a head crowned with thorns. The eyes were closed, the hair matted and bloody on either side of a long face, the nose sharply etched in death; the lips full, slightly parted, high cheekbones still bearing marks, cuts and bruises. De Molay and Branquier leaned forward, faces to the ground, chanting the prayer: 'We adore you O Christ and we praise Thee; because, by your holy Cross, you have redeemed the whole world.'

Corbett could only gaze. The image was so life-like; if he could stretch out and touch it, the head would surely move, the face would live, the eyes would open.

'Is it . . . ?' he whispered, and then recalled the stories and legends about a sacred cloth which once covered the face of the crucified Jesus. Some said it was at Lucca in Italy. Others in Rome, Cologne or Jerusalem. De Molay straightened up. He let Corbett stare for a while before going forward; he extinguished the candles and covered that haunting face behind the tapestry. He then sat down on the dais opposite Corbett.

'It is what you think,' he murmured. 'The sacred Mandylion. The cloth which Joseph of Arimathea and Nicodemus used to cover Christ's face in the tomb. Somehow the cloth took on the imprint of his face. For centuries it was hidden but when invading armies sacked Constantinople in 1204, it came into our Order.' He gestured with his hands. 'This is what we venerate in the dead of night. This is the source of the garbled stories about Templars worshipping severed heads or indulging in secret rituals. This is our Great Mystery, and it is this which Philip of France would like to seize.'

Corbett leaned back on his heels and nodded. Any king would give a fortune for what he'd seen. If Philip owned it, he would use the cloth to underline the sacredness of his rule and, if circumstances demanded, sell it on the open market for a fabulous sum. All of Christendom would bid to own it.

De Molay came over and helped Corbett to his feet.

'Only the chosen few in the Order are ever allowed to see what you have seen,' he explained. 'Now go, Sir Hugh, but *never* utter a word about what you have witnessed.'

Corbett rose and left the small, mysterious chapel. He returned to his own chamber in the guesthouse. Maltote was already asleep, but Ranulf was eager to congratulate his master and ply him with questions about what had happened. Corbett just shook his head. He took off his boots and climbed on to the bed, wrapping his cloak around him.

'Surely, Master,' Ranulf wailed, 'you can tell me.'

Corbett half rose, resting on one elbow. 'I'll say one thing, Ranulf, and you must not question me again. I am a singular man: in one night I have looked into the heart of evil and the source of light. I have glimpsed both heaven and hell!'

And, with Ranulf's muttered curses ringing in his ears, Corbett lay back down on the bed, praying daylight would soon come and this business would be finished.

The next morning Corbett, with Ranulf and Maltote in attendance, stood outside the front door of the manor house. The sun had not yet broken through the cloying mist which hung heavy amongst the trees, shifting under a sharp cold breeze which gave the manor gardens a ghostly appearance. De Molay had insisted that every Templar be present, formed in a square around a crude wooden platform on which a block had been set with a large, two-headed axe lying on one side. On the other stood a small basket filled with straw and coated with sawdust. The grand master stood on the platform intoning the '*De Profundis*', the psalm for the dead. He moved aside as a Templar soldier, dressed in black from head to toe, a red mask covering his face, stepped on to the makeshift scaffold. A single drum began to beat as Legrave, dressed in boots, hose and a white linen shirt, was led out through the main door of the manor. He looked pale but, apart from that, showed no sign of fear. He went on up on to the scaffold and knelt before the block. De Molay approached and whispered into his ear. Legrave smiled slightly but shook his head, refusing to listen. De Molay stepped back. The executioner lashed Legrave's hands behind his back and thrust his head forward over the block. For a few seconds the prisoner remained motionless, neck extended, eyes closed. He then abruptly lifted his head. The executioner was about to thrust him down again but de Molay shook his head. Legrave looked up at the sky and then round at the host of witnesses to his death.

'It will be a fine day,' he declared in a clear voice. 'The sun will rise, the mist will burn off. Brothers . . .' His voice shook a little. 'Brothers, remember me.' He laid his head on the block, the executioner pulled back his shirt a little then moved back. The drum beat began. The great axe went up. There was a shimmer of light as it swooped, cutting the air, piercing Legrave's neck, veins and sinews. Corbett closed his eyes, murmured a prayer and moved away, back through the crowd.

In the solar of the Archbishop of York's palace, Edward, King of England and John de Warrenne, Earl of Surrey, sat in the cushioned windowseat staring down at the scene in the courtyard below. Corbett, Ranulf and Maltote were preparing horses and two sumpter ponies, loaned from the royal stables, for their journey south. Corbett was on his horse, staring out through the yard gate, lost in thought, as if calculating how long it would take to travel from York to his manor at Leighton. The king stifled his annoyance and, opening his hand, stared down at the Secret Seal.

'Your Grace, I am going,' Corbett had declared. 'I wish to be on the road by midday. I kept my word and now you must keep yours.'

The king had fumed, sulked, shouted and pleaded, but Corbett was obdurate.

'Your king needs you!' Edward yelled in exasperation.

'So does my wife and family,' Corbett retorted and, taking the ring from his finger and the Seal from his purse, he'd walked over and thrust them into the king's hands.

'My Lord King,' the clerk had whispered, 'even a good dog gets his bone as a reward.'

'But why now?' Edward grasped Corbett by the front of his tunic.

'I . . .' Corbett had glanced away. 'I am tired,' he whispered hoarsely. 'I am tired of the blood, the violence. I resign my office. I wish to sit in my manor and count my sheep. Go to bed with my wife and stop sleeping with a dagger beneath my pillow whilst Ranulf and Maltote guard the door.'

Corbett had closed the king's fingers around the Seal and ring, then strode out of the royal chamber, shouting at Ranulf and Maltote that they were leaving. De Warrenne followed Edward's stare.

'I could stop him,' the earl offered. 'Give me ten good archers. I'll seize him at the city gates and bring him back.'

'Oh, for the love of God, don't be stupid!' Edward groaned. He leaned over and tweaked his earl marshal's cheek. 'You are a good man, John. If I told you to mount a destrier and charge the moon you probably would.' Edward tossed Corbett's ring and Seal into the rushes, though he made careful note where they fell. 'I made Corbett what he is,' he muttered hoarsely. 'What I fashioned once, I can fashion again.'

Even as the words were out of his mouth, Edward knew he was lying. He would miss Corbett: dark, secretive, with his wry sense of humour, his love of law. Corbett, his shadow-master or 'guardian angel', as the king had once referred to him.

'He did well,' de Warrenne grudgingly conceded. 'Do you believe Master Hubert Seagrave?'

Edward grinned. 'No, I don't. Truth comes in many guises, but a rich vintner coming to confess his sins, his chests full of ancient gold, craving the royal pardon for a momentary lapse . . .' Edward shrugged: he jabbed a finger at the courtyard below. 'Corbett's brain may be of steel, but he has a heart of wax. I suspect he had a hand in it. However, my coffers are full, my Exchequer clerks are dancing with delight at the profits, not to mention the low price Seagrave will charge for every tun of wine delivered to the royal household.'

'And de Craon?' the earl asked.

'Huffing and puffing,' Edward replied. 'Shocked, outraged. The lying bastard protests too much. He'll go back to my sweet brother of France and I'll have letters! Oh, by the moon's tits, I'll have letters! Angry protestations, fierce denunciations, then Philip will scuttle back to his spiderweb and plot again. He's set his heart on the Templars and the Templars he will have; but not while I sit on the throne at Westminster . . .'

Edward rose and went across to the table. 'Legrave is dead,' he continued. 'De Molay will return to France to accept Philip's protestations of innocence. He will even offer the French king a loan.' Edward sat down and began to leaf through the books Corbett had borrowed from the Archbishop's library. 'But this fire . . .'

'You had heard about it before, your Grace?'

'Oh yes,' Edward lied, snapping his fingers at de Warrenne to join him. The king leaned his elbows on the table, cupping his face in his hands. 'In the summer,' he mused, 'I intend to cross the Scottish march. I will teach Wallace and his rebels a lesson they'll never forget.' He tapped the pages of the book. 'I want my Clerks of Stores to read this. What Corbett discovered, so can they. That rogue Claverley, whom I'm going to reward, can help. Let us, my good Earl, take this fire north. I'll set the very heather ablaze!'

Edward heard a sound from the courtyard below. He pushed back his stool and went to look out of the window. His heart skipped a beat: Corbett was gone.

Author's Note

The events of this novel are based on historical fact. The city of York is as I described it, though sometimes I have used other spellings of well-known landmarks, e.g. Botham Bar for Bootham Bar.

The introduction of gunpowder into English warfare is well described by Henry W. Hine in his book *Gunpowder and Ammunition, Their Origin and Progress*, published by Longmans (1904). He gives a scholarly analysis of gunpowder, talks of the '*Liber Ignium*' as well as the secrets of Friar Bacon's work mentioned in the text. Even today scholars are puzzled by the complex anagrams and cryptic language in which Bacon conceals his formula. Perhaps the good friar realised the latent dangers of his discovery! Greek fire was used by the Byzantines and, for a while, was their jealously guarded secret. Edward I's remarks at the end of the novel are probably based on fact: the events of *Satan's Fire* are set in 1303: according to Hine's book (page 50), Edward did sweep north in 1304 and used this fire, for the first time, in the siege of Stirling Castle. By 1319 the Scots had learnt their lesson and also had the secret from a Flemish engineer.

The fall of Acre and the consequent effect on the Templar Order is also well documented. Philip of France did attempt to join the Order and was repulsed. There is evidence that he tried to stir up Edward's agitation against the Templars, but was prevented from carrying his designs through. In 1307, however, after Edward I had died, Philip launched his notorious attack on the Templars, accusing them of witchcraft, sodomy and of worshipping a severed head. The English Crown was one of the few institutions to raise a voice in defence of the Order and, for a while, Edward II tried to resist his father-in-law's demand for the destruction of the Templar Order in England. Philip, however, had his way: the Templars were destroyed and, in 1313, Jacques de Molay was burnt alive before Notre-Dame Cathedral in Paris. Before he died, the Templar grand master protested his innocence. He summoned Philip of France to meet him 'before the tribunal of God within a year'. He also cursed the French monarchy 'until its thirteenth generation'. De Molay's curse was prophetic: Philip IV was dead within the year. His three sons died childless; his grandson Edward III of England claimed the throne of France and plunged Western Europe into the Hundred Years War. Louis XVI, 'the thirteenth generation', died on the guillotine, his family's last prison being the Temple in Paris.

The Templars undoubtedly held the Mandylion, the cloth which covered Christ's face. This not only gave source to the legends about worshipping a severed head but figures prominently in Templar art, as recent excavations at Templecombe in Dorset prove.

© Paul C. Doherty
14 September 1994